THE DREAM

HENRY DE MONTHERLANT's earliest novel, *The Dream*, first appeared in 1922 when he was twenty-six, and at once established his reputation as one of the most brilliant young French writers of the period. *The Dream* is ostensibly a war novel and contains some extraordinarily vivid impressions of warfare on the Western front; but it is less concerned with the drama of war itself than with the relationship of its three main personages under the pressure of their war-time life.

The Dream is a highly characteristic and deeply interesting piece of work, containing episodes that only Montherlant could have handled, and descriptive passages that illustrate his peculiar blend of harshly astringent realism and intense poetic feeling.

THE
DREAM

HENRY DE MONTHERLANT

Translated from the French by
Terence Kilmartin

with an introduction by
PETER QUENNELL

THE MACMILLAN COMPANY   NEW YORK
A DIVISION OF THE CROWELL-COLLIER PUBLISHING COMPANY

C. 3

First American Edition, 1963

INTRODUCTION

Le Songe, its author's first novel and second published work, made its original appearance in 1922, when Henry de Montherlant was twenty-six. Seriously wounded in 1918, he embarked upon its composition early in the following year; and his recent experiences furnished his story with its atmosphere and scenic background. Because his widowed mother, a somewhat possessive invalid, had begged him, so long as her life lasted – and she knew that she must very soon die – not to join a fighting regiment, he had begun by allowing himself to be enrolled in the auxiliary services of the French army. His play, *L'Exil*, which, although written in 1914, remained unpublished until 1929, describes both his personal dilemma and the clash of temperaments that his mother's attitude provoked. But Madame de Montherlant's death at length released him from his grudging promise; and he immediately applied for permission to serve with a famous infantry corps, the Twentieth, '*alors célèbre pour sa belle conduite*'. He obtained special permission to serve as a combatant; at the same time, he retained his auxiliary rank; and in this role he had far more freedom of action than would have been granted to the ordinary infantryman. Then a shell-burst ended his military career; and, having been cited for his courage in the field and received the cross of the *combattant volontaire*, he returned reluctantly to civil life.

Just as his experiences had been those of a *franc-tireur* – a part that, in literature and in life, Henry de Montherlant has very often played – so his account of them bears little resemblance to any of the other war-novels, French, English or American, that depict World

War I and World War II. There the protagonist tends to merge his identity in a cumulative impression of human suffering: here the author focuses our interest upon the private fortunes of a single character, and war is introduced merely as the outward crisis that, by sharpening his sense of his own identity, helps to stimulate his individual growth. Not that the novelist's pictures of the front line lack distinction or dramatic verve. Henry de Montherlant, when he chooses to employ it, shows an extraordinary descriptive talent; and in *Le Songe* he employs it much more freely and abundantly than in his later, soberer and less lyrical books. A passage may be selected at random. Warfare, through a soldier's eyes, is a combination of violent, terrifying activity and mournful, deadening inactivity; a shell explodes, scattering destruction; but, under the light of a livid summer noon, its sluggish smoke, as it hangs on the air, recalls the foliage of some huge unruffled tree:

> *La plaine en avant de la forêt de C—— s'étend à perte de vue comme un océan dont les lisières de la forêt seraient les falaises. Ce 23 juillet 1918, la chaleur accable. Il est midi. Le ciel sans un nuage n'est pas bleu mais grisâtre, comme si, de même que le fer rouge, il avait pâli à force de chaleur: la lumière est livide et les ombres sont faibles; on dirait que se prépare une éclipse. A l'ouest, l'horizon, que la poussière rend indiscernable, est bouché par un tapage incessant de mitrailleuses.*
> *Vers là-bas s'en va la route (qui ignore tout), blanche comme de l'ivoire ou du lait. Au loin, en bordure de cette route, trois, quatre obus éclatent. On voit la fumée du dernier rester un long temps immobile avant de se défaire, noire comme l'encre, si dense et si nettement découpée qu'on croirait un grand arbre solitaire dans l' étendue.*

This fantastic infernal landscape is not devoid of human figures; and just as vivid are Montherlant's impressions of soldiers in a village behind the lines, or of a farmyard crowded with French and enemy wounded, most of whom already bear the mark of death. But it is among the living, rather than among the dead – in passion, ambition and the will to survive – that the author finds his true subject.

6

Le Songe, above all else, is a discussion of love, and of the various divergent forms that love assumes. We are confronted with the hero's carnal affection for his undemanding, ever-satisfying mistress – *tant que je serai sûr de celle qui a nom Douce, sûr de pouvoir établir le contact avec elle, me charger d'elle comme d'un fluide électrique, je serai soulevé et porté par l'esprit de victoire qui brise toutes choses; tout me sera possible, tout me sera permis.* But we are also told of his exalted attachment to the beautiful young athlete Dominique, who only loses her hold on his imagination when she attempts to step down to the level of the senses. Montherlant's hero, Alban de Bricoule, is both an aesthetic hedonist and a Nietzschean man of action; he lives feverishly in the present, but no less feverishly in the past, which gives the present day its real meaning. '*Partout, dans le livre* (wrote a contemporary critic) *les grands exemples du passé . . . doublent le récit. Alban de Bricoule vit . . . avec un peuple de fantômes qui, tour à tour, l'excitent ou le découragent, le secourent ou l'accablent.*' He is fascinated particularly by the frieze of the Parthenon; and in that frieze, as an austere Athenian virgin, Dominique seems to have her proper place. She forfeits it by attempting to become his lover and ensnare him in her sensual-sentimental toils; at which he refuses her love and roughly reasserts his independence. For Alban welcomes the carefree, uncomplicated sensuality that he enjoys between the arms of Douce, and cherishes the pure unexacting friendship that binds him to his naïve companion Prinet; but he rejects the spurious blend of passion and sentiment, which is all the unhappy Dominique can offer.

In every good novel, there appear to be certain episodes that form the imaginative nucleus of the story; though they are not necessarily the chapters or paragraphs that, on the surface, make the greatest show. Such is Montherlant's description of how Alban, Prinet and a fellow soldier plod wearily towards the front, across the torrid and breathless landscape portrayed in the passage I have already quoted; and how Alban shoots Prinet's dog because its barkings and gambollings may perhaps attract a German plane. Wounded to the heart, Prinet leaves his side and walks off into the hostile distance; and Alban, as he watches him go, is ashamed momentarily to call his friend back:

> Il eut l'impulsion d'appeler, de courir. L'image: 'Moi courant après Prinet' l'emplit de honte, le cloua au sol. Il resta immobile, les yeux fixés sur cette toute petite chose vivante dans l'étendue ... 'Il ne se retournera même pas!' A l'instant que jaillissait de lui ce reproche, il vit le garçon se retourner vers lui, grimaçant contre le soleil, mais sans s'arrêter, sans s'arrêter. Il ne bougea pas, le masque illisible, avouant toutefois par sa seule attitude: 'Oui, j'attendais quelque chose de toi.' Une seconde encore ils furent face à face, non cœur à cœur; puis l'aspirant se détourna. Et plus jamais Alban ne devait voir son visage.

In the construction of Montherlant's story, Alban's quarrel with his friend, and Prinet's complete disappearance amid the gathering storm of battle, strikes me as far more significant than his troubled relationship with Dominique. For Prinet represents a theme that reappears in many later books – the theme of masculine friendship and martial comradeship; to which Montherlant opposes the contrasted theme of love as it exists between the sexes. Dominique, like Soledad, the heroine of his next novel, remains always a romantic lay-figure; whereas Prinet seems to have emerged from the deepest regions of the author's memory. *Le Songe* is a young man's novel and shows some of the accompanying defects. Here and there, the style is rhetorical and declamatory, and reveals the influence of d'Annunzio. But it is also a remarkably original work; and, when it appeared, it was welcomed by critics as a lasting contribution to twentieth-century French literature. '*Dans l'ensemble,* (wrote Daniel Halévy) *j'y trouve la volupté, et elle est vraie, la combativité, et elle est vraie, la pitié, et elle est vraie.*' Jean-Louis Vaudoyer added his own analysis of the novelist's peculiar approach to life: '*Comme un artiste grec idéalisait des corps, M. de Montherlant idéalise les impression physiques, ce qu'il regarde, ce qu'il touche devient la nourriture de sa pensée.*' It is this gift of poetic assimilation, shown in the fusion of sensuous and intellectual imagery, that gives the book its literary value. No one, I think, can fully appreciate such mature novels as *Les Célibataires* or *Les Jeunes Filles*, who has not begun with a reading of *Le Songe*, which foreshadows the novelist's future triumphs, and sketches out, in experimental shape, so many of his most passionately held convictions.

PETER QUENNELL

PART ONE

PART ONE

I

He Rejects the Crown of Thorns

LIKE A sick man trying to raise himself on his elbows, Alban de Bricoule leaned out of the wrought-iron chair and gulped for air, literally suffocated by his soul. And once more he was in communion with the world, with all those soft and tender things that live in gentleness of spirit. He caught the scent of the roses diluted in the moist air, the minute trembling of the grass, a branch of wistaria which hung there, translucent, like some divine hand, the finest of the roses, deep red, with the leaves on its stem reddened as if the flower had bled upon them, or as if it were light itself and they reflection. He wanted it to give him more. He took it out of the basket, inhaled it deeply, and when he had exhausted this sensation, desire was overtaken by desire, as one wave overtakes another, and pressing his mouth against the firm, sweet heart of the flower, he bit into it, and remained there motionless. Moment of stillness. Then, joyless but satisfied, he crushed the spent thing.

> *Fall of Troy, year of the world 2820; 1884* BC
> *Foundation of Rome, year of the world 3254; 754* BC
> *Marathon, year of the world 3154; 490* BC

He smiled with his eyes. So that was what he had been transcribing, sitting at the little garden table on this mild day of March 1918, when a sudden need for relaxation had made him take up the brochure which had arrived with the morning mail together with the Provençal flowers he had just so harshly misused – this gazette

13

from the college where he had completed his studies five years ago. He glanced swiftly through the obituary notices, through the letters from servicemen, his schoolfellows, through all the names which were the names of living people, of people who could struggle, desire, calculate, make others weep. He who so often had spoken of his 'soul-obsession', who had called himself a 'guardian of souls', how quickly he skimmed over all these souls! 'Poor fellows, did I love them? Yes, as Caesar loved his legionaries. But I hated them sometimes, I'm sure of that, hated them when I saw them bent over their books, improving themselves, in other words arming themselves against me.' And now his eyes went back to an item which he read again, as though not quite understanding it, or as though it were his own name he read there:

TO THE MEMORY OF
JACQUES DEJOIE
Lieutenant in the 152nd Infantry Regiment,
Croix de Guerre,
Chevalier de la Légion d'Honneur
Killed in action June 12th, 1917,
aged 22

At school, he had hardly known this dead youth who was his own age. Since school, how often had he spoken to him? Three or four times, perhaps. They had never written to each other, he had never known his address, he could not remember a single word they had exchanged which had not been banal. And now here he was, having known of his death for six months, yet with his hands trembling over this miserable booklet, and his cheeks burning.

'And I? And I?' For the fourth or fifth time, as one's eyes irresistibly stray back towards a corpse; for the fourth or fifth time, as we take up again, to die therein, the newspaper which merely prints the name of the woman we thought we no longer loved; for the fourth or fifth time, he took up the gazette and started reading again . . .

Here were the struggles and hopes of this boy Dejoie, the memory

14

of the day when he first took up a machine-gun, and all the expressions of a twenty-year-old – 'When I get back, I'll have to . . .', 'I know I'm protected' – all those affirmations of life which are invariably engraved upon tombstones. As he read, it seemed to him that every line written by the good Father had been written with him, Alban de Bricoule, in mind, had been written *against* him, and when he had finished he shook his head as though he had just drunk something bitter. A sentence stood out in the forefront of his consciousness, clear, indisputable, isolated from all others as by the frame of a phylactery: 'I am horribly jealous of this dead boy.'

Ah! holy jealousy, and with what love in it! This dead boy who was no friend of his had entered into him as a wasp enters a room, and was making an enormous noise there. Everything was stirring, everything was catching fire again. The names of the boys in the list of *Addresses at the Front* looked like the names of the runners in a race-card. 'Who will be first? Who will fall? Who will refuse a jump? Who will be boxed in by his rivals?' Heat emanated from them as though he were leaning over a forge. He felt a lump in his chest choking him, a feverish impatience as if the shade of the dead youth loomed in front of him, barring his way; and he flung himself at it, he riddled it with revolver shots, but it remained intact and he could not take another step. Ambition, like a vampire, had suddenly pounced on him, clamping him down with her claws, and he struggled impotently beneath her; motionless in his chair, no longer able to lift his eyes, no longer able to look at anything but the gravel, the legs of the table, the earth in the flowerbeds, no longer able to lift his eyes. And through his impotence flashed like lightning the most absurd moments of his malady.

He saw himself again as he was on those evenings when his reading of Roman history literally went to his head, when he really felt that the grandeur of it all was unsettling his mind. At these moments his movements would lose their assurance, he could no longer eat, the whole of the lower part of his face became paralysed as though with terror . . . 'What can I do against this disease? Pre-eminence is indispensable to me; I see nothing attractive in it: it is simply that I can't imagine life without it. I am not interested in happiness.'

Names on a card, a race ... Ah! If it had been a race at this moment, he would have overtaken them all; had it been a fight, he would have strangled them all, flung them all broken at his feet! But what could be done against a Dejoie, a monstrous ghost who plays Charlemagne, who goes off, his glory already won, leaving you with no chance of ever being able to humble him? What could be done against the simplicity of his action when you yourself were at your work-table, when you could only oppose him with a certain power of mind, or knowledge, or memory, or genius? His elbows on the table, holding his head in his hands like a rotten fruit, Alban squeezed the thing enveloped in bone and hair, his brain, limp as a sponge, taking up no more room than a billiard ball, but the only weapon that might enable him to conquer all his peers. When one measures one's own limitations in cold blood, one feels something big rising up inside, something grave and sad as after a failure, something which does one good. But when it seems to you that your brain is contracting at the same time as your eyebrows in an effort to increase its power, in an effort to gain something extra, there and then, as tangibly as when one adds something to a pair of scales, and when it fails to do so and you rush madly in every direction, and on all sides must pull up on the brink of your failings as on the edge of an abyss, surely this sensation could lead to madness ...

Suddenly, he pushed the table back, got up and took a few steps round the garden, where a crowd of little hopes began to flower. His two familiar cats, stretched out flat on their backs amusing themselves by flicking their bodies over from one side to the other with a jerk of the loins, got up as he approached and walked in front of him like pages: two blue persians, of the same size, with the same iron-grey fur, and both nameless.

'I have been mad,' he thought, sitting down on the grass and stroking with tenderly skilful fingers one of the soft, rounded heads (the beast's eyes were closed and she wore the imperceptible smile of one remembering something delicious). 'Why this self-distrust? I rely on myself alone and take only my own advice.' He knew very well that everything he wanted would be his, that all his ambitions would be achieved, one after the other; and the calm with which he anticipated his victories made him worthy of them all. 'Nothing can stop me – except illness . . . or death . . .' Unthinkingly he echoed the ancestral phrase: 'Unless the heavens fall upon me.'

In the grass, a pair of battling ants caught his attention. The bigger one was dragging the other away, swallowing it alive: part of the body had already disappeared, while the legs still struggled. He flicked them away: 'You bore me; go and suffer elsewhere,' then got up again.

'I must get away. Enough of Staff clerks and the wretched Ministry. (Following a badly-healed appendectomy, he had been assigned to the rear and sent to a ministry in Paris). 'Prinet, dear boy! *Amice primae admissionis!* He is with the . . th Infantry regiment; I shall join him' – (already he could not have tolerated anyone speaking ill of this regiment in his presence) – 'My brain has exhausted itself whilst my body was reviving. Henceforth I renounce thought. I reject the crown of thorns! Now I must take my rest in action.'

How many hours he had walked in this garden, imagining a certain presence at his side, imagining the questions and the answers! How often he had plunged his burning face in the jet of the fountain to soothe the perpetual fever which made him keep always on his table, close at hand, a jug of cool water! He looked about him. It seemed to him that the shoots in the neighbouring garden were more advanced than here. It seemed to him that because here he had exposed too much his heavy-heartedness, had thought, desired, hated and raged alone too much, the grass had burned up, the buds shrivelled, the wistaria scorched; and that even now, as he walked on, each sprig of green was imperceptibly drying up as he drew near, as if he were the sun.

'A dug-out, misery, death . . . But all purified, all simplified! The simplicity of action, the simplicity of war! In order to establish my intellectual and social influence, how much patience, work, skill, how many pitfalls! And I shall be criticized, not encouraged, by those I love; my best friends may well become my enemies; left to myself, who can assure me that I am on the right track, who can deliver me from doubt? But out there! To stand on a parapet, to go and look and then come back, to press a trigger – there's something clear and straightforward and immediately redounding to one's honour. There, values are sorted out and graded; everyone agrees about each one of them. How infinitely superior! And how restful!'

Suddenly he stiffened, his whole face instantly alive:

'The panthers!'

Raucous growls were coming from the Bois, on the edge of which Alban's villa stood. He had heard them many times, these panthers from the zoo; and when their irritable yawns, echoing through the silence of a summer night, reached his ears as he worked at his open window, an uneasy exaltation swept through him, his whole being soared towards Imperial Rome on the eve of the games. But today he only thought: 'So the wind is in the south,' and the words kindled his eternal nostalgia for the south, which merged with a feeling for the spring. He realized that behind his sudden need for war there was the fear that his life might not match the beauty of the spring, might be unworthy of the spring, that the beauty of the spring might remain unused, wasted. At this very moment, perhaps, roused by the same emotions, others were deciding to leave for Lake Maggiore.

'A dug-out, misery, death . . . I shall show that I can endure the extremes of misery as I have endured the extremes of pleasure – like Alcibiades, and Caesar, and Catilina. I shall suffer, I shall atone for my sins. I have sinned, O God, I have sinned! I have caused suffering and I have not suffered. I have raised my hand against a priest. In the confessional, I made a firm resolution to do my enemies every possible harm. And I confessed it! And I received absolution! But this time, all shall be washed clean. I shall seek more suffering,

18

as when, after leaving the woman I loved, who had just been cruel to me, I telephoned her with the sole object of hearing the harshness in her voice at the other end of the line. I shall volunteer for the most unpleasant duties; I shall bury the dead; and I shall take each one of these ordeals and offer it up to God for my salvation and the salvation of those I love. And all these trials, through the mere recital of the words "I offer it up", will be set down and used on my behalf . . .

'And what if I should die?' he asked himself suddenly. 'Certainly, death for death, a violent death is the most worthy of me.' Then a voice spoke, which was not quite his voice, but a voice speaking within him and saying: 'I am indifferent to death.'

Through his fever passed the girl whose name was Douce, the little silent girl who never refused herself to him and never caused him suffering – useless except for love, and then set gently but firmly aside. She was all around him like water, above and beneath him, and he lived in the midst of her as in the midst of a swift-flowing stream. 'Once more I shall kiss your forehead, on the little spot above the temple which always burns as if you were thinking! Once more I shall listen to that thing beating inside you, as if you had a heart! Once more the taste of your eyelids and your palms! Once more the smell of your hair!' The sudden overflowing of his sensuality tinged his thoughts with tenderness and infinite gratitude towards the healer of all pains. 'O you who lightened my heart! Even when my desire made you open your eyes so wide that the pupils no longer touched the rims of your eyelids, even at that moment of utter heaviness when the alcove of dawn is like a huge, grey-white moonstone, even when we so deliciously lent death a willing hand.'

His study was on the ground-floor, its windows open – a room assailed by the night as a ship's cabin by the sea. Climbing two steps, he went in.

He saw himself coming in the mirror, his hair ruffled by his habit of burying his hand in it in meditation, his dark face with the minute lines on his eyelids and in the faintly swollen flesh below the eyes;

there was something in him both burning and burnt out, a continual exhaustion in his body which was yet as strong as iron, which today might be steeped in pleasure and tomorrow would outdo the most ascetic in austerity, just as his voluptuous soul had mingled with the populace and given itself up to the most vulgar concerns in order to demonstrate its flexibility and affirm its mastery over life.

And all around were the books, some of them lying open on easels like the Gospel on an altar. All around were leaves of paper, the naked or half-naked gods, the chlorine solution for cleaning antique marble, the blanket which he wrapped around his legs when he was working furiously by lamplight at five o'clock in the morning, in the cold. Then there was the extract of vervain which he dabbed on his forehead, eyelids, neck and wrists; the table in the same disorder as the night before when sleep had overcome him, with that rather withered look of a place where one has spent a long time thinking but which has been unable to keep the thought alive; on the wall the bull's head between two banderillas, the iron points of which, blackened with dried blood, still had some of the brute's hairs clinging to them; Greek and Latin dictionaries on the floor; and here and there, a dead leaf from last winter that the wind had blown in through the window or a cat brought in stuck to its tail, looking, for the moment, like some little Dionysian creature. Above this battlefield of his victories and defeats, higher than the books, higher than the works of art, towered a huge anatomical figure. The human flower. The music of the world made flesh! Let us pause awhile.

Meanwhile, Alban's eyes had come to rest on an ivory crucifix which stood radiant in the middle of his table. It was a Louis XIII crucifix framed in oak, with the shimmer of something streaming wet, small vertical cracks in the ivory suggesting trickles of sweat and blood.

He looked at it. 'Why is your breast swollen like that, just as ours are in the stadium, when we stand panting after the four-hundred metres? Are you, too, consumed by your own heart?'

Often he had pressed his lips to this image of Christ scarcely knowing what he was kissing, whether it was the face of his God, or the miracle of art, or simply the beauty, the softness and the desirability of the substance, so full of warmth it seemed to him to give out an aroma akin to that of human flesh. He had kissed it, he had named it the presiding genius of his work and object of his *veni creator's*. He had asked it to make him more worthy, begged from it the power to create the secret phrase which would bring to his altar 'those who call God the secret of the woods'. And such was the arrangement of the room that, sitting at his table, the young man could see himself beneath the outstretched arms of Christ, reflected in the glass of his bookcase against the dark background of the bindings. And beside them, suspended in mid-air, true ghost of a world grown cold, a diaphanous female face, glowing with a mysterious whiteness that made a translucent aura of the shadows round it: the marble sculpture brought back from Achaie which, foaming like the froth on beer, sparkling like the sparkling crystals of sodium borax, came from the other end of the room to cast its reflection, like a head leaning over a shoulder, beside those of Alban and the cross.

On the table stood a photograph. Alban picked it up and let his eyes linger on it.

The girl stood looking out at him, upright, unsmiling, a finger marking her place in a book, without jewel or ring, with only an ivory bracelet on the strong young wrist; upright, with her straight nose, her tightly twisted hair lying close to the head and low over the forehead, her mouth a little hard, her eyebrows slightly knit, her serious eyes in which you seemed to see a soul, and beyond it another, and beyond that yet another. And the look in the young man's eyes, as he met hers, was one of the most beautiful in the world. A male look, a noble, manly look, full of admiration, of respect, of comradeship, of gratitude, a look neither sensual nor lingering, like a frank handshake. Plato said: 'A lover is a friend in whom one senses something divine.' The eyes of the young man defined the girl, although she was not a lover, as a friend in whom one senses something divine.

Alban tilted the picture. On the cover of the book held in the bronzed hand, the two words of the title glowed triumphantly: *Taciti Opera.*

'Dominique . . . Ah yes, it is good that she exists. How glad I am that she does! My beautiful girl, how satisfying you are! What a joy for the mind! O invulnerable one!'

'Am I going to die?' he asked himself.

'No, of course I cannot die.' The existence of this girl preserved him from death. 'Even so?' He looked at her once more. And a voice rose, emanating not quite from him, coming from someone else, a voice born in him but not entirely sanctioned by him: 'I am indifferent to death.'

Down in the garden again, as he was closing the college gazette, Alban noticed that earlier, while he was deep in thought, he had absent-mindedly made a little sign opposite the name of a school-fellow, then of another, then another. A sign? What sign? Suddenly he recognized it: it was a printer's delete sign: 'Let him be destroyed' – 'Let him be destroyed' – 'Let him be destroyed.' And with a shudder of shame, he covered the appalling signs with ink.

2

Sister of Victories

'I MUST *hold fast*, Alban,' said Dominique Soubrier, leaning on the table in her father's drawing-room – and with a light tap she smoothed a crease in her pearl-grey dress. 'Can you understand how much those words mean: hold fast? When you told me so bluntly, I might almost say so rudely, a few moments ago, that you were leaving, you did not see me either falter or complain – that would be contrary to our code,' she added in a lower voice, as if she wanted the words to be said and not heard. 'But now I understand more clearly the threat this news of yours holds for me. Why should I pretend to ignore it? Are we the sort of people who need to pretend? No, nothing will be altered by my telling you quite simply that I have reached a higher level of being with you beside me. And now you are going, and I have no idea what will become of me on my own.'

'Is that a question?' the young man asked.

'Yes, if you want to answer it.'

'Then it's not a question.'

'Ah,' she said regretfully. 'And why not?'

'Because I deny myself the right to advise you while I know you so little. People think I am perceptive. They do not know the extent of my blindness.'

'Your indifference to people is appalling. How could you ever make the effort to understand them?'

'It's true, I only like the people I like. I don't like those who mean nothing to me; it's inconceivable, isn't it? But what darkness there is in those I love best! I see in you many things which I assume are easy to grasp but, if I try, I come up against something straight away, as a trapped bird might kill itself against the glass of this bay window by plunging into what looks like the open sky.'

The large bay window, one single pane rising to the full height of the drawing-room, made a screen between them and the Ranelagh gardens so transparent as to be indeed invisible. Beyond it could be seen the spring lawns, the women, the babies, all the nicest things, and a group of little girls engaged in those games and pummellings that always end in embraces.

She said:

'Where shall I turn for advice?'

And suddenly to discover that she, the stalwart girl, with her square shoulders, her helmet of hair, her heroic hands that flung the javelin in the stadium, with those strong features so often clenched against the wind of a race, clenched until they assumed a splendid ugliness, with her tough, chaste, wild soul – suddenly to discover that *she* could be troubled by something coming from *his* mind, something which his mind could choose whether or not to call into being, made him feel embarrassed and displeased, as though this corporal marvel, by depending upon the product of a mere intellect, had fallen short of the divine plan through his fault.

'Where shall I turn for advice?'

Absent-mindedly, he was fingering some scattered art albums. In one of them, which he half-opened, he saw the reproduction of a naked form, and his heart beat faster, as it always did at the sight of uncovered flesh. And he spread the book open, as if from this spring of human freshness they might receive sympathy and sustenance.

She understood his meaning and sat down wearily; art was indeed like life: comforting when one was happy. And then, propping the album on the edge of the table, they bent their separate heads over it.

Across the wide photogravure plates rode the horsemen of the

Parthenon. Page after page they rode by, all alike, now jostling each other in a wave, now one by one like men of quality. And the little horses reared up in the same rhythm, so nervous and quivering and yet so well-behaved, even the one who kicked up his heels towards the sky with a kind of peaceful exultation; and the boys rode on their backs, 'suckled among flowers', their calm brows slightly bent beneath the light-hearted science of Silenus; and as they bowed their heads a little, while gazing steadily straight ahead, their half-veiled pupils were lost in dreams. And all looked straight ahead, save one who tore his face away from the semi-darkness of the collective profile, and stared straight out at you, as if it were from the stone itself that he wished to wrench his face, from the stone, from oblivion, from death, from one knew not what terrible bondage, in order to fling it alive into eternity; and Alban felt such an affinity between himself and this figure that he threw back his head, overcome with emotion. Had he, too, not tried, by means of art, to wrench from his life the moments of beauty and sweetness and turn them into something that might preserve him from death? And, as the girl was looking at the opposite page, he grasped her arm above the elbow in a comradely gesture, to call her attention to the touching figure. And he felt the arm stiffen in an impulse of withdrawal, try to free itself from him, struggling like the wing of a bird. And he smiled, and was filled with pleasure as though, instead of making this gesture of refusal, she had suddenly fallen into his arms, all loose-jointed and weak with love.

The solitary horseman had passed by; once more they were all on the move. Great scars in the stone tore gaps in the dream. Now one glimpsed only a streaming mane, or a swan-like neck, or a hand resting idly on a crupper as earlier it might gently have fingered the fleece of a lamb, or a long human leg, smooth and supple, divine in repose. And now here they all were facing in the opposite direction as though they were coming back, as though they had reached their goal and were coming back, and there was something inexpressibly strange and moving in seeing them return like this with dreamy eyes and bowed heads, animals and men in the same rhythm, all equal in this brotherhood of grace. And as page followed page, the young man's heart swelled, as a symphony swells with the entry of each new instrument, and his voice was no longer entirely his own when he raised his head, bursting with music as a full view of the temple appeared, and said:

'Purity, Dominique! How many of us who render homage to the Blessed Virgin dare remember that the most famous pagan monument was dedicated to purity? The Parthenon: the temple of the Maiden! Look at it,' he said, blushing as if it were not an idea he had just stumbled upon, but a mistress unexpectedly glimpsed among the indifferent crowd. 'Its columns, having no base, seem to spring up out of water. They are the strength of Man, rooted knee-deep in the earth, supporting the world on its shoulders ... You know, what I find so remarkable is that this temple of the Maiden is built in the Doric style, as if the Athenians, since the guardian of their city was a woman, had wanted her abode at least to remind them constantly that she was also part of the male order.'

He stopped, for his heart was pounding in his throat, and looked at her breathing gently, bowed over the album, the topmost sheet of which, slightly raised, flattened against the one below each time she breathed upon it.

'If only you knew how I have wandered from woman to woman before reaching you, the patience, the goodwill I have shown, all the allowances I have had to make for them, all I have had to forgive them! And then, one day, there would be something, I don't know what, a phrase, a laugh, a way of clapping their hands or playing the piano, and they would fall back into their own paltry world, back inside that little circle of pleasure out of which I struggled to drag them. So that when I am with you, I am like a scientist facing the solution to a problem which has baffled him for years: amazed, incredulous, a little anxious because of that terribly delicate balance ... My dear, how mysterious it is that you satisfy me so utterly! As one moves around a statue which is equally

26

beautiful on all sides, I can move around you always at the same level of happiness . . .'

He stopped, and was silent. A flower was born from his silence, as in Indian music-notation the drawing of a lotus indicates the end of a song.

The girl's black hair, tightly twisted over each ear, then falling over the forehead to the eyebrows, framed and clasped her head. And the face emerged from it like a fruit half out of its husk, the moist mouth resembling the wound in the pulp at the place where it has been bitten. But the dark skin was smoother than the skin of a fruit, which is always ribbed and veined. Tightly drawn, polished as by some delicate varnish, it had the uniformity of metal or sky, pink on the cheeks only and darkening towards the neck where the frontiers of the body already introduced something animal, making one want to squeeze it with both hands. The mark of an old scar above the lip was like that of a fingernail on wax. And every time some feature of this face provoked in Alban a wave of desire there came, too, a wave of gravity, beginning further away, deeper down, in a vast sea glittering somewhere far off; and this wave would override the other and destroy it, as the ground-swell overrides and destroys the foam of the sea as it dies along the shore. Each beauty as it rose was instantly laid low, replaced, and the new one felled in turn, like soldiers on a rampart.

When he had first seen her a year ago, at 'Palestra', her knees flashing round the stadium in the thousand metres, she had given him a supreme joy with the majesty of her stride and the grandeur of her style. He had wanted her, warm and dazed with exertion after the winning-post, amid the panting of victory or defeat, with the glow of the venture gathered on the still unflushed face. But his desire had gone no further. For, as he came to know her better, she had revealed to him a feeling which at its peak of perfection excluded desire, which desire would have distorted and cheapened. Why then continue to seek in this girl, who could only lose by it, that pleasure which so many others would gain by giving him?

All the blood had risen from the depths of his being into his brain.

27

For hours he would remain enveloping her with his eyes, empty of desire, and then on leaving her would overwhelm, destroy the child Douce, so admirably stupid, and always desired the more in proportion to her stupidity: precious girl, who had enabled him almost to relive the sensations of the ancient demi-god marrying a fabulous goose. During this same period, Alban became aware that what was peculiar to his genius was comradeship. He knew that he was capable of friendship, he knew that he was capable of desire; he knew that he was not capable of love; but comradeship with young men of his own age, this he had developed to perfection. Clearly distinguishing it from friendship, he had made of it something more attractive than friendship, because it was not self-regarding, whereas friendship is, like love. And between Dominique and himself he had fashioned this, his own creation: a comradeship full of wonder. They had wanted and made themselves equals, equals yet with an element of piety underneath it all, no matter what they did, because one was a man and the other a woman.

Meanwhile, a little girl, who had just crossed the garden with her nurse, came hopping into the drawing-room.

'Oh, Dominique, I found such a lovely pebble!'

She held out a very ordinary, pinkish little pebble.

'I don't want your pebble, it's horrible,' said Dominique. 'Who is she?'

'A little cousin of mine. She comes here from time to time and creates havoc in the garden.'

She was overwhelmingly sweet in her rejected offer, this slender Psyche, so like the one on sarcophagi who represents the soul descending to Hades on the speckled wings of a butterfly. Her wondering eyes devoured the narrow face, her skin was fair as the tender wood of a freshly felled tree; the sumptuous, tawny hair, flowing in a compact wave, parted a little at the nape of the neck, and a pink ear emerged from it like a tiny rock of pale coral from the middle of a golden torrent in some enchanted valley.

As she insisted, begging for the acceptance of her gift:

'Do leave me alone,' Dominique interrupted angrily. 'Leave me alone!'

'Dominique,' said Alban (who could feel in his fingers a growing desire to stroke the child's hair), 'Dominique, how cruel you are!'

He would have liked to question her playfully: 'Have you never walked beside her, holding her by the belt of her little sailor's coat? Has she never walked around the lawn on the croquet hoops, resting her hand on your bare neck? Have you never had a secret to tell her, lifted her curls away from her ear and whispered it to her, then lightly tapped the curl back over her ear?'

But he merely said, looking at the heart-rending frailty of the small body:

'What I find moving about her is the promise of her power.'

'Her power . . . how shameful!'

That a man should throw a woman into a state of emotional turmoil was all very well, thought Dominique, since women were only too happy to have emotional disturbances to help pass the time. But that a woman, the silly bird this little girl would one day become, should influence a man's life! Would it not be inconceivable for a man even to speak to a woman if desire were not involved? She looked over towards the Ranelagh gardens, and saw the women hanging on the arms of their lovers like spineless creatures who would otherwise weakly collapse like great, dressed-up slugs; and on the gravel in front of the benches, the patterns made by the umbrellas of the eavesdropping old ladies; and the benches and the bowers and the statues, all marked by the hopes and memories, the schemes and torments of the heart. Once she had caught a couple kissing, and thought: 'How stupid and ugly it is, a face offering itself, that tilted, straining thing with its look of happiness . . .'

And yet at the same moment she remembered that two days before, as the workmen were coming out of the factories, she had overheard the remark of a young apprentice on his way to some open space, his football kit under his arm. 'Half-wits!' the youth had muttered as he passed the entwined couples. And she had been shocked, and had shrugged her shoulders, not at them, but at him!

Whence came this contradiction? And since the main goal of her inner life was to escape from her sex, particularly through sport, how was it that she could not sympathize with this new generation of athletic young men who took no interest in women, despised romance and even jeered at sensuality?

Now more than ever, upset as she was by Alban's departure, she could feel this contradiction within herself, the implacable opposition between the universe of sport and that of the heart, an opposition which was confirmed by the fact that amongst her comrades at Palestra all those who reached the highest class in athletics were heart-free, and which perhaps could only have been dispelled by some loving friendship nourished within the stadium and identified with it.

As a dog or a child will remind you of its existence in order to earn a caress, a puff of air came in bearing the fragrance of grass at dusk. A pigeon flew up from the doorstep, and there was a pink sheen on its belly and under its wings from the rays of the setting sun.

A clock struck the half-hour. Alban said:

'I must go.'

'Ah! So it's now . . .'

A wave of anguish washed over her. The fear of seeming to weaken, the fear of being like everyone else in this leave-taking scene already experienced by millions of others, made her dumb. She sat there, fighting for breath, with one leg crossed over the other, staring at her foot which quivered with each heartbeat.

And Alban, too, was looking at her leg, at the warm, strong pulp, its delicate strength stretching the black silk of her stocking. How that leg, bare in the stadium, had tormented him! He would have liked to keep it for ever, to possess it totally, a possession compared with which kisses and caresses are nothing; seeing it there in front of him he realized his powerlessness, he was tortured by the impossible, and it gave him a sense of the infinite . . . And once again he felt, as he had felt earlier, an angry protest of his whole being at the idea that this girl, so magnificently consummate in her body, could be injured by a soul, could depend upon a soul – yes, *that* body,

30

upon *his* soul! And his only reaction to the girl's cry was: 'Victory, sister of Victories, are you not ashamed to need me?' And he worshipped life at the front, immersion in the elementary, the utter annihilation of intellect and heart.

He gave her his address, which she wrote down in silence, and they exchanged a few words. Then they gave up the struggle against silence.

It was the silence of the antique hour which men once called the hour of Hermes, because this god presided over everything that flows away and passes, the road, the twilight, youth, the sweetness of the flesh. People were now getting up from the benches. Above the children's playground, the sun was dying behind bare trees, like a red balloon caught in the branches. A swallow flashed past, swept round a tree like a chariot on the race-course. Was it an uneasiness she had always felt (which perhaps all women feel), as the shadows thickened? Was it because this rising wave of darkness foreshadowed the change coming over her life? As she stared at those great blocks of flats so pale against the lifeless blue of the western sky, those great gaunt buildings covered with a strangely livid glow, she felt as if she were entering an eternal night, alone, forsaken, as if in the depths of a forest. It was a physical sensation so unbearable that she stretched her arms out in front of her.

She put her hand on his shoulder as though she were blind. Facing him, close to him, closer than she had ever been, almost touching his chest, she looked at him fixedly, her hand resting on him; he did not move. Often, when alone with him in this drawing-room or in the street, amid all the appearances of love, she had felt, and he had felt with her, the necessity and the exquisite pleasure of denying the appearances and of asserting their detachment. Now, once more, she sensed keenly that he was right to make no move-ment; that no doubt he was even struggling not to make a gesture that might destroy the equilibrium they had vowed between them; that he was true to what he had always been, to what they had always prided themselves on being. And yet she felt chilled at the thought that he could emerge victorious from this struggle. And she remained there, with her hand on his shoulder, as though someone had caught her stealing from a drawer, and she had not attempted to run away, giving up all pretence, accepting everything.

Suddenly she looked at him in horror, with her clear eyes which would have remained dry beside a death-bed. She had the sudden feeling that together they had begotten something monstrous, like some mis-shapen child. No precise reason occurred to her, it was simply an uprising of the depths of her being, but so violent that her eyes avoided him and dropped with a hitherto unknown embarrassment, and she drew her hand away in shame.

He moved towards the door. She followed him.

'Good-bye, fidelity,' the voice said.

'Good-bye,' she said, lifting up to him for the last time the sadness of her face, like a silent prayer.

He grasped her hand, her fine hand so muscular and limpid, soft as a horse's muzzle. After a few seconds – how did it happen? – she felt that it was she, Dominique, who was holding his hand. Scarcely had she become conscious of it than she freed herself, glanced at her wrist-watch, said: 'Ah, five to six, I must hurry,' and Alban found himself alone.

3

In Love with the Front

'As long as I can be sure of the girl whose name is Douce, sure of being able to establish contact with her, charge myself with her as with an electric current, I shall be uplifted and borne by the spirit of victory which breaks down everything; all will be possible for me, all will be permitted. My certainty that she will always consent – that is my mainstay, my guiding light. Dominique, with her mind and her soul, is an inestimable boon to me. But you, Douce, with your body alone, you are the very legislator of my life!'

The train ran on, carrying towards the front those who had left their homes at the appointed hour, taking with them their thoughts, their memories, their loves, all their invisible possessions which moved with them through space. In a corner of the carriage Alban gently put his hand to his face, smelt on his fingers a faint odour of gum, the odour of a young flesh that was not his own. Clinging odour of caressed bodies! It sticks to the fingers like the dust of a butterfly's wing. Alban had deliberately refrained from washing his hands that morning; as much as possible he had avoided touching anything, so that nothing might disturb this odour which lingered on and on, as though the body of the girl whose name was Douce had torn from itself this secret fragment which prolonged her presence for a few hours beyond their parting.

Vaguely, through the window, he saw the thin clusters of bushes fly past, and the deserted plain with its long pools of greenish water. Vaguely, in fits and starts, the men around him existed for him.

Then he was filled with the desire to pass them his wine, his food; to make room for them so that they might be more comfortable: the great brotherhood of sport had put him on a level with the people. And then his inner life would shroud them and devour them, his own life, that hung so heavy in that train.

'I am going to the front line, to join an infantry company, in the Hautes Vosges, for the pleasure of it. I hope I am going to enjoy myself. Even so, I'd have enjoyed a journey to Spain even more.' An hour ago, before the barrier which kept the civilians away from the platform, time had stopped for a moment, six couples petrified at the pinnacle of their embrace, while the crowd whirled around them. Two hours ago, at home, with the haversacks shut and the car expected, there had been a moment of silence and emptiness, all having been said and done. Defenceless against the sudden inaction, his mother had fallen on her knees, sobbing:

'Will you say a *Hail Mary*?'

He had knelt, tense with displeasure at having to yield to pathos. She had got up and had asked:

'Did you say it?'

He had answered 'yes' with the faint little voice of an unhappy child.

And four hours ago . . .

'How wonderful you are, Douce! How wonderful you are!' Time after time the phrase had sprung from him, involuntarily driven from his flesh to his mouth like the cry of a wounded man, amid the little groans of the child, limp and stiff and ah! contorted with pleasure. No part of his intellect was ever set to work by the child; no part of his heart either, except this false tenderness, the froth of lust. But a reality different from that of the intellect was contained in the words: 'how wonderful you are!' – 'O you, desire I am always sure of! O you, so frank and easy to please, so perfect, so aware of your purpose!'

Here, in this carriage, his body tinged with the fragrance of another body that was as much a part of him as his own, it seemed to him that a faded universe was floating in the half-light below a great sunlit peak. No light from this Limbo could seem luminous, none of its joys could be a joy for those who had once been transported to that peak. To him who had been able to tell Dominique in all sincerity: 'you satisfy me completely,' it appeared nonetheless, at this moment, when he was still stupefied with pleasure, that art, knowledge, the intercourse of minds and souls, offered only deception, inanition, dull suffering, a world full of insipid plains, of barriers, snares and mirages. Pleasure alone fulfilled its promise. Pleasure alone proved its case, attested beyond doubt that it was fulfilled. And that was why, when on the threshold of his ordeal he had had to stock up with strength and peace to last him four months, his instinct had made him choose, between the two women, to see Douce last. And he had made his way to the healer of all sorrows.

Suddenly he gave a start, as though in response to a musical summons. A camouflaged locomotive passed them, then a gun on a truck with the gunners sitting round it as in a *tableau vivant* on a carnival float. Leaning out of the window, he saw that they had left one world behind and reached another. No longer a single woman, no longer a single child, no more enemies in black and grey, but a people of blue men, blue like him, all of them his equals, all of them his brothers. He was overwhelmed with conflicting emotions, and ready to give his heart, which was now beating against the lowered window frame. He sniffed the air, and it seemed to him purer and as it were sacrosanct, like the air which bears the presentiments of the sea. But what presentiments were borne upon this air? Into what new country was he penetrating, with the sensation of moving forward to meet the night? Where was he going? He was plunging into a dream. He was going to the land of the front line, he was going *up there*. Up there . . . As words uttered in a tunnel reverberate endlessly, so the ancient words resounded, dragging long bow-strokes over the raw nerves of the soul. *Up there . . . depart . . . return . . .* What were the trains saying to each other, what dangers were they warning each other of, when they raised into space such long-drawn-out laments? Were they afraid? Did they think they

might never return? The gleaming length of the rails, their hallu-
cinating length, the panting of the engine, the vanishing smoke,
suggested things struggling, pulling free, getting away, irrevocable
things. Right and left, other trains ran alongside his, overtook it or
were overtaken either at once or else after having run side by side,
one knew not why, with the same mysterious purposes that puzzle
one in the patterns of a ballet. And all were going eastwards, sucked
along by that great gaping void behind the last perceptible line,
the invisible valley of death which fascinated them, drawing them
along their network like flies across a web towards the spider –
towards *there*, towards the calm horizon, with its woods, its houses
and hills, like all the horizons of the earth.

'Révigny!'

Some of the men got off: those who were going to Verdun. He
watched the faces of these men of Verdun, the grocers, the lawyer's
clerks, the roundsmen of tomorrow, men who do not belong to
'your class,' who live, suffer, bestir themselves without your being
aware of their existence. He put his fingers to his face, but
Douce's smell had gone. He felt his chest contract. This really was
their farewell. Or rather, it was as if Douce were rejecting him,
leaving him without hope. Childishly he looked at his wrist-watch,
and the gesture brought back Dominique's last gesture. He felt
alone, having broken away from everything that made up his life,
thrown by his own will into a huge machine where his own will no
longer counted, where Dominique and Douce and all his suprem-
acies no longer counted, a poor despised thing, manipulated by
ferocious hands which spread out all his flesh and all his soul so that
everyone might know that not a single particle of either was exempt
from the possibility of injury. And he was filled with a sort of sad
eagerness, a melancholy enthusiasm, a nostalgia whether for yesterday or for tomorrow he did not know, an exquisite self-pity. He
was going, he wanted to go; with all his might he was straining
towards the new land as towards a new happiness; and in the same
moment he experienced this long-drawn-out regret, this prolonged
lamentation in a minor key, this apprehension of misery and death.

Ah, was it not, this mixture of attraction and hate, was it not really love?

In love with the front . . . He remembered the words of Socrates: 'I can only love.' And he, too, was there nothing he could do without that madness? His fanatical patriotism, his passion for the Christian thing, his love of valour, his craving for knowledge, had all the characteristics of love; his exasperations and absurdities had something sensual about them. He had wanted these abstractions, panted after them, seen them laid out in front of him and adored in a delirious, wordless pleasure. And he accepted the front in the same way as, twice before, on the threshold of love, he had hesitated and then, by a deliberate act, had accepted love with all the confusion it brought: the obsession, the waste of time, the slackening of his rhythm of life and work, Penelope's purple night which would destroy the patient work of his untiring intellect.

The idea intoxicated him. Without any military knowledge, ridiculously out of training, having even lost the habit of walking, the madness of his action saved him. To this brilliant and irrational nature, anything justified itself by being extreme enough: the strong man finding rest in the extreme. The countless forseeable sufferings became for him but variations on the beauty of living, opposed to happiness, but no less desirable than happiness. For the thousandth time, the strong man interchanged values, melted down the barriers, recomposed quite arbitrarily a world fitting and favourable to him. All was resolved in exultation. Not for an instant did he feel that he was doing his duty, for he did not feel unhappy.

On the platform, hunched beneath the heavy load which yet lifted him, as though with wings, up to an heroic sense of selfhood, Alban stood motionless for a while. He had felt, in front of this rough village of the Vosges, the same pang of love as for a being of his own blood. A fallen house, the mouth of a shelter, helmeted men on guard, no hint of frivolity or comfort: only life stripped bare and arched, ready to wound, to defend itself, to face the adversary. 'Holy order of Manhood, holy kingdom of the strong, you have been mine since I was at the breast, being rocked to sleep on a bronze shield. Let me die if I must, since I shall be dying in a world I accept.'

Then he saw Prinet standing up in a car parked in front of the station, Prinet looking round for him, and his heart leapt. With his raincoat revealing only the black collar of the *Chasseurs* (he had retained the uniform of his old regiment), with his 'tank' beret over his forehead, he was indeed the same tall, rather gawky boy who had walked up the Rue Soufflot two years previously, his books wrapped in a small cloth cover under his arm. Their year together as students came flooding back to him. And he stood there without making himself known, letting the harmless deception go on awhile, watching with an obscure pride the look on another's face when he is expecting you, you alone and no one else among the crowd, and longs to see you, and his face will light up when he sees you . . .

He moved forward, they saw each other and were soon exchanging empty words: 'A car?' – 'I've borrowed the divisional car, we'll go down to Granrupt . . .' while Prinet held his hand, shaking it a little in that same funny way as when they had said goodnight in the Place de l'Observatoire, with the glowing street lamps hanging like drops of brightness in the rainy air.

Then Alban said, with friendly impatience: 'Go on, tell me about yourself!'

But, without giving them any time, the wind carried them away. A thousand tiny wings lashed at their faces, covering them as with a quivering mask. They dashed headlong into a forest: the forest engulfed them; the trees erected a triumphal arch for the man who was entering the kingdom of Death under the sign of Spring. And Alban felt himself come to life again amid this wild excitement. The sensation of rest in motion, of cutting through air while still lying down, filled him with childish pride. With tight-shut lips and stiffened features, he felt his soul revitalized. The future whipped him like the wind. The life of desire was born again in him. Everything in him aspired to outstrip the car in speed.

They sat silent and motionless, yet he was rediscovering his friend, as a forgotten tune comes back to you. He had found him again, he had found himself again when, at a level-crossing which was bound to give the car a jolt, he had slightly raised himself while Prinet, ignoring this caution, took the shock with his back. And he had thought he could hear him again as when, on that winter evening, they were looking for the church of St Séverin: 'Now, do we go right or left?' Alban asked, and the resigned voice in the dark behind him had answered, with the slight lisp caused by the tongue pressing against the teeth: 'Oh, it doesn't really matter, since we'll get lost anyway . . .'

And he saw him again, standing before St Séverin . . . and before St Germain des Prés, his overcoat collar turned up against the evening rain.

Prinet had, at the back of his head, that funny spike of hair which nearly always denotes a pupil of one of 'our houses'.[1] But the two boys had met on the Montagne Ste Geneviève, during the first year of the war; Alban was completing his studies for an arts degree, and the younger boy was starting to read law.

An only child and an orphan, living with a melancholy uncle in the depths of remote Auteuil, Stanislas Prinet was a solitary person from birth. By what chance did Alban happen to speak to him between two lectures? Nothing that Prinet said to him during those five minutes was of any interest whatsoever. Yet when they separated, a small but significant thing had occurred: Alban felt warmly towards him.

How delightful this feeling is! How everything thenceforward falls naturally into place! How it makes up for everything else! Once the feeling was born, various reasons could easily be found to justify it: Prinet's decency, his purity, his touchy sensitiveness, his reticence, that brittle freshness of adolescence . . . But how unnecessary was all this to one who gave himself freely, recklessly, without expecting anything in return! Being biased and knowing it, what would have irked him in someone else increased his affection for Prinet. Prinet had no memory and would fail in his law

[1] *Nos maisons*, the phrase used by the Jesuits in referring to their schools. (*Translator's note*).

39

exams, which he had accepted the necessity of reading for as every-thing is accepted in France, as the soldier accepts war, as civilians accept the price of butter. Prinet said that Racine bored him, Prinet did not understand the philosophers, knew nothing about politics, nothing about history, nothing about art, nothing about music, nothing about business. Prinet was not serious, though he was often grave. He was intelligent, but with the intelligence of a child, inadequate except for a child, made up of sudden flashes of intuition. 'Is it not true that I would despise him if he weren't my friend? Only the best counts for me. Is it not true that he is second-rate? But what does it matter, as long as I'm fond of him?'

Indeed, this artlessness tended to bring the two youths closer together. Exhausted and bored by intellectuals, Alban maintained only the most obligatory contacts with his contemporaries. They would meet to 'exchange ideas'. Alban, the college cat on his lap, used the little pulsing body as an antidote to the stupidity and tediousness of these thinkers. Sometimes, from these exchanges, an insignificant companionship of minds sprang into cold life; then some minor incident, like the 'friend' going to live in a remote suberb, would bring to an end, without a pang, the community of interest in Debussy or Beyle. But with Prinet it was different. Alban could let his fifty-year-old soul sink in order to allow his fourteen-year-old one to rise to the surface, the soul of an apprentice on the spree that was always straining towards the light beneath the con-straints and the absurd preoccupations of modern life. And this alone would have been enough to bring them together.

The departures on winter Thursdays, one o'clock at the Porte Maillot, on their way to a football match! The joy of it! The madness of youth rose in the two boys as they hung on the running-board of the little tram speeding along the Bois, the wet branches dripping on their bare heads as they passed. The joy of it! Blessed is the joy that springs not from a clear conscience but from a collar that is soft and loose! And the laced shoes, and the mud from the avenues on the trouser-legs! And not to have to think! Not to have to disguise the gaps in one's culture and the weaknesses of one's mind! Not to have to justify one's opinions! To be able to make wild criticisms, to contradict oneself, be incoherent! And then the thousands of questions on which one has no opinion at all! Ah, the havoc they wreaked, the massacres of prophets and poets! Knowledge, intelligence and genius all burning together in a splendid *auto-da-fé*! Sometimes the younger one would laugh, seized with dizziness at the peak of divine Amusement: 'We really are idiots!' 'Ah! If one could be an idiot always! Always!' poor Alban passionately exclaimed, remembering that this same evening he would have to start again to be a person of consequence.

A hill slowed them down. They were able to speak.

'It's tough here,' said Prinet. And the other haughtily rejoined: 'Would you want me to be subjected to second-rate ordeals?'

The wind carried his words away from his lips and he said to himself: 'As death, perhaps, will carry them away,' little thinking that life itself would render them one day so vain and obsolete.

Upright, motionless, stiff-faced, each of them trembled with excitement at the great things happening within him, and at having beside him this living echo which would multiply them. The first barbed wire they passed was like an explosion of desire or music.

'You see the camouflage?'

A curtain of leaves ran along the narrow headland thrown up between life and death.

'Are we in sight? Are they there?'

'You'll see the shell-holes along the road.'

Suddenly he heard: 'Douce,' whispered his flesh, 'Douce'; and then, shaken, his mind, his heart, everything repeated 'Douce'. His life was full of things which remembered and repeated: 'Douce'. The smells and the colours of her body, all varying with the place, the time and the season, like the smells and colours of the earth; the idea of slowness in kisses and love-making; the narrow strip of neck between the hair and the high collar, where the lips are hemmed in, circumscribed, much more exquisitely than in front where there are no limits – all this filled him with the pride of life. Because she was his, everything was his, the power of self-sacrifice, the taste

41

for responsibility, quick decision, a god-like certainty. The fleshly creation might well be the liberation and the safeguard of the spirit to the point where there would be no Dominique, no, there would be no Dominiques if there were no Douces; he felt that from desire alone was born a universal power, a superhuman faculty of understanding and invention. At this moment, everything he offered up, everything he was capable of was nourished upon the memory, the hope and the certainty of pleasure. At the summit of the pyre fluttered the bright flame of his country. As in old biblical pictures, from the woman's womb rose the vast tree, bearing the fruit of all the gardens on earth.

'Now we are really at the front, aren't we?'

He would have liked this to be clearly perceptible as when, going into Belgium as a child, he expected some sign (the sky suddenly red?) to show that at last and without any possible doubt he was 'abroad'. The road was winding round wooded slopes. To their left, above them, to their right, descending steeply, the pine-forest stretched as far as the eye could see, a mass of fresh, grey-green leaves with now and then a touch of purple. Through the gaps, one glimpsed the thick depths, the pine-trees blue against the skyline as if the watery sky were flowing over them. Twice, by the roadside, they passed the new orchards planted with white, symmetrical, cruciform trees each bearing a single tricoloured fruit.

'And now, is this the front?'

Dug-outs opened in the slope.

'This is an artillery shelter,' explained Prinet.

'And that one?'

'That's a command post.'

'You do know a lot,' Alban thought, intoxicated by these technical terms, and remembering the diffident student who had once said to him: 'I must talk to you . . . Look, it's pretty silly . . . You must plan my life for me, give me some ideas.'

Huddled at the bottom of the car, he could see the shoulder-blades raising his friend's raincoat a little, the dark hollow behind the over large ear, his cheek which had sunk in as his own used to sink when as a small boy he lost weight in the heat of summer; and the wind-reddened cheekbones, where the freckles had disappeared, made the rings of tiredness under his eyes show paler, icy and blueish like mother-of-pearl. Suddenly the boy turned his head slightly and his eyes shone, staring fixedly. Alban followed the direction of his gaze.

Above the dark woods, already merging with the falling dusk, one single ridge was still lit by the weak sun, a stretch of raw, upheaved earth, the colour of a lion's coat, with a scattering of bare trunks like masts in a harbour. Impossible to tell whether it was quite close, or an hour's walk, or else a mirage which moved away as you advanced and which would soon vanish into the dead turquoise sky. Impossible to say whether this mass of scars and warts was a kind of leprosy, a disease of the world, or else a sacred plot, purified by the burning winds of the spirit, the chosen peak raised up, offered up even higher by the whole mountain. On the slopes below, figures were bustling round houses, a breeze bent the tips of the grass-blades as though a layer of gas had drifted over them, and from the thick of the woods rose puffs of thin blue smoke, telling of the soul and all its promises. And, crowning all this, the devastated earth, stuffed with living creatures, lay still. This plot of earth on which for years a multitude of men had suffered, hoped, struggled and died, appeared deserted like a place that has never been inhabited, or inhabited only by titans in the dawn of time, when the rivers were being born from the silence. Impossible to know whether it was a refuge of the damned, isolated on these heights so that the disease might rise without spreading, or whether it was the face of the world, the face of dead Prometheus turned up to the sky. Impossible to decide whether it was the city-wall of Dis, that Dante saw, or Calvary.

4

Bread of Beauty

So closely did Dominique follow in Suzanne Kestner's wake that she had no difficulty in keeping her eyes fixed on the blue vein across the back of the girl's knee. She had adjusted her stride to Kestner's; their movements had meshed with one another like the teeth in a piece of machinery; their pace had become as regular as the five compulsory steps between hurdles. And the pursuer's head fitted so exactly into the gap created in the air by the leader's that the displaced wind did not touch her face.

It was her favourite race, her 'beloved thousand metres' as she called it, and they were nearing the end of the last lap but one during a morning's training. At first she had let the mad young things take the lead, but they had soon been run off their feet and overtaken, and now she no longer even heard behind her the feeble padding of their feet on the turf. She had run the first lap at the rear of the bunch, feeling an odd pleasure in such proud humility; then, with the collapse of the others, she had found herself, without having forced her pace, behind Kestner, the old, tough rival, and between these two evenly-matched girls everything now boiled down to a battle of wits.

How she loved it, this intellectual aspect of sport, the mental excitement which mingles with the physical excitement in a matchless combination! Instinctively she had tended towards the branch of athletics which demands it most: the medium-distance race; sprints, jumping or throwing did not excite her in the same way, because they only call into play one's physical and technical abilities. At this moment she was conscious at the same time of her perspicacity, her technical knowledge, her bearing, her presence of mind, her vastly organized powers of endurance; and then the freedom and the strength of her legs, the close grain of her cheeks which never shook as she ran, her ease of movement, all the potentialities in the muscled body, the deep reserves of strength and breath as yet unused in the heaving chest. Although she knew she was beautiful, she also knew that in a race she was transfigured; and the sense of this perfection was such that a sadness overcame her at the thought that it could not survive. Vainly, time and time again, she had had herself photographed in the stadium: what was the point? 'Though I land so very lightly on my toes, though I seem to be moving in oil rather than in air, though I exert myself with such cool deliberation, though my action is so admirable (I have seen it in photographs and anyway I can feel it), yet what will be left of it all? Only a few hundred people have ever seen me, most of whom did not even appreciate the perfection I had achieved . . .' And, intoxicated by her physical prowess, she had the same feeling as if, in the middle of the desert, she had drawn from some divine instrument a music nobody would ever hear.

Now they were starting on the last lap. Dominique regretted having stuck to Kestner's heels. She had to get back in her lane, as the end of the race was near; sensing that she was disengaging, would not Kestner break away for fear of being caught unawares? Dominique hesitated for a few seconds; then she made up her mind and took to her lane, but slowed down at the same time so as not to cause her rival anxiety. A risky move, which nevertheless seemed to achieve its purpose since Kestner did not increase her speed, though it cost Dominique a couple of yards. Thus they entered the 'back straight', the last straight line before the run-in.

It was not her strength she was uncertain of, but her tactics. The eternal question: at which moment should she make her effort? She always had a wicked inclination to leave it to the very last moment, the swaggering recklessness of the hare in its race with the tortoise.

45

But this time she was somewhat disturbed by the wide gap between Kestner and herself. 'I shall join her at the bend. Then I'll see what she does.'

But as they approached the bend, voices rose from a group of friends crowded at the top of the oval: 'Come on, Kestner!' 'Suzanne has won!' And suddenly she reversed her decision. Ah! Suzanne has won, has she! Well, I'll show them! And, governed by her anger, she did not try to overtake the leader, wishing to maintain the little friends' hopes to the last moment, so as to extinguish them the more brutally.

The tape was now in front of them, the empty grandstand on their right. She thought: 'When we get to the showers, I'll speed up.' And as they passed the small building, calmly, in full control of herself, she lengthened her stride. Intoxicating, how intoxicating it is to appeal to oneself and to feel oneself answer, to feel oneself gaining ground, to feel that one can do even more and yet be strong-willed enough to resist the temptation! The track hypnotizes you, carries you forward as though it sloped downwards, reinforces you as the slipstream reinforces the cyclist sticking close behind a motor-bike. Your feet spring back from it like rubber. It is a mystery to you that you can go so fast without effort . . .

Suddenly, on the eighty-metres line, she bounded forward. For a brief instant, she glimpsed the girl at her side. Then she found herself alone, facing the great empty space, the figurehead of the whole bunch. Nothing left to go by. What are the others doing? This ghostly threat behind one. The one desire: to decrease the distance between oneself and that stupid post. The limit of strength. The eyes glued to the spot from which the green line of the finishing-tape will loom up. Her eyes fixed there, Dominique yet saw, as though she also had eyes in her temples, the other back again, once more at her side. Side by side, shoulder to shoulder they flew on, side by side and equidistant like the two horses of a chariot, like the two wheels of a chariot. The girl had overtaken her. By a chest. By fifty centimetres. The noise now was shattering. The limit of strength? There is no limit. She drew up the dregs of her

46

strength. She could not catch up with the girl, no more than if there were a wall of compressed air between them. She was oblivious of everything. The darkness of the extreme effort, when one hardly feels oneself running any more, when one is no longer absolutely certain that one is running, when one feels no movement in oneself below the waist . . . Awareness only returned with the realization that her mind was no longer in control of her body, that there was no art now but only rough nature; her waist swayed, her arms thrashed, she pulled herself forward as though pulling reins. Another six yards. The girl was in front of her. She drew in her chest and gave up.

But hardly had she given up when Dominique was emptied of everything. Her chest, drawn in, jerked violently forward; she cut down the track in three heavy steps, as if running to catch up with her chest, three steps on flat heels which made three dull thuds; and she collapsed on the grass, stretched flat out on her back, arms out, legs apart, flat like something non-human. The sky above her flowed into her closing eyes. Her breast heaved up from the ground.

She felt close by her the strange warmth of fresh skin, with its faint tang of vanilla. She recognized it as Kestner's. She opened her eyes. The girl was by her side, as red as if the blood was going to come spurting out of her nostrils, her mouth, her ears; and the green line of the finishing tape was still floating about her shoulders. Laughing, they shook hands, their 'handshake' extending right up the forearm to the elbow. She could not speak for lack of breath, while a burst of love rose in her for her conqueror. They were still laughing. 'Soubrier, the strain has cured the sunburn on your nose . . . Quite white, your nose is, quite white . . .'

Sitting close to each other on the sweet-smelling turf they gazed, softly inert, drinking in the morning which seemed to have been created and designed for them, the beneficence of the grass, the frugal atmosphere, the well-loved comrades, the air which itself had something feminine about it, a whole mode of life in which nothing jarred. In this dedicated and exclusive club, most of the thirty girls were charming; five at least, having mastered a great style, were really beautiful. At this very moment one of them, who was practising the high jump, was rejoicing Dominique's heart. So young she looked, her strong but delicate legs evoking the Homeric expression 'charming virility'. Starting her run very close in, almost contemptuously, she set off with a dry, nervous little flicker of her leg which sent a quiver down into the muscles of her toes. And each time she was above the bar, suspended at the pinnacle of her effort, Dominique noticed a half-smile playing upon her mouth, on the grave, serene face which expressed in that instant nothing but the full enjoyment of physical perfection. And she also, looking at her comrade, overflowed with joy.

She saw other girls passing the finishing post, often in a single line like a wave, their heads thrown back, their eyes closed, with an expression of ecstasy; and their movements were like those of a dance, but she did not find them ridiculous because strength, not charm, was the aim of this dance. Others were running, their bent arms holding the javelin neck-high; and as they threw, the hollows of their armpits following each other, pushing each other like the swell of the sea, they were most beautiful, most worthy to be loved. All of them glowed with an invisible flame. Not one of these bodies would have been cold to the touch of a finger.

They appeared to her perfectly intact, perfectly fulfilled in their noble calling. As they were almost naked, they were purer than fully-clothed women.

'The best of them', she said, 'are exactly similar in clothing and in body to the fighting Amazons one sees on the pediments of Greek temples. Believe me, Kestner, I really have those bas-reliefs before my eyes, and I tell you that Jarrier, Pluvinel, young Lemaître, are identical with those figures. But who cares? Who gives them credit for it? Who acknowledges the patience, the energy, the courage needed to achieve this?'

Then, her ideas moving off in a different direction:

'Battalions of women! The first time I ever saw you marching past all together in the stadium, in rows, with little regular steps,

I had a revelation of what an army of women (the idea seems ridiculous at first) could be, made up of women like us.'

She paused, dreamily. A javelin gave a tremulous rustle through the air. A discus fell echoless on the grass.

'Were you in the ambulance service, Kestner?'

'Yes, old girl. In 1914 and 15.'

'You didn't stay?'

'Six months, then one gets tired of it. But why do you ask?'

'Because the idea occurs to me that girls like us, healthy and honourable, not fake women, could not find a better place than the ambulance service.'

'Has it taken you three years of war to find that out? Your fiancé hasn't been wounded, by any chance?'

'I have no fiancé,' she said; her right leg was bent and she was pricking her left calf with the long iron spikes on the sole of her shoe.

On the winner's legs, the colour of milky coffee, on the front only, little fair hairs glistened, minute fibrils of pure gold. Dominique's legs were brown as a perfectly ripe olive, smooth as wax, with the earth from the jumps on her knees, and grazes showing here and there, the more recent ones brownish, the old ones glazed pink like strawberry ice with a bronze grisaille like a patina above, and on top of that, stuck by perspiration, bits of freshly-cut grass. Her left leg, its ankle bound with a crepe bandage, was spread out in such a way that the calf-muscle, forced back upon the inside of the leg, traced along the fibula a deep shadowy groove. She stroked her knee, which was chequered with those little cells of skin which rasp a little at the touch of the hand. And she admired the strength of her wrist and her wide, fleshy palm; she admired her dirty hand, with no more rings on it than on those living, moving sea-plants which are visited by the gods.

'Aren't you coming to the javelin,' shouted one of the girls. 'No, I'm dead.' But Kestner got up and pulled her by the hand. Then she became herself once more, aloof and on the defensive, standing before her inner fortress like a fierce angel with a sword.

'I said no. Now leave me alone!'

49

Kestner went away, and the muscles rising to her knees gave a curious effect as of leggings. She suggested nothing but her own beauty.

No sooner had Dominique finished speaking than her thoughts, as though they had been watching for this gap to steal into, turned to Alban. 'He has been gone twelve days, and no letter. An absurd army postcard, open, and what outrageous words: *Capital. Have learned lots of things. Would not change places for anything. All the best. Alban.*' She recognized in this his familiar mixture of cruelty and artlessness, harsh and fresh like the source of a fountain. 'How ridiculous and offensive he is! How natural for everyone to hate him! That is why everywhere he goes he has made himself intolerable by his impudence and his lack of human kindness. And yet in every place he has been to there is one being who will never forget him.'

She lifted with a finger the narrow band which held her hair, twined round the coils at her ears, and a little air, passing underneath, bathed her forehead.

'He is alive! He is alive! He feels himself becoming better! He has often told me that he only had to escape from society in order to begin liking it, to become good, to want to serve society; that if society wished to make use of him, it should first provide him with a retreat, a place of solitude, if only the solitude of a prison . . . Yes, he is happy there! Yes, he has *learned lots of things*! He really is gone, lost to me, caught up again in this male world which, whatever I do, I shall never enter, and which is his kingdom. *Would not change places* . . . He is clearly in his element out there! In fact, I can't imagine anything in that life that could hurt him. He is tough, heedless of comfort (he even finds comfort repulsive), delighted to be among ordinary soldiers and not officers. I believe he feels a kind of physical repulsion for refined people; he could not befriend anyone who was sensitive to cold. He says that geniuses, more than other men, have certain of the qualities of beasts because they value nature more and are closer to it; that there is something uncouth in all conquerors, whether they be conquerors in war, or in thought and art. There are all kinds of refinements and re-straints he ignores, or rather despises, or rather even hates as being fetters, wasters of time or strength, washing out life's colour. He himself is coarse, coarse as his scrubby hair, his eyebrows that meet in the middle, his large square-fingered hands with their thick knuckles, unattractive hands which seem indeed made to hold a gun rather than a pen. He is strong and healthy, healthy to the point of naïvety, healthy in all his pursuits and always pure because of this health and this strength. One day I happened to be with him on his way to a reconciliation with a priest he had slapped for having wounded his pride, and he was so full of passion that his nose started bleeding; well, I never saw such a beautiful, clear, bright red, really intense like the colours one sees on prisms or glaciers.'

Once more she was torn away from her thoughts by what she saw. Twelve girls were dancing soundlessly, and grace enfolded them utterly. A spirit of freedom danced also amid their steps. The young sun flowed over the young skins, and one might have thought the early hour had been chosen solely to produce this harmony. Rhythmically, with rapid feet, the young girls beat the ground. Their movements seemed to contain nothing beyond their beauty; yet each one of them was so composed as to vitalize this muscle, to liberate that organ, to throw this into relief, to make that articulation more supple, to bring to perfection a particular point in the economy of the human miracle; each movement, as it were, fulfilled creation. Sometimes they threw up their arms as in an invocation to the sun; sometimes, in the serenity of their souls, they threw back their heads with the classical movement of frenzied Bacchantes; and it was endearing in its ambiguity, this Corybantic gesture coming from these calm virgins. In their midst, satyr-like, danced a tubby little man in shirt-sleeves, with thick calves and short curly beard, whom you might have imagined behind a counter, working at some lowly task, but who now, with his arms stretching and relaxing some invisible threads in the air, appeared handsome, light as a bubble, skipping like a little horse, and sowing delight in your heart. And, in them as in him, beneath the kind sun, there was not one atom of their bodies which for a single second ceased to die.

There was indeed something *new* here, something which was an *advance*: time-worn words, which here found all their youthfulness again. What had been lost, obliterated by the distortions of fashion, by the sexual fantasy of the male, by the error of artists in taking that fantasy for their ideal, by centuries of conventions born of ignorance and stupidity, was here restored by these ordinary young women: the pure feminine body as Nature first created it. The order imposed on their bodies had penetrated their whole lives. Lit up by candid laughter, they were both happy and serious in their short black tunics, serene and simple as blades of grass. Prurience, men's ridiculous curiosity for the body's hidden but unsecret sanctuaries, were disarmed by these half-naked maidens, who could laugh but who never smiled. Had one of them pulled off her stockings on this lawn, eight out of ten among the coarsest boys would not even have thought of making a joke, so natural would the gesture have been. And Dominique, thinking of the 'refined, affectionate' war-godmothers in the advertisements in *La Vie Parisienne*, those nauseating creatures one would not even touch with a pair of tongs, thinking of the miserable hags, crazed with impotence, who lose their balance and claw you in the underground, looked upon her companions in the stadium as the true female sex, such as it existed in the beginning – while those typical Parisian ladies were not women but monsters born from some infamous contact, fit only to be stoned to death, as the hermaphrodites of old, for being an insult to nature.

The clock struck eleven. She gave a start. A friend was expecting her at eleven! Quickly she went to the dressing-room; then, putting off her shower until she got home, she left the stadium.

The notion of war reappeared to her, confused, full of gaps, and at once she stumbled against her own incompetence. Alban himself, if she closed her eyes, she could not even evoke; much too concerned with herself to be observant, she could not have said how a greatcoat was cut or buttoned . . . This silly detail pulled her up short. She felt more acutely how effective an obstacle the smallest incident could be against what they had intended to share, how heavy was the task of continuously toiling to make up ground, and, exaggerating these ideas with the ineptitude of one cut off from reality, she imagined strange studies which she would have to undertake in order to share in Alban's preoccupations, as though to achieve this she must learn by heart, for instance, the position of every regimental depot in France. She planned to go through the illustrated magazines at her father's to see some more photographs of the front. She looked along the avenue for a passing soldier, as once, when a little girl, she used to look for a nurse or an under-taker because if you met three nurses, three undertakers and three horses on the same day, something good would happen to you. She saw one and crossed the street to have a look at him.

Alban was like that. Other soldiers passed her; she watched them intently, with a new sympathy; she was discovering them. It struck her that Alban, when he was present, sufficed her. In his absence she became curious. Regretful too. Regretful that she did not know more about his past, his ideas, his pleasures, that she had not questioned him more.

The friend having been disposed of, her uneasiness returned when she went into her bathroom to submit to the pleasures of water.

She admitted frankly that his departure had unbalanced her life, and she loathed this colourless solitude into which she had been sinking during the past twelve days. The thought of offering her services to a hospital at the front or in the back areas began to assert itself. To go away! So doing she would get away from herself; she would enter that male world on the boundaries of which she had always enviously hovered; for the first time, she would seal her moral freedom by an act. If she asked herself: 'Would I be *running after* Alban?' the spectre of her weakness did not rise to paralyse her, since she would not be joining him, would not be at his side any more than if she stayed here. But the fact that she would thus provide herself with preoccupations similar to his, memories they

53

would be able one day to compare, the mere fact of getting nearer to him, ministered to a desire which in any case provided no cause for alarm.

She undressed thoughtfully, stirring the aroma of lavender with which her underclothes and her own freshness perfumed the whole room; and her apprehensions, her uncertainties, the gap between what she possessed and what she wanted, between what she was and what the world is, weighed heavily in her breast, numbed her vitality, made her so slow, so halting, that when, suddenly, she found herself naked, she was taken unawares.

She saw herself, and instantly her heart beat faster in front of this beauty of beauties. 'My beloved body!' she exclaimed in a burst of emotion and tenderness, 'my beautiful muscles!' And the earnestness of her voice, her childish gravity, her emphasis on the *beloved*, had an overtone of love which jarred upon her lips like a questionable joke in church. The cells of her *rectus abdominis*, one upon the other, seemed to form the drums of two pillars of which the breasts were the capitals and, just as the torus widens out at the base of the capital, the breasts did not emerge suddenly from the *recti*, but were part of their actual mass, which gradually swelled, supported and lifted by a torus of flesh. She had never worn a corset, but the development of the pectoral and dorsal muscles had given her a natural 'waist', so much so that her hanging arms did not touch her hips and it would have been her shoulders, not her hips, that met the circumference of the 'egg' in which the hermaphrodite was inscribed. She radiated light and warmth as if there had been inside her a gentle flame, or else the flower of life.

She was golden as ripe corn, darkening towards the nape, the loins and the armpits, brick-coloured on her arms and legs, so often exposed to the air, flame-coloured on the narrow rectangle left bare by her sports tunic and which, like her nose, had been sunburnt. Her suspenders had printed a rosy lace-work on her thighs. And as she thus was, so varied, she was yet cast all in one unbroken piece.

Without altering her attitude, she contracted her muscles, pulling

54

them upwards. Then there appeared a whole world hidden under the skin, in the same way as, if a sea were half sucked dry by its bed, a world of new continents would appear on its surface. Her whole body was like delicately beaten metal. And suddenly, through this enrichment of the body – through the broadening of the neck, too – the face lost its importance, all its spirituality ran down into the torso which it illuminated; the knees themselves, so finely modelled, seemed to have acquired the intelligence of faces. The lateral grooves of the abdomen curved and rose, drawing away from each other, sliding beneath the breasts which they proffered, in a curve which was the curve of some flowering thing; and the three fascicles of the *serratus magnus* sprang out from beneath it, resplendent, like the rays of a hidden sun. The *antero-rectus* stood out on her thighs, a light, well-defined fascicle; and under the knee the tibial muscle, at the same angle, similarly shaped, seemed a smaller reflection of it. The lower extremities of the quadriceps bulged, breaking almost too abruptly the line of the thighs, as in the legs of dancers. Their strength justified the exclamation they had once drawn from Alban in the stadium: 'As long as these columns of your legs uphold your life and all your living things . . .' And the whole body tapered down from the broad shoulders, the whole great marvel of flesh reposed and stood erect on the two feet standing close together, long and well-made like the feet of angels.

With the pad of her middle finger, she stroked her slightly protruding ulnar vein: her eyes having taken in everything, her sense of touch would now discover new values. She turned slowly in front of the triple mirror, knitting her brows in the subtle game of distinguishing fat from muscle, and recognizing in passing all the sweet and pleasant things: the charming grooves between the three fascicles of the deltoid muscle and between the two visible parts of the triceps, and the shadowy valley along the thigh which separates its posterior masses from the quadriceps – all velvety and fused in the unity of youth.

She named each muscle in turn, inventing for each a little god for it alone, like the gods of small objects in ancient Rome. Monotonous litany! She named the protrusions! She named the overlayings! The *fascia lata* like a magnificent great stream, stretching across the whole outside of the thigh, from the hip down to below the knee; the sartorial muscle sweeping right through, a lonely, proud headland; the fibres of the muscular masses visible here and there, as if the skin were delicately worn; the digitations of the *serratus magnus*, each one set over a rib, like one step above another; the deep *coracobrachialis*, invisible, very secret, but which shoots across the armpit like a rope when the arm is raised; and above the raised arm, where the deltoid enters the shoulder, that wonderful tumult, that great stormy gulf, like some great vortex of the sea . . . All grief was banished. The thought of Alban came back to her. She knew that this thought was meant to be rather sad, yet she did not feel its sadness; as when we drink certain draughts with our nose stopped up, knowing they are bitter, yet not tasting the bitterness. All grief was banished. Feelings, thoughts, words were fleshless shadows. This well-being rose up in her almost until it hurt. She was overwhelmed by her body. All grief was banished.

5

The Dancer at the Fête

THE HILL called 'the Dancer at the Fête' was waking amid the
morning clouds, dominating everything, remote and isolated,
yet peopled and alive. The shafts of the trees were hardly visible
yet already a noise of hammering could be heard, frail and light as
air in the immensity. The altitude, the isolation, the virginal purity
of the air, the clouds rolling beneath you on the slopes, the slow
brightening, the confused murmurs, the mountain apparently
suspended in water, suggested a world in its infancy, changing
shape from instant to instant in a moonstone-coloured dawn, the
deep vague world of Wagnerian mystery in which the music swells
and subsides.

'Prinet!'

In the half-light of the dug-out, he saw the youth lean over a
dark pail of water in which the flame of a candle was reflected, then
emerge, his head dripping, to stand before the rising sun which was
like the reflection of the gold at the bottom of the Rhine. Alban
thought he could feel the cool caress over his own face, so vividly
did he feel his friend's pleasure as his own.

'Shall we go?'

They had spent the night with the reserve company, in the
heart of the woods, a mile or so below the advanced positions on
the crest. And now Prinet, assigned for a few days to the battalion
commander, was going to accompany his friend to his post in the
firing line.

The air was intense. With their mouths shut they absorbed as much of it as one absorbs by slowly inhaling the air of the plains. The morning was in the palms of their hands, on their eyelids, inside their eyes, between their necks and their collars, between their wrists and their sleeves, surrounding them and penetrating them on every side like the girl Douce before or after giving herself.

Prinet's helmet, worn well forward, hardened his features, hid his forehead, hid his mind, transforming him into a mere juvenile killer – with the gas-mask hanging at his side, and the revolver in its handsome holster, and the stick in his dry hand, and his dirty leggings! Alban too was carrying all these things. And together they climbed, like the rising day.

A silent, breath-taking climb. Alban did not speak or raise his eyes, and it seemed to him that because of this his pent-up strength was multiplied: 'My life! My life! How beautiful it is! How I love my life!'

From time to time he opened the holster of his Browning and slipped his hand inside with a gesture that was almost sensual, imagining the suppleness, the slackness of his arm relaxed when taking aim. He had the same feeling as a young Catholic who has abstained from love until the night when marriage places in his arms a woman, and every liberty. 'The dead killed by those beside you,' he thought, 'must shatter your nerves, but the most hideous dead body is not ugly when you yourself have killed it; just as a woman can weep without seeming ridiculous if she is weeping because of you.' But his readiness for killing was no greater than it used to be in Paris by night when all he awaited was some provocation to commit a legal murder.

On a ledge, Prinet paused. ('But *I* am not tired,' Alban thought to himself.)

The sadness, the softness of the pale green trees against the milk-white sky! They were like pale flames of chlorine. And they plunged down below them as far as the eye could see, the light in the underwood seeming pale-green too, as if it radiated from the trees themselves. The barbed wire could be seen glistening with dew, like the long trail of some monstrous snail. A little grey bird like a mouse could be seen threading its way through, as though it could not fly.

'Ah! Cloud!'

A cloud was closing around them. They were in the cloud, lost in the cloud. They were detached from the earth, borne up, no longer real. They were in the thing we see, compact, high up in the middle of the sky.

'No one can see us any more! We are free, free!'

He stretched out his hands, and a thin mist frayed between his fingers. And Prinet, a few steps away, was sometimes visible, and sometimes drifted away, as a memory fades, as a body floats away, motionless, over the flooded bank.

When the mist had cleared, they saw each other again, and the morning light was on their faces.

'Look!'

Sitting on the ground, Alban rubbed his leg in the dust. A large, yellow stain appeared on his trousers.

'I can do this! Do you realize how tremendous it is? See how dirty I am. Yet no one will say a thing!'

He repeated:

'No one will say a thing . . .'

He got up again as though he were floating on air, as though he were about to rise off the ground. And what pervaded him was not only the intoxication which the countryside gives to the town-dweller, not only the wild and sombre spirit which drove him furiously to shun a society he had failed to subjugate, but a feeling that this great community of the front, born at the level of the rivers and the fields, was closer to truth and to nature. And he remembered the reply given by Julius Caesar to the tribune who reproached him for pillaging a temple – a reply that so often would seem to him an irrefutable justification: *war is no time for law.*

'Haven't you a commando platoon here, where the leader's rule would more or less be: "I'm sending you out first to face danger. In exchange, I'll shut my eyes to everything else"? Each man liberated according to his merits – like the saying of Paul III: "Men of merit . . . must not be restricted in any way." Ah! if he were to make me free, you have no idea how far my courage would go! I shall join the commando platoon.'

There was a rattle of machine-gun fire – a series of sharp, quick raps like those behind the theatre curtain before the 'three knocks'. Alban straightened up as if his soul were carrying his body up into the air to meet this exalted summons. Then, on the opposite side, another machine-gun rattled, and he felt as if a deadly screen were being thrown up between the world and them, protecting them. He had an impression of protected solitude, as in a park.

'Ah, yes! You'll soon get disillusioned.'

'Have you been disillusioned?' asked Alban; but in such a bored, uninterested tone of voice that Prinet did not answer. Alban was relieved. The soul seemed to him a kind of sickness. The image of Dominique, which came to him suddenly, was deemed importunate.

They had started walking again, and although Prinet did not tell him so, some mysterious instinct warned him they were nearing the summit. The machine-guns went on rattling and the two distinct sounds, different in tone, fell silent, then started up again, now singly, now overlapping, like two quarrelling people trying to shout each other down. And thus, because of the sun, they went towards death with a feeling that they could not die.

Some men were digging a trench. 'Fatigue party,' explained Prinet. A sergeant kept an eye on them, revolver at his side. As they went by:

'Watch out for the asps!' muttered one of the men, bent over his labour, without looking up.

'Yes, they bite!'

Alban paid no attention to the remark, but after a few yards, looking at his friend's face, he saw a shadow there; the eyes were less clear, the corners of the mouth drooped a little. He remembered his words: 'You'll soon get disillusioned.' Could there, he thought, be a correlation between *asp* and *aspi*, short for *aspirant*?[1] A pun meant to wound him? And why did he always look so unhappy? What was at the bottom of it all?

They walked a few more steps in silence, then: 'You're having trouble here? Why don't you want to talk about it?'

The sentence had formed in his mind 'talk to *me* about it?' but he had rejected it as being too intimate, and, just as he had spoken curtly, Prinet answered curtly:

'Because.'

From this harshness, Alban guessed that he would talk.

He knew it, the younger one, he knew that he would talk. The very moment he said 'because' he knew his refusal was absurd, since he was only waiting for a word to start talking and in one minute *would* start, since from the moment when, standing in the car, he had first seen his friend, he had suffered from not talking and slyly and timorously had sought for an opening. And he needed to talk; yet he wondered how he could bring himself to do so.

'Aren't the chaps friendly?'

'Oh! I think it comes from myself really.'

'Everything always comes from ourselves, you know that. What, in fact, is the matter? You're not liked here?'

'It's obvious I'm disliked. There's something wrong.'

They were out of the forest now, and had sat down on the grass and removed their helmets. Prinet was tapping one of his leather leggings with his stick.

Around them was the naked ridge beneath the sun, the stubble ploughed up by the shells and, even more, by farm-work suddenly interrupted. But, between the great outrageous scars, the grass of old pastures could still be seen, fresh with flowers.

'I suppose I'm awkward. It's strange: the people I talk to for the first time are always very pleasant, the second time they're a bit less nice, the third they give me the cold shoulder; there is no fourth

[1] *Aspirant* = (approximately) officer cadet. The French for 'asp' is *aspic*, which is pronounced the same as *aspi*. An untranslatable pun. (*Translator's note*.)

time: they pretend not to know me. Now, I am the first to hurt, to make it plain that I don't seek anyone's friendship.'

'I am the first to hurt,' Alban repeated to himself. 'The anguish in these few words!' He pondered further: 'His phrase: "the people I talk to for the first time . . ." is too well shaped, too well balanced; he gave it this shape long ago. All he is about to say is finding expression only now, but it has been turning over in his mind and heart for days. Putting it all into words is going to be an effort for him, like walking for an invalid on his first outing.'

'In Paris, and here too, I see people adapting themselves to an environment in which they can move easily and cordially while I'm always on enemy territory. Here, at the beginning, I thought it was going to be all right. Then, I don't know how, I've irritated those who showed some friendliness towards me. I can't really blame anyone. I know it's all my fault.'

'Alas,' thought Alban, 'demon of souls, what do you want from me? As an animal is invincibly drawn towards the hole in which another is dying, I thought I was going to find peace yet an obscure instinct was driving me towards this wound and this distress. Even though twenty different places offered me a life of adventure – the African Rifles, the Zouaves, the east, the Venetian front – I chose this one because I would find here a being whom I trust. I must therefore accept the obligations of this trust; on the brink of one of the greatest joys I have ever imagined, I must pause and suffer, because of this suffering which is not my own.'

And in spite of everything he found it a heavy burden, because for all the affection one may feel towards another person, it does not alter the fact that this person is not you.

'I am compelled,' said Prinet, 'to eat with the officers. First I ate at the field kitchen with the men, but the officers were furious; they thought I was trying to make myself popular. As for the men, they thought it was a kind of affectation. One of them asked "what I had done that I had to make up for". At the beginning, I could not express an opinion on some military point without being shown that it was idiotic. If I read the *Platoon Commander's Handbook*, they would sneer: "Book knowledge . . ." Now, I can't even utter one syllable on any subject without being criticized. Ah, yes! It's people who kill you, not shells.'

'Yes, and people can save you as well.'

'When I am with them, I feel dizzy, I feel like a man in the Dead Sea, who can't lift the water around him. I feel as though I'm empty inside . . . as though I can't even move . . . But then, once I have let it all settle down, I find I'm just the same. I need a long time alone to recover some of my self-confidence.'

He felt in him an inner volubility, the outpouring of one who has long kept silent. And yet he did not speak quickly. For a year, he had not once spoken at all profoundly; he was no longer very adept at it. And he laboured a little, was sure he would have a headache that night and would have to take an aspirin. And, unburdening himself thus, with diffidence, with difficulty, he was like two hands holding a heap of sand, but unable to prevent a little of it escaping though the fingers.

Alban listened to him, and shivered in the bright sunshine as at the hour of dusk. He felt him all tensed up, constricted and compressed as were his forehead and ears beneath the tight beret which devoured his eyebrows. In the end the beret seemed to him a kind of symbol, which he found unbearable. He did not take it off himself: familiarity was a physical impossibility to him; strangers called Prinet 'Stanislas' or 'Stan', but he never called him anything but 'Prinet'. He did not take the beret off, but he advised Prinet to do so as he, Alban, had taken off his helmet, in order to get some air. Without noticing, the other bared his head.

But then, when he saw him dishevelled, his untidy hair falling a little over his ears (which were too large and translucent against the sun), he no longer seemed constricted and tense, but on the contrary all confused and lost. And he watched him in terror, as though he had not removed a hat but a mask, and revealed the dark abysses of his soul.

And he was filled with pity, and his pity did him no good.

Prinet was still speaking, chewing at a stalk:

'At the end of last year, appalled by all my inner failings, I decided that, as from January 1st, I was going to reform my nature, to have more drive and daring. From that moment would date the full possession of myself. Until the New Year, I could be as I liked; my inferiority didn't count.'

Stray words, left unfinished by the one, unanswered by the other. But with young people it is the unexpressed that counts; they communicate in fits and starts.

Then he went on:

'I have remained silent so long! I think it has been very bad for me because now, the first time I try and express myself, I shall attract so much attention! It will have to be really good.'

He added quickly:

'Since you're here, I rely on you to help me.'

It was an echo of his astonishing remark of old: 'You'll have to give me ideas, plan my life for me.' He was still tapping his legging with his stick. Not once, for the past ten minutes, had Alban caught his eye. But after these last words, he saw him brighten up, like embers blown upon. He said:

'You are nineteen, it's only natural for people to be jealous of you. And then you are disliked because you seem not to like things. Tighten your tie up a bit, it will bring the blood to your cheeks, and people will think you're happy.'

He saw Prinet turn towards him the saddest little smile in the world. His ears rang with the children's cry: 'Oh! please don't laugh at me!' He hated what he had said, and anything that might make this boy distrust life.

'It's strange,' said Prinet, 'I'm like the Boches' (and still he smiled). 'I don't really know how to make myself liked even by those I seek out. I have to make an effort, even with those to whom I think I'm really close, to make them remember me. Sometimes, when I see all that there is inside me . . . anyway, all the same . . . so many things . . . I'm . . .'

He hesitated.

'. . . I'm astonished at how indifferent I can be to other people.

64

Ah, how can I tell you this! How can I be sincere with you to this extent! You see, one of the things which keep me from confiding in a person is the fear that, afterwards, he might be exactly as he was before. Before, one can think: "He doesn't know me," but afterwards: "Now he knows me, yet he remains the same." And you, perhaps tomorrow you'll behave as though what I'm telling you now had never existed.'

Alban's lips stiffened. 'What can I do to reassure him? How can I cure him?' He saw him suffering, a foot or two away from him, as he might have seen him wounded, on a hospital bed. 'Then there would be injections, drugs. Matter can cure matter. But is there anything in the mind that can cure the mind?' There was a depth of emotion in his friendship. Since his tendency towards people was boredom and dislike, this emotion had real validity.

'I can do nothing for you. Can one ever do anything for anyone?'

Painfully he assessed the dark areas of his intellect, the impotence which prevented him from discovering both Prinet's real disease and its remedy. He himself always in the end stumbled against those very beings who were his curiosity and his torment, or rather against his own shadows, with an eternal 'I don't understand.' The hypertrophy of his personality, the ardour he brought to his passions, his thorough exploitation of himself while asking but little from the world, his over-awareness of his own special emotions, different from and often opposed to those of other people, had eventually created in him an inability, sometimes dramatic in its consequences, fully to understand anything that was not part of himself. And the cruel words of Epictetus vibrated in his heart: 'When one is deceived about someone, do you think one really loves him?'

'I too, for six years, from the age of sixteen until last year, was in the dark, calling for help, lonelier than you could ever conceive. Hard, brusque, intolerant, I would not deign to communicate with people whom I did not admire, and made enemies of them all. And as for those I did admire, none of them would have anything

65

to do with me. The champions of what I revered kept me at arm's length, and those I wanted to serve were afraid of me.

'Everything, everything, I've done everything alone, always – wandering from place to place, suffering perhaps, I can't really remember . . . I seem to recall that such and such a person behaved badly towards me, but I would be quite unable to say precisely how. Today I say to them: "You were my salvation." What a farce politeness is! From my past only the joys remain. I have suppressed everything that hurt me. If only you knew how good I am at forgetting! And I can say quite happily that I have never had either help or advice – except from those who were gently urging me to impale myself on what they knew to be my errors . . .'

He saw Prinet's eyes gazing at him, his face lit up; and he realized that he had found, unwittingly, the healing words he had sought in vain, since in loading himself with all this distress, he was taking it away from the other. Just as Alban, earlier on, had felt vaguely reluctant to share in his friend's trouble, Prinet now felt vaguely happy because his friend had suffered. And their friendship, reaching its limits, turned back upon itself and seemed more close-knit. From all this, some good was born.

He concluded:

'And yet, here I am, at peace. It's strange: I have gained nothing so far, yet I have something of the calm of those who have gained everything. Yes, calm, Prinet, very calm.'

'You have hurt others. You have caused suffering. Do you think those things don't come to light in the end?'

Alban raised his eyebrows. He did not remember very well . . . Whom had he made to suffer? He saw an odd, painful expression on the cadet's face. Then Prinet said:

'I have a feeling that you are often wrong. But I don't know enough to be able to answer you. Ah! I would love someone who knows to say all that has to be said to you.'

'It would be quite pointless.'

'Pointless? And what about the truth?'

'What is truth?'

There was a silence, then Prinet said:

'Let's go.'

They got up, and walked on in silence. Something had snapped between them. 'Is it because I said "I can't do anything for you"?' Alban wondered. 'Could he be dull enough not to have recognized my distress?'

'Why are you sulking?'

No answer.

'Look here,' he said impatiently, 'we're going to have enough suffering. Don't let's add to it just for fun. If I have hurt you, tell me how.'

'You'll think I'm stupid. You'll say to yourself: "what an imbecile he is . . ." '

Suddenly, in Alban's mind, an absurd idea took shape.

'No, it's impossible, it can't be because I said "What is truth?" '

'Yes, it is.' Eyes lowered, voice a little ashamed.

Behind them, the thunder of a ·75 rent the sky. A wave of sadness descended upon Alban, a sense of back-breaking discouragement. At this moment, hundreds of thousands of men were living with the sole aim of controlling matter or defending themselves against matter. Human intelligence was centred upon the trigger of a gun, on the placing of a stack of branches, on the resistance of a wire; lives hung upon a sliver of metal in the numb, impassive flesh, and the fate of nations, perhaps, upon a few feet of rubble lost or taken. But on these heights besieged by death, tensed even in repose under the flight of death which might swoop at any moment, two people once united now found themselves divided – because of truth! Thought, that awesome ghost, had slipped between them, under the rustling dome made by the shells above them. And the men who died by fire and sword, the men who fought against the veiling night, against smothering space, against the sucking mud, the crushing earth, the drowning water, made a grotesque and scandalous farce of the drama between these two, fighting against something which did not exist.

'You make me pine for a dog's life,' Alban was tempted to say, shaking off his melancholy at last. But he did not want to hurt the boy, and merely said gently:

'You know, having problems is nothing to be proud of, any more than being ill. We all have more troubles than we are worth. As for me, I'm not ashamed of finding my strength in calm.'

'And anyway, I was wrong to worry, because you are not so calm as all that, oh no, not so calm . . .'

'Calm and free, if you only knew! Listen, do you hear? Well, whatever is inside me is as serene as that . . .'

From the bottom of the valley, from Granrupt, the tenuous chimes of the church clock broke clearly into the air, like bubbles. The crystalline spirit soared into the light between two bursts from the ·75s, an extraordinary echo of the good life reaching out to this desolate plateau. What could it evoke in these wretches, prisoners of the death-zone, this voice repeating twenty-four times a day: 'Peace is only a mile away'? A painful bitterness? Or a feeling of solace, an absurd belief that, so near to safety, it was almost impossible to die?

Suddenly the two young men turned simultaneously and looked at one another, their eyes wide . . .

'The band rehearsing!'

Smothering the chimes from the church, an unearthly symphony burst out beneath them. Down in the forest, protected by the angle of the slope, the regimental musicians, every man for himself without a thought for all the others, were rehearsing their parts, and the mountain echo, exaggerating their proximity, gave the illusion that they were playing a few yards away. An unearthly symphony it made, this discordant concert of cornets, trumpets, oboes, all playing off-beat and out of time, sometimes surging up together and sometimes fading to leave only a faint ethereal modulation, sometimes a mere cacophony and sometimes a barbarous rhapsody reminiscent of Russian music, strange, frightening and distorted, far, far beyond beauty. It was like the voice of another world, as if (to what end?) all the spirits of the mysterious Dancer at the Fête were shouting their answer to the nine strokes of the bell. Yet in this tumult that had so brutally replaced the limpid chant in which he sought to recognize his soul, Alban heard many other things: summonses, heroic clamours, voluptuous sighs, lingering human laments, childish trills, sounds of crystal and sounds of purple, the whole of Greece in the luminous oboes, the whole of Rome in the praetorian brass, all the voices of all the passions, each listening to itself alone and furiously refusing to acknowledge the others, all the voices of the vast orchestra of the world. And they looked at one another, and a frozen hand gripped the lower half of their cheeks, and in the depths of their hearts a small voice pulsed like the fragile pulsing of the oboe: 'Not so calm as all that, Alban, oh no, not so calm . . .'

6

The Body's Torment

THERE ARE moments in his sixteenth or seventeenth year from
which even a strong man shrinks as he would from a ghost. Poor
boys, why are people not nicer to them! Faced by this powerlessness, this distorted vision, these untearable paper chains, this
pusillanimity beneath the insolence and all the noise, the strong
man feels ashamed of what he once was. Memories, if only we could
kill you!

Such was Dominique's reaction whenever she chanced to remember her week of training at the hospital – that week when, for
the first time, she came to grips with life.

Made for solitude, having lost the habit of verbal intercourse,
she had come back worn out from her first interview with Mme
Verlet, the matron; worn out, telling herself that she would never
be able to bear this change in her life, since a single hour's conversation was enough to prostrate her, and agonized at feeling so incapable of rising to the occasion. How unbalanced and disorganized
she must be without knowing it, in spite of her body's achieve-
ments, since the slightest unaccustomed experience washed her out
so, leaving her with a bitter taste in her mouth, no appetite, feeling
sick even. All the snags she had been warned about, the fear of
these 'absences' into which she slipped when she was in company,
the distaste, the hatred she felt beforehand for the other nurses, the
prospect of finding herself amongst young men, the questions she
would be asked, the necessity to impose herself in a way alien to

her nature, to force herself to laugh, to be interested, to know 'how to deal with them—' all this combined to make a thorny future, which she shuddered to contemplate.

Was she then only strong in her own room, with the door closed, sitting in front of her diary, since she now admitted that to regain any self-confidence she would need some uplifting event, something to inspire her a little? Was she strong only on the track? She recalled the stock-phrases with a derisive laugh: 'the control of the body, acquired in the stadium, leads to the control of the mind,' etc . . . Her mind, virile and wise within its own boundaries, and whose only knowledge came from books, revealed its childishness on the threshold of action, like an awkward schoolboy. Over-impressed by words, taking everything equally seriously, full of scruples and seeing contradictions everywhere, she attached an exaggerated importance to the clichés repeated by the excellent Mme Verlet with the conviction of a father confessor: 'Your role . . . not only the care of your patients, but moral influence . . .' She was staggered. 'Moral influence,' she thought, 'when I don't even know whether I'll be able to cope at all!'

'Shall I adopt an open, vote-catcher's manner?' she wondered. 'Or a serious, imperturbable one? Or shall I look stupid so as to pass unnoticed? Or shall I cultivate bright eyes and puckered brows, so that they'll say: "She's remarkably intelligent"?' Then, flaring up, monstrously distorting reality, she cried: 'My failure here will be the proof of my failure as a person. That is what makes this such a solemn moment: I am about to find out whether or not I can still be like everyone else.'

These were the thoughts that agitated her as she sat in the little white office where the matron received her on the first day. Suddenly she had seen through the open door some 'light casualties' walk across the ward, talking loudly and laughing, and when she realized that she was looking at them now, not as the detached spectator she had been all her life, but as a participant, she had experienced the febrile intoxication the dictator feels at the stir of the crowd. 'I shall hold them in the palm of my hand,' she had muttered to herself, together with other such phrases of pathetic little boys wasting away in giants' dreams.

The next day she stood there uncertainly amongst the lolling men, speaking to no one, not being spoken to. She took refuge with the matron and held forth about the psychology of the French soldier, remembering bits from the *Revue des Deux Mondes* where she had looked for ideas before leaving home. They shuffled round together, with frequent stops. After a prolonged silence, the old lady said: 'Do you know what you ought to do now? Go and talk to them, take the plunge.' Led in this way to the fence, without a trial jump, Dominique swerved and balked, shuddering. With some vague excuse she fled up to the first floor without once looking back, as if pursued by some demiurge. Leaning against the window-pane, she looked down at them in the courtyard. Sophistry came to her rescue, but in vain: 'I have been told to exert a moral influence. In order to do this, I have to know them. But by living amongst them one doesn't get to know them; one only watches oneself. I can learn more in a quarter of an hour at this window than in a whole day's silly chatter with them.' The words were those of Sordello to Dante's pilgrims: 'From these heights you will be able to observe their actions more easily than if you were down amongst them.' But the very element of truth contained in such thoughts did not comfort her, as she knew only too well that it was a defeat: it was not the element of truth which gave them so much power.

She saw herself as timid and incapable. For a whole hour she wandered miserably through the large, noon-empty house, going from room to room, haunted by the noises she heard, wanting to go downstairs, ordering herself to do so and being unable to obey, afraid of suspicious orderlies, afraid above all of good Mme Verlet, of reading in her eyes that she despaired of her. Her lips parched with thirst, she rejected them all, drew back, fought shy of the effort, unable to lift this weight, and the feeling of time wasted filled her with gloom. Yet she could not be said to be really suffering, for the act of refusing a duty, even if the duty was not an unpleasant one, filled her with an obscure satisfaction.

Then, her whole soul trembling beneath this extreme tension, her thoughts flew back to the life of calm, the little room overlooking the Ranelagh gardens, reading in the tram, the conversations with Alban. She thought of giving up. She imagined a spurious telegram calling her home, a hasty departure, and afterwards a long letter to Mme Verlet: like everyone who is incapable of talking, she needed to write long letters. She would say to her: 'Forgive me. I made a mistake. I have no right to persevere in something which goes against my nature . . .' She imagined four pages full of this kind of thing.

At half past five, for no apparent reason, she felt a little better.

That week was made up entirely of alternating days of hope and of despair. She described the former in detail each evening in her diary. About the others she wrote merely 'Bad day'. And as she wrote very fast in order to think less about it, her handwriting became practically illegible.

However, she had now been here for a week and she felt . . . well, yes, good lord, she felt happy. She was surprised, almost indignant at this. As she sat playing a game of *manille* with the greasy cards, she thought: 'What! Me! And actually enjoying it!' But she added at once: 'People only see the commonplace surface. They miss all the overtones, they don't realize I'm making something immense out of nothing.' The idea lulled her, magnificent in its unconscious insincerity, all the more so since she could not admit that the services given by these women, the younger ones in particular, were entirely gratuitous. This was not only because she had always found it almost physically impossible to express admiration, as if to praise a quality in someone else was to deprive herself of it; she also had a desire to belittle and debase them. If one of them held a boy by his coat-button, or gave him a tap on the cheek, she would sneer, and assume that there was something between them. She knew of course that she herself had the same small feminine impulses. But hers were deliberate, long pondered, heavy with meaning. She would, for instance, take someone by the arm, or put her hand on his shoulder (the shoulder nearest to her, not the

73

other, which would mean an embrace). Such gestures were intended to mean: 'I am a comrade, a brother to you, nothing more . . .'

She also realized that she only did this with a few of them. But why couldn't one have preferences? Who hadn't? Had not Mme Verlet herself said to her: 'There is so-and-so and so-and-so, and young Bouchard, for instance . . .' She had looked at Bouchard. His eyes were small, his nose too big, his mouth too wide, in fact he was charming. She had gone and looked at the patients' list: 'Bouchard Marcel, class 1918, Eighth Engineers, electrician, recruited in the Seine department, bullet in the thigh.' She had jotted it down in her notebook, smiling at his name: Marcel, such a proletarian name. She had not tried to find out the name of his soul.

At dinner one evening, one of the medical officers, speaking of the heavy losses on the Oise, remarked: 'Sacrifices are sometimes necessary.' At the time she scarcely noticed the remark, but two hours later she remembered it with a thrill: 'There are, in any hospital, men whom a nurse must neglect if she wants others to be well looked after. Everywhere there must be sacrifices: in helping others, as in strategy or art . . .'

The idea excited her, and a thousand thoughts came flocking into her mind: 'Are they really dedicated, the girls who take equally good care of Tom, Dick and Harry, without putting anything personal or intimate into what they do? How nice it must be for Tom to think that the attentions bestowed upon him are a kind of supply dump constantly available to the hospital, and from which the next man to occupy his bed will benefit equally! Then of course, by looking after everyone one can't concentrate, one ceases to know any of them. Yes, there must be a choice, there must be a kind of physical attraction; one ought to be able to say "my soldiers" as one says "my soldier". Anyway, one leads to the other, because the whole lot will soon benefit from this feeling even though it was originally addressed to only one of them. If you are asked: "What do you think of your soldiers?" you will not answer "One of them deserves to be loved," but "They deserve to be loved." And when you have repeated it several times, it will be true . . .'

Lying on the small, hard bed, breathing in the strong smell of carbolic, hearing the muffled noise of lorries unloading in the yard, Dominique Soubrier reached that climax of cerebral pleasure when intelligence flies to the rescue of instinct. 'Intelligence flying to the rescue of Instinct,' what a splendid allegorical subject for the ceiling of Alban's study! And if a voice challenged her with: 'But what you're asking for is love!' she would answer herself in a scholarly tone: 'Yes, love as the Greeks understood it when they spoke of the love between the iron and the magnet.' As always happens when the ideas we give birth to are worthless, she felt a need to rationalize her emotions, to build a whole dogmatic system around them, as intellectuals are wont to do. All this on her small, hard bed, breathing in the smell of carbolic, hearing the lorries, hearing also, in the next room, the groans of the wounded. And each of these groans did something to her which was not altogether painful; no, not painful.

The next morning, as she came into the ward, she felt uplifted by an extraordinary feeling of freedom. Everything had become easy, for she could now admit to herself without compunction that she was indifferent to three-quarters of these youths.

Their recovery, their return to the front, their post-war fate – for all this she cared nothing, but she liked their ways, she liked their cheerfulness, she felt happy among them; grateful to the humblest of them for even speaking to her, she felt pleasure in her own weakness, in giving these insignificant creatures a power over her. When they were all together, she would choose from their faces those to whom she might have dedicated herself and those she would have left to die. She was full of pity and anxiety for this one, that one and that one – buzzing around them like a wasp buzzing against a window. And it seemed to her that her attachment for these three spread its influence over the entire bunch. Every time she touched on one of these three focal points, her attachment took on new strength and radiated out towards the rest. Because of these three, and because of them alone, Dominique felt capable of helping them all.

Beneath this mild fellow-feeling a total detachment persisted. This detachment maintained the link between her former life and her present one. Because of it she was not disturbed to see these unexpected feelings and preoccupations spring up of themselves. There she was, involved in what had always been an object of repulsion to her, but finding it quite easy to accept because she felt securely shielded behind the thought: 'My heart is not in it.' But the thought of Alban frightened her – from which she deduced that the less her emotions were engaged in her relationship with the soldiers, the more faithful she would remain to her ideal. Strangely enough, the safeguard of her dignity was in the end a kind of cynicism.

One day she was watching Bouchard and the others peeling potatoes: watching them was always her favourite pastime. They were playing, pelting one another with the peelings. Bouchard was often hit; quickly he would bend down, pick up the peelings and throw them back. He was laughing, overexcited, out of breath, and suddenly a swearword escaped his lips like some inarticulate cry, and that word, uttered as if in spite of himself, took on a marvellous intensity of passion. And, for the first time, Dominique was roused.

At the same moment Bouchard saw her; he came towards her and asked to see l'*Illustration*, in which there was something about his regiment (there were books and magazines locked up in a room for the soldiers to read at certain specified times). She said it was too late, access to the room was now forbidden.

With a slightly vulgar movement of his head, he indicated that this did not matter. She smiled. They went to the room.

She gave him the magazine. They exchanged a few words. Vaguely she tidied or rather untidied the cupboard. He turned the pages and read.

She came towards him, laid her whole forearm on his shoulder and, leaning over him, pretended to read. Some article! She never even knew what it was about!

She could see his dry hair close to; she liked the way it stopped at the back of his head, high up, newly trimmed, showing most of the young neck and thus giving an impression of nudity. She thought to herself: 'If I bent down a few inches, my mouth would touch his neck and he would hardly feel it.' She was conscious that, in order to do this, she would have to turn her head so that her face could fit into the hollow of his neck; she thought that his hair, the trace of the scissors still visible in it, must be a little prickly, and she imagined herself stroking it upwards with her finger, or perhaps scratching it a little to see whether he would purr like a cat (he had the eyes of a little cat, she decided). She had the impression that he would say nothing, that perhaps he might smile. She felt he almost belonged to her, so near, so unsuspicious, right up against her and quite odourless.

A simple, tender moment. Around them, what silence! What real solitude! Yet the air was fraught with danger, the bay windows open on to the courtyard, the door open on to the rest of the house. They might be watched from anywhere. But even if she had noticed it, she would not have had the strength to tear herself away. She could not even imagine a situation in which she would have wanted to.

He moved a little, and she drew away her arm. When he was still again, she immediately put it back. She did this several times. It was an odd mixture of caution and temerity.

His reading over, 'I must go,' he said, and got up. Then he asked: 'Are you coming?' and they went out.

She had never believed that sensuality could be bad, only sentimentality. The pleasure she had had from Bouchard amused her without disturbing her. Had she seen a pair of lovers holding hands, she would as always have reviled them.

'Should I, perhaps, have said something?' she wondered; 'asked him not to breathe a word? Or would that have been a clumsy way of attracting attention instead?' She felt a little apprehensive when,

77

the following morning, they were all assembled for the doctors' round. Sitting up in bed, with his breeches on the counterpane still moulded to the roundness of his thighs, Bouchard was talking with his friend Carton, and Carton looked at her several times. She was terrified that he might have said something. When the medical officer addressed some remarks to the ward in general and the two friends had to stop chatting, she breathed again; but when he started his round of the ward, stopping in front of each man, and Bouchard turned again towards his friend, she became frantic. Could she really go and beg their silence? Would it not be an admission of something which otherwise might not even have existed?

When she had come in, he had smiled at her in front of everyone. She had met his smile without returning it. But with what an effort! Moreover a waste of effort, since her look had been like a handclasp.

Now he was looking at her – lingeringly. She was already well acquainted with that intensity in the way he looked at people which gave him at times something of a squint. Her eyelids lowered, deeply absorbed in a temperature chart, she tensed every muscle in her face in an attempt to keep it impassive, but she could feel the blood pulsing up to her face, clouding her brain like a pall. She sensed around her the hooded, foxy eyes of these young country lads whom she feared so much at this moment. She thought: 'How does he feel about what I did? Does he even know it happened?' It was a rhetorical question; little did she care whether or not he was intelligent. She thought he was 'a little above average'. Yet sometimes, at some remark of hers, he had turned towards her with a disconcerted, almost shocked look and she had felt embarrassed by his lack of understanding.

But when, on getting up, he passed by her, he began to whistle in an offhand way. Then she realized that he knew and would keep the secret, and she felt a burst of love, not for Bouchard in himself, but for Bouchard the keeper of her secret. 'But what a child he is! He whistles so as to look natural. He will betray us with his artlessness.' She foresaw an education to undertake. She was blushing to the point of tears. She bent down and pretended to tie up a shoelace, to justify the rush of blood to her cheeks.

That afternoon, at 'closing-time', there was a whole gang of them in the reading-room. Gently she pushed them out. When she saw the young electrician quite naturally stay behind, thus showing there was no question of his leaving, this complicity filled her with satisfaction. Eventually the men called after him:

'Hey, Bouchard, are you coming?'

She said:

'You know very well that Bouchard helps put away the magazines.'

It was the first time she had misused her authority. It is not a potion one can sample with impunity. All her life she would be poisoned by it.

But when she saw him sit down to read, as he had done the other time, and when, turning her back to him, she started shifting the books round the cupboard at random, she had a violent sensation of the tedium of these identical circumstances and the need for something new. At the same time, what had left her cool yesterday, had even rather amused her, disturbed her deeply today. She was quivering with agitation and her fingers were all thumbs. Looking at these fingers covered with dust from the old books she said:

'It's wonderful how filthy one gets here!'

'You find that wonderful!' he exclaimed, as startled as befitted a well-washed boy. Yet she was awfully fond of his hands, never quite clean, a little swollen by work, with lovely rectangular nails.

'It's stifling,' he sighed after a moment – it was a close, stormy day. Suddenly faced with these words, she saw her opportunity. Her reaction was admirably instinctive and opportunist. She said firmly:

'I advise you to take off your coat. You know what the doctor said: "You're still weak, you know. Avoid anything that may tire you." Nothing weakens you more than perspiring . . .'

'That's it!' he exclaimed, and she had no idea what he meant. Then she remembered one of her maids who used to say in the same way, for no apparent reason: 'That's it!' She felt towards him an exquisite distaste. 'At certain moments,' she thought, 'there is something ugly about his face which I adore.'

And then she saw him obey at once and take off his coat, and seeing him do this so submissively, forgetting that she had practically ordered him to do so, she took it as a sort of provocation. And sensing his presence there in the centre of the room, a prepared and utilizable thing, with his bright little animal's eyes, she went from cupboard to cupboard as though she were being pursued, without once turning towards him, like a billiard ball ricocheting from cushion to cushion, intersecting the corners.

As he read, she asked without looking at him: 'Is it interesting?' and other pointless questions, thus preparing her move, to come and read over his shoulder. Suddenly she came.

Without a moment's hesitation she closed her fingers over his braces, then boldly slipped her hand between braces and shirt. Her hand moved up his back, wandered, then stopped at last, enchanted. She inhaled the clean smell of the shirt; she felt the human warmth penetrate her firmly pressed palm through the material; and this spreading warmth created an atmosphere which held her within its radiance. She spoke to him laughingly about a mole on his neck. With a charming gesture he touched it with his finger as if to make sure that it was still there. And as he lifted his arm, she could feel a hollow deepening under her hand with the swift displacement of the muscle. Calm almost, with a certitude of a protracted pleasure of a kind she had never suspected or approached before, she stood there silently and passionately thanking him for remaining so still, for doing nothing to free himself, and nothing to underline the occasion. And what she had experienced, what was now coming to an end, and what was just beginning, were fused together in this burst of joy.

All this she felt without looking at him, or knowing the expression on his face.

She heard the sound of footsteps and hastily withdrew her hand.

'Ah, Bouchard. So that's why we couldn't find you!'

The doctor! She waited for what must inevitably follow. But, as a bull sometimes rushes upon an ungarded *torero*, stabs the air with its horn and goes by without having touched him, so the doctor, after that first glancing blow, went on to give a fatherly technical dissertation. Dominique would always remember the scene. While he was speaking, she appeared to be staring into space beyond him as people do when they are trying hard to understand something. But in fact she was not staring into space; her eyes were fixed passionately upon Bouchard who was standing behind the other man, and this communion across danger, all this talk about dressings to which she nodded while at the same time her whole self went out through her eyes towards the source of her joy, intoxicated her. All three left the room together.

Because she was afraid to show that she was secretly enjoying it, her whole hospital life became gradually infected with suspicion and constraint. After having trumpeted her enthusiasm and demonstrated her zeal, she now thought it wise to affect a certain indifference: a subtle indifference which, she meant people to understand, applied not to her task but to the men's personalities; her devotion must be known, but thought to cost her a great deal. So she no longer spoke of the wounded except in clinical or administrative terms. She watched her own behaviour, exaggerating, in public, her coldness towards those she liked best, as if everyone were thinking of her what she thought of the other nurses, that her motive for being here could only be shameful. Nevertheless, instinctively she nosed out the pure of heart, and her own inhibitions increased her animosity towards those who could do anything with impunity. At the same time, of course, she consorted with those girls, made overtures, gave tokens of friendship, provided herself with friends against any contingency. At least, she made an effort to do so.

Yet God knows what a penance it was for her! She loathed them. She found less difference between herself and the hospital dog than between herself and these women. Needless to say, their kindheartedness, their devotion, their sacrifices, even their courage, did not exist for her.

Mme Verlet herself, whom she had liked at first, was the cause of an amusing incident. Dominique had written to her father: 'This Mme Verlet is very nice. Who is she? etc . . .' When she received the answer, 'I am so glad you like Mme Verlet . . .' she read it with a sneer, for in the short time it had taken the two letters to travel to and fro she had already managed to develop a loathing for her. She flouted her openly, aped her tearful manner – for the poor woman had just lost a son. Furthermore, Mme Verlet was pious, and Dominique, as a free-thinker, regarded Catholicism with nausea rather than indifference. At the table presided over by the old lady (blowing her nose, coughing, sniffing and sighing, audibly moistening her dry lips), Dominique would turn away so as not to see this ravaged mask of Saint Monica, with that recoil of the whole flesh which caused the Greek gods to turn away from corpses: 'Corpse! filth! corpse! I loathe your suffering!' She hated the old lady's suffering as much as she loved the men's. Then something would rise within her, a sort of half-caress, and her hand would come down to rest on anything as though it were human flesh, the neck of a bottle, for instance, where it remained as on a human neck.

Ah! the wonderful, the adorable first contact with life! Each day she learnt a little, changed a little, adapted herself a little more to *life as it is*, feeling a new flexibility and adaptability in all that part of her which was rigid and self-contained. At home, when there was talk of some intrigue or other in the Parisian social world, or when she was reading certain novels, she used to think, not being able to imagine the situation, that in such a complex life she would always be manipulated, never a manipulator herself. Yet now that she was immersed in such a life, she found herself manoeuvring instinctively with the cunning and flexibility of the old foxes who used to amaze her. There was just one small detail to correct: she still lowered her voice a little when she was lying.

She loved, she blessed, the rendezvous, the anxieties, the little signs (oh, the signs!) the whole petty strategy: as when one of the men, from the other end of the room, would raise both hands with the fingers spread out and smile, meaning: 'Ten . . . I'll see you at ten o'clock'; or when she volunteered to run an errand (how helpful Mlle Soubrier is!) simply in order to be able to get into Ward B and catch Hérivel's eye; or when she was completing some papers and Bouchard came and said: 'I'm going for a stroll; would you like to come with me?' and she would ruin a whole hour's work, pushing the carefully sorted papers pell-mell into the drawer . . . Far from feeling humiliated by the pettiness of all this, she took pride in it: 'I'm alive! I'm alive!' she cried. 'I'm the only one among all these idiots who is really living!' She choked with scorn, and her impulsive disgust rendered her satisfactions the more acute.

How delightful they were, these escapades with her boy friend! She would drop everything; the others could cope. How agreeable not to be involved, to be outside it all, watching other people work. Always putting things off to the next day, pushing everyone around, as if intoxicated by her lack of conscience, she rushed through her duties with one obsession. Everything was dropped as soon as her pleasure was at stake. But it was not even pleasure; it was simply her passion for rejection. To reject! To reject! This was her fundamental impulse. To escape, to slip away, not only from duties, responsibilities, obligations, but from *everything* not pleasurable to oneself!

She resented wholeheartedly every order she was given, regarding it as an imposition. The mere fact of having to fold up her own things at bedtime seemed to her almost a form of persecution, or at least an insufferable waste of time for which the twenty-two idle years of her life were not sufficient compensation. In the end she had only one single rule in her work: to do as little as possible. 'I have the soul of a servant,' she told herself. And it was only her remoteness from the others that prevented her from broadcasting it, so thrilled was she to discover in herself an instinctive baseness and vulgarity. Thus, in this house of suffering to which her colleagues came to give themselves, she let herself drift happily along like some dead weight upon the efforts of others, consuming without producing, taking all and giving nothing. But what, after all, could she do against her utter inability to take an interest in anything outside herself? No more than those who have self-sacrifice in their blood can do to remain indifferent.

Her behaviour became odd and capricious. Her high-handedness, her passion for favouritism, her inability to put up with what she disliked, the way she repudiated her strongest convictions according to circumstances, in all this she was giving vent to the harsh and extreme side of her nature. She became more than ever changeable, dependent on the moment, without any guiding aim. Had there been anyone there who loved her, she would have made them suffer dreadfully. She did in fact feel that she was going too far. And as she was inclined to exaggerate everything, she imagined that her most insignificant action was the object of gossip. And yet, just as she had gone on leaning over the young soldier although she knew they might be observed, so now nothing on earth would have induced her to give up her pleasures.

If anything, she began to regularize them. Now she delighted in bringing Bouchard cigarettes and sweets and then, as time went on, anything he asked for. He did not fail to ask, and she soon realized that he regarded these small gifts as his due. But what did she care, Dominique, what the devil did she care if this was the only kind of interest he had in her! Her reward for these acts of generosity was the satisfaction of pleasing him, of asserting her social superiority, of spending money, etc . . . It was also the satisfaction of binding him by a deal, a *quid pro quo*, a means of pressure. Far from shocking her, the introduction of a mercenary element in their relationship delighted her. It made everything simpler and freed her from any scruples by a quick settlement of accounts. Above all, Dominique reaffirmed thereby her scorn for sentiment, thus allowing herself to feel that she was still emotionally intact. And then, what fun it all was! All those little secrets about cigarettes, and the smell of chocolate lingering about the pockets of his trousers when she brushed them . . .

In any case she cared less and less about whether she were intact or not. Her behaviour with Bouchard was exactly what she had always despised? Well, that made it all the more amusing! 'If I saw another girl doing what I am doing, it would make me sick! Running after a soldier! Giving him power over you! But from them it's bad. From me, it's good.' These drastic simplifications delighted her. To lose an occasion of pleasure out of loyalty to one's principles was for her the act of a dangerously sick woman. Granted, she was inconsistent, constantly veering from one thing to its opposite; but the impulse of yielding to both without compunction, because they had sufficiently justified themselves by the pleasure they gave her, was always the same impulse, giving unity to her disparate states. 'But this is straight from Alban!' she told herself, and immediately realized how much he had affected her, how much he had influenced her development. Then she felt unhappy, no longer sure of herself.

Sometimes, too, she watched the other men. When, during the reading of the communiqué, she caught some of them making jeering remarks she thought (curious psychology!) that they must be morally equally base all the way through, and that perhaps, if the occasion arose, they would behave as Bouchard did. 'Dear little scum,' she thought, melting with love, or pleasure, or something . . .

It is understandable that in these circumstances, being continuously on the brink of a misdemeanour, she avoided the doctors, and got as flustered as a schoolboy if she ran into one of them, always expecting to be told that 'her presence in the hospital was no longer desired'. She saw herself on the day of the storm, behaving like one of those rubber-stemmed punch-balls in a gymnasium which bend in all directions under the rain of blows, but always straighten up in the end. 'In view of this, Mademoiselle, we must give you back your freedom. We thought we were dealing with a well-bred young lady.' 'Doctor, I promise my behaviour will be entirely satisfactory from now on. Could I perhaps stay on probation for a week . . .' She realized that there is an excessive servility of which only excessive pride is capable. Remembering the Japanese proverb: 'Victory belongs to him who can hold out another quarter of an hour,' she modified it thus: 'Victory belongs to him who can bear to be insulted for another quarter of an hour.' And every day, every time she got a fright, the scene sprang to her mind, almost as if to her memory, with the vividness of something already experienced, half ecstasy, half nightmare.

Here again she showed, in an extreme form, that pliability she had now incorporated in her whole life. Dominate by yielding. Yield to preserve one's peace, yield also because 'they are too stupid, I shall not oppose any of their wishes'. This last reason gave her the further satisfaction of contributing to an injustice, the victory of the second-rate, also observed by Alban at the front (where, for instance, a cowardly officer must of course be sent back to the rear).

Yet, more often than not, from the bottom of her fears, Dominique recalled the words of the Duc de Guise: 'They would not dare!' She reviewed the Soubriers' connections, assessed their importance in society: the Minister had dined at their house two months ago ... The general ... She now felt the great importance of all this, which she had scorned before she became involved with the world and its ways. Not only did it postpone the scandal by removing suspicion from her; but also, if and when the scandal broke, it might well be hushed up by one of these men on whom, only yesterday, she had so impudently turned her back. And the necessity of flattery was revealed to her, suddenly instilling a new flavour into her whole future. Nothing is more calculated to open our eyes to the ways of the world than the daily expectation of a cataclysm.

This state of affairs lasted until the morning when, as she came into the ward, Carton came up to her and said: 'Bouchard is out, you know.' What did he mean? Why talk to her about Bouchard? What was Bouchard to her? So she picked on the first-comer (it was Mainadier), went about publicly with him, asked everybody whether he deserved to be helped, promised him a gardener's job at her uncle's after the war. At the same time, she was seized with a frenzy of hypocrisy: 'You know what the hospital means to me ... One big family ...' etc. What a splendid noise these words made, drowning her sniggers! In this way, her life became a series of lapses and recoveries, alternating fits of rashness and play-acting.

At times she reflected that the war would come to an end, that within a week this pleasant comradeship with the lower classes would become abnormal and 'out of place' in the eyes of the world, all the bridges between herself and these people would be cut, she could never again use the familiar form of address to them and put her soul into it; all this freedom, this healthy candour would no longer exist. And she felt an anticipatory nostalgia for this promiscuity, and an ingenuous wish, which she accepted and approved in the very midst of all the blood and misery, that the war might continue until the inevitable day when she grew tired of all this.

Who will not condemn her: wicked Dominique! Yet all of them, some by nursing, she by living thus, helped others to live. Let us thank them all!

*   *   *

On June 20th, she was overcome with a desire to kiss him. A kiss from behind, on his neck; because it was his neck that she knew best and most closely; and because she felt (being a woman after all) that not seeing at that instant the expression on his face would make the kiss less momentous. She could perfectly well picture him letting himself be kissed, laughing a little, perhaps. He never made advances and he never rebuffed. He had a style all his own.

The idea of the kiss began to ruin their meetings. She told herself that such favourable circumstances would never come her way again, that time was running out and soon everything would be over. Both during and after their meetings she cursed herself. She *must* have the will or the courage to do it next time. She must. It must be done at all costs. She would even fix the time and the place . . .

She realized, however, that her timidity was not the sole culprit. She pictured herself doing the thing with blind, ferocious vigour, but the sensation she imagined was never one of pleasure. She realized that this act represented itself to her – but why? – less as a physical pleasure than as the accomplishment of a kind of duty which would assuage her intellect only: what would be satisfied would be not the desire for a face but the idea of not wasting anything, of not having anything to regret. She was restless at not doing it, yet the only benefit she would derive from it would be relief from her restlessness. 'How hungry I shall be,' she thought, 'once it is over.' Precisely, it was an obsession, not a temptation.

On June 23rd, a small incident of the kind fate provides moved her to take a step she would never otherwise have considered.

At dinner Mlle Roselier, one of the nurses, spoke of the teams from the Soldiers' Institute who put on shows for the benefit of neighbouring regiments in towns near the front. The day before, the Lunéville team had gone to give a performance at Gemaincourt, and on the 28th the St Dié team would be going to Granrupt ... Dominique gave a start.

She knew how difficult it was for women to get to the real front line. And moreover, she had never felt a strong desire to go and spend a few hours with Alban. But this time (all the more since a liaison car on its way to Ch ..., halfway to Granrupt, passed by the hospital every morning), could she turn down the opportunity?

She made inquiries, spoke of a close relative, her childhood playmate ... Everyone was most kind, so much so that she felt slightly ashamed at having snubbed them so. She could have a four-day leave; and as for using the car, nothing easier! But would she find another car at Ch ..., a biggish town? How much fuss and bother would it involve? And how long would it take?

She spent the whole of the next morning weighing up the pros and cons. On the one hand it was a rare opportunity, and furthermore Mlle Roselier, who knew someone in the St Dié set-up, would give her a letter of introduction. On the other hand, the prospect of difficulties at Ch ... and also the fact that she had planned to go out with Bouchard on Sunday made her hesitate. Sunday ... She pictured herself, as soon as she was alone with him, holding the point of his elbow and playing with his funny-bone, or squeezing his arm high up under the arm-pit, squeezing his strong arm. She found it somewhat hard to bring her mind back to Alban. The other pleasure had dulled her universe.

At midday she met Bouchard. As he was leaving her for the day to go to a mechanics' readaptation centre a few miles away, she said goodbye to him. He, after his goodbye, added 'Think abah't me,' then corrected himself and pronounced carefully as he had been taught in school: 'Think about me.' She was touched by this. As it was, only a few moments before, he had sneezed in such a child-like way that she had been overcome with tenderness, and over-come with joy at being thus moved. And she made up her mind to stay.

Then suddenly, at seven o'clock, perhaps only because the thought had crossed her mind of the large empty car arriving at Ch . . . , she decided to go. In a second it was all settled, irrevocably. Mme Verlet could not be found. She had to rush round looking for her. She would have been heartbroken if a hitch had occurred.

The next morning she was speeding along the road to Ch . . . The driver was a nonentity.

7

An Endless Thursday[1]

ONE MORNING, Alban's company was seriously shelled for the first time. Alban put up a good front; but time seemed to stand still.

When all was calm again, he reflected: 'When the shells came whistling towards me and I might at any moment have been plunged into eternity, I had no thought of religion, no feeling of repentance, no burst of tenderness towards those I love.' From the day he had decided to go into the firing line, he had not paused once to think of death, he had not written to anyone or made a will of any kind.

Yet he had gained from this baptism of fire both a knowledge of danger and an appetite for danger. He rejoiced at having at last felt the fear of death. It was a most beautiful, most moving feeling. A man who has been living for a long time in an environment foreign to him becomes used to it and no longer minds, but if one day he comes into contact with his native element, his present state becomes unbearable; in the same way Alban now could only survive in the morbid excitement that danger brings. This was for him the most favourable, the most productive atmosphere.

No doubt he had not altogether kept his composure during his his first taste of battle. But that was only because he had been taken

---

[1] Thursday is a holiday for French schoolchildren, and this chapter heading suggests that the war is an endless holiday for the school-friends Alban and Prinet. (*Translator's note.*)

by surprise. Through danger sought by an act of will came a wonderful exultation of life, for this truly was the real thing.

When he picked out an exposed track on the map and chose it rather than any other; when, seeing a shell land two hundred yards away, he hurried towards the spot; when he intentionally lingered in a place raked by machine-gun fire, he felt, unbelievably enough, something similar to what some artists seek from drink – an acceleration of thought, a rush of memory, a burgeoning of images, flashes of insight into minds which had up to then been obscure to him, explosions of creative joy in which he exclaimed: 'I shall have lots of children!' – a plenitude he experienced with his eyes lowered and a smile on his closed lips, as though he were doing something wrong. And it is true that this kind of courage often has some of the characteristics of sin. It is not simply a form of curiosity for life, as a taste for sacrifice is but a form of life's prodigality: it is the invasion of the whole being by the temptation to an act and the suppression of everything that might stand in the way of it, and in this case heroism no longer consists in running to the call of danger, but rather in resisting it. Moreover, all this rapture was steeped in blood. War will always exist, because there will always be twenty-year-olds to bring it into being through sheer love of it.

The closer threat of death awakened his sensuality: 'Once more before I die! Once more and I'll agree to die!'

Several times, in the course of his duties, he had had to spend a night in the village. He never knew on his way down who would give him his pleasure that night.

When night fell, the hunt would begin. As certain animals take on a distinctive demeanour when hunting, so, simply from the manner in which the young man moved, one could have guessed his preoccupation at a glance. Leaning forward with dangling arms, walking fast with his feet turned in a little like a man who has spent a long time in the bush, his face set in a pose of splendid gravity and his head absolutely still while the eyes swivelled from right to left and back again, unconsciously he aped the appearance of our earliest ancestors as they plunged into the many-hued forest. And what impelled him, what impelled all these men who went off on their own at nightfall, was not only the desire for a brief moment of pleasure, but also an obscure need, in men so long and so exclusively bent upon destruction, of a simulacrum of creation.

Sometimes the woman would insult him: mere breadcrumbs aimed at a fortress, for he was strictly incapable of being humiliated. At other times it was a sudden darkness, sprawling bodies, blind mouths, the upturned yielding face. Then the quick departure, the desire never to know either Christian name or surname, or even the precise features of the face, the desire for there to be nothing in common save this one high moment, blind, devoured. 'I do not know whom I loved in the night.' And true enough, he would often have been unable to recognize next day these spirits of the night.

Once it happened in the tall, concealing grass. Once in a barn where they were shrouded by the dust rising from the hay (Ah! he would give his whole life for this single moment in the hayloft, this terrifyingly happy moment!). Once in the back of a cart, amid the smell of hemp from the empty sacks, behind the huge and motionless back of the father pretending not to understand . . . How the horses whinnied!

Thus he secured himself against the terrible question posed at the moment of death: 'Have I had my fill of earthly pleasures?'

Yet beneath his joys a regret persisted: he had never killed. To think that the opportunity of war might go past in vain! It left him with a vague feeling of inferiority similar to the feeling he had had during the amateur boxing championships, when he had defeated some of his opponents in the ring on points, had forced others to retire, but had never managed a knock-out.

One night they were attacked. The redoubt was held by a bunch of kids who, being under fire for the first time in five days, fought like little devils, throwing grenades with the same shouting and scuffling and excitement as, not so long before, they had bombarded one another with snowballs at school. Alban's exertions were rather muddled and ineffectual.

Another time, making use of the freedom given him by his liaison duties, he advanced into the German lines for the fun of it and came upon three old conscripts who were completely unaware of his presence, as he was hidden behind an embankment. Longing to kill them though he was, he prudently retreated because of their numbers. But he shook with frustration.

Yet another time, when he was in the front trench, a bullet whistled past his ear. Furious, he leapt on to the parapet, but a fellow-soldier, seeing his lunatic behaviour, grabbed him by the feet. He toppled over. At that very moment a bullet tore through the space he would have occupied had he still been standing.

He had incurred such distrust from the officers as a result of having admitted, on his arrival, that he had voluntarily transferred from the auxiliary services to the armed forces and then from the rear to this front-line infantry regiment, that he soon realized that secrecy must be the condition of his 'superfluous heroism'. However, one minor incident was observed by a witness, causing him to be mentioned in the regimental dispatches. This gave him pleasure.

One morning, the cook brought him three letters at breakfast: 'The catering-sergeant brought these back for you from St Dié.'

He took them, looked at the envelopes, and slipped one of them into his pocket. There it remained all through the meal. He enjoyed these little exercises in will-power which told him whether everything in him was running smoothly. He had recognized Dominique's small, so intelligent hand. Ah, yes, it was obvious at once that the letter didn't come from Deauville!

He read the others. One was from Marseilles, from a confraternity of penitents – one of the last in France – who accompany the bodies of men condemned to death to the common grave. The letter invited him to attend some ceremonies. He could not refrain from thinking that here, too, he belonged to a vast lay-brotherhood, perhaps even mightier than the other, that here, too, he was living with condemned men. And he saw his greatcoat as a monk's cowl.

The meal over, he took out Dominique's letter – and reading his name on the envelope filled him with smiling astonishment, as though he had just learnt that she knew his name!

My dear friend,

This is rather absurd. I had no particular reason for coming to see you. But an opportunity has arisen and I am coming.

As you probably know, the 'Soldiers' Institute' from St Dié is giving a performance on the evening of the 28th in Granrupt, for your regiment.

I shall come with these people. We'll talk a little.

Best wishes from your friend,

Dominique.

Surprise mingled with pride! She, the proud girl, coming here for his sake! But a moment later his face fell.

Wherever he was going, wherever the river of his life was leading him, her sudden emergence there, with all that she stood for, represented an obstacle. In his relationships with other people, always he had taken care that the initiative came from him alone. How often had he rebuffed with cruel wisdom those he loved most, because the moment was inopportune! So he was vaguely resentful of this girl who offered herself, as of a threat to his freedom.

Nevertheless, as he read again: 'Yes, proud girl indeed!' he thought. 'It's the right word for her.' He liked the curtness of the note, and the short paragraphs, each 'indent', he knew from experience, being a pressure on the brake; and underneath the text, so voluptuously cold, the Christian name alone putting an incontrovertible seal upon their intimacy.

He went along the main trench, through the communication-trenches, treading on cartridge cases, following at random the astonishing maze of these advanced lines, where one could walk for ten minutes without meeting a soul. The ill-will of the men, who could not tolerate that the relieving troops should find clean what *they* had found dirty, the monstrous carelessness which always made them prefer danger to the trouble of organizing shelters, would have transformed these 'defences' into the most appalling death-traps, had not the enemy been equally concerned to justify the sector's designation as a 'rest-area'. Here and there the trench was blocked, and in order to proceed one had to climb over debris, exposing oneself above the parapet; sometimes it was so wide and its banks so eroded that it looked more like a small path where one had to walk bent double; sometimes a tree trunk had been wedged across it to hold up the slipping walls.

Here it was that Alban found himself, enclosed between four walls of dazzling azure and gold: yellow of sun and earth, blue of sky and shadows. And the contrast between the icy shade into which he plunged his face when he bent down and the scorching sun which hit him when he walked upright was so intense that he sneezed every time.

The desire to read the letter again welled up in him, violent as a summer thirst. He read it again in the half-light, and found it much more wonderful than in the full light of day. Then, gradually, the fact that the girl had come, that she was there, ten minutes by car from this wild kingdom, no longer seemed a violation, but filled him with that pride of life he knew only too well. He towered above the world, watching things move and arrange themselves around him like filings round a magnet; and the summits of his life broke into flame one after the other as the signal-fires of the cohorts answered one another in the Roman night. He saw that he had indeed fought hard, but had obtained with more or less perseverance all that he had desired; that his most extraordinary mad dreams of happiness had been realized, years after, without effort (without joy either, sometimes) – all the mad dreams and aberrations which came to him at dawn. He saw those he loved and who did not love him, those who loved him and whom he did not love, the enemies brought round by his virtues and the friends whom his virtues had alienated, and they all blended together, comple- mented and compensated for one another, were all equally neces- sary; and the purity of this or that friend, the impurity of Douce, Dominique's strength and Prinet's weakness were also necessary to him, and none was less valuable than another; and the riches of his nature had reconciled the irreconcilable, enthusiasm and calculation, brutality and culture, devotion and dissoluteness, friendship and love; and from good and bad, from pleasure and suffering, from each he took the amounts he needed, as a painter takes a dab of paint from his palette . . .

That night, the battalion went down to rest.

In Granrupt, they found changed faces:

'We're going up to the Oise.'

'This time we're in for the real thing!'

'We're going to be under Mangin.'

Then a voice was heard to exclaim:

'Mangin! That's terrific!'

It was Prinet, whom the sergeant from the posting-section would willingly have murdered for this exclamation.

Around them, the colonel's stay-put boys looked very downcast indeed. But the men of the battalion were unruffled: 'They say we're in for it this time. Well, we can't complain; we haven't had any for four months.'

In every group, the only subject of conversation was 'the real thing'. The impending danger seemed almost like a game because of the catch-phrase it had produced.

Would the show be on tomorrow? asked Alban. Yes, of course it would.

They spent the day with the company staff-sergeants. In this village that had been systematically spared and was unpurified by death, there was an atmosphere of gross mediocrity. And indeed, in the whole of the French Army, there is nothing so stupid, lazy and malicious as a Staff NCO. Here, you are in society; it is Sunday at the *concierge*'s. Much astonished disapproval because *Monsieur* de Bricoule has not had fancy pockets sewn into his coat. A company sergeant-major imitates Mayol. One says: 'Say hullo to the boys for me!' There is talk of *lady-friends*.

Alban was stupefied. For the first time since his arrival at the front, he made a conscious effort not to appear *stuck-up*. Gone was the healthy freedom of 'up there'.

'Lousy half-gentlemen, who look down your noses if one doesn't apologize for passing in front of you, or if one forgets to clink glasses before drinking, you are as revolting as dance-hall dandies. Ah! To be up there again! Up there!'

Here everyone knows that the most disagreeable comrade – colleague, one should rather say – may after all, should the occasion arise, save one's life: one dare not, as one would in civilian life, make enemies for the fun of it. And so, coffee, cards, bagatelle, France is lost, there are no American troops, all officers are murderers; above all one must waste one's time. Yes, life here is a permanent Sunday; Sunday, the dullest day of the week, the day when, more than ever, one kills time. (O Time! Kill them! Kill them!) Everything will be forgiven you if you waste your time as blatantly as possible. Alban, who gets a book out, is a 'seminarist'. Someone even suggests: 'quite probably an officer reduced to the ranks.'

The next day, a real Sunday this time, the band played.

Alban would always remember the blazing sun, the brilliant music, and also the impending menace, the serious faces. He was with Prinet, among the groups in the courtyard of the chateau. The whole of the staff was present. 'These handsome uniforms, these stripes, are we going to see them fleeing along the road, routed? What will the faces look like then? Will the lieutenant cry? How does he look when he cries?' The brass made their feelings heroic. The trumpet call was like the sound of the Roman trumpets greeting Caesar's arrival at the entrance to the arena. A young peasant-soldier, sitting with dangling legs on one of the castle walls, was the very image of the young legionary who used to watch the show twenty centuries before, perched on a buttress of the *spina*, the same who once ran naïvely to the aid of Nero when the latter, for a joke, had himself chained up by one of the actors in the play.

Prinet was amused to see how Alban's eyes kept going back and fastening involuntarily upon the rows of medals worn by the high-ranking officers.

'Let's hope you'll get the *Légion d'Honneur* one day,' said Alban.
'Yes, if I deserve it.'

'One of my cousins, on the Army Staff, might perhaps . . .'

'Oh, no, not that!' Prinet interrupted with a start.

And Alban regretted his blunder. Did he not remember the ridiculous affair of Prinet losing his head during his examinations, being ploughed, having to study for another year after having exhausted himself with ineffective swotting, and all this because he had refused to allow anyone to pull strings on his behalf when nothing would have been easier. Alban was touched to the quick by such delicacy of feelings, but at the same time worried at seeing it combined with such helplessness. Yesterday again, in the course of a day spent in the company of new people, he had been able to observe how low the young man's credit stood, how incapable he was of making people appreciate him: nobody listened to what he said, he was continually interrupted, nobody turned to him in conversation. His rank made him half-officer, half-NCO, and it was disturbing to notice that the boy always veered towards the latter, disturbing to feel that he was already resigned to spending all his life in subordinate positions, that he would be the sort of man who only deals with secretaries, that an obscure instinct drew him for preference towards those who were least successful. 'In ten years' time, shall we still know each other?' Alban wondered, suddenly overwhelmed by a wave of sadness.

The music stopped, and they saw Captain Véran suddenly emerge from one of the doors of the chateau and stand in the empty space between the band and the audience, like a bull arriving in the arena. Restless, feline, his body slightly bent, looking up from under his eyebrows, his eyes moved ceaselessly and he gave a start when the colonel signalled to him, for he was consumed by one thought: 'Will the big show make me a major?'

Alban watched him with childlike admiration. He knew that the red ribbon on his breast was the blood of his men. But he stood silent, gazing intently with eyes full of love, fascinated by the domineering brute. Prinet attacked him under his breath.

'And yet,' Alban replied, 'can you imagine, can you actually imagine him saying: "F . . . ! I've really made a mess of it"?'

Prinet did not answer, and these words seeped into him. And he too began to look in childish wonderment, tamed and full of love for this man of worth.

Now the music started again. It was obvious that the smooth-faced band-master, with his handsome profile, had his orchestra well in hand.

'I'm sure he would make a good commander,' said Prinet knowingly.

Alban thought: 'He thinks the chap would make a good leader, just because he controls his band well and has a Napoleonic profile! Yesterday, when we were having a go at that German plane, he shouted: "Oh! It's on fire!" when it was only the glitter of the sun on the propeller! What a child! And a good half of this battalion are like that! And France's throbbing life is in these schoolboys' hands!'

He thrilled with ambition as, in a loud burst of music, the groups parted to give way to a splendid car which glided swiftly and noiselessly into the courtyard. Gold-spangled officers stepped out, were seen speaking to the colonel, then hurried into the castle. Then, while Brahm's Hungarian Dances released above the doomed heads a thousand silken streamers, the men turned round and stopped listening, and voices rose:

'What are they saying? What's up?'

'Things are bad.'

'Ah! Again!'

Again! Always! The heart tightens.

As everyone was leaving, Alban went up to Father Perrin, the colonel's secretary. Never would he forget the despair on the face of this man at the end of that festive day.

'Will the performance be on all the same?'

'Yes, but you know, we've had it.'

'She will come!' thought Alban.

And that night it was only after a savage struggle; the furniture was overturned and the frightened cat jumped out of the window, and they throbbed together as at the climax of a fire . . .

Calm at last, the young man fell asleep. He had killed. He had possessed. Now Dominique could come. He was ready for the soul.

8

Music at Night

BEHIND THE curtain, in the silence and the half-light, a woman's voice rose, then another, then another, like fountains being turned on one by one, then the whole choir, and all heads were bowed. Privates and NCOs, old and young, lowly workmen and clerks, the most obscure, the most under-privileged, all had felt a supernatural presence descending upon the humble barn. And heads had bowed as though to the elevation of an invisible monstrance; and their wretched life had been transfigured as a landscape is transfigured by the fall of the first shell, as a drawing-room where a man has been waiting is transfigured by the woman's arrival; and the lukewarm song had lifted the roof as the steam of boiling water lifts a lid, and had spread outside; and the sentries, raising their heads to the drifting music, thought it was God on night-patrol over the lines.

On arrival, while the ladies of the 'Institute' were making their way towards the building already buzzing with voices in the twilight, Dominique had searched for Alban among the crowd. She had not found him, and had been the last to get into the barn, miserable at the thought that she might not see him. And now, leaning against the back wall near the door, having spotted him at last among the boys, she looked at the man for whom she had come.

Clear-sighted and accustomed to self-examination as she was, she realized at once: her experience at the hospital would in any case have sufficed to enlighten her. As she watched him, as she learned again the features of his face, suddenly sensing those infinite depths of sadness, sensing this cruel well-being which had overcome her like an attack of fever, no doubt remained: she realized that, for the first time because of him, something more comprehensive than her intelligence was stirred.

'This is terrible!' she said, for she had seen the lioness, which, like Cybele, she had held sleeping in her lap, open wide its jaws. 'But is it possible?' Her eyes widened, she shook herself, body and soul, straightened up, body and soul, as a pilot straightens up his pitching aircraft. 'With him as with Bouchard?' In a flash she imagined him in the same circumstances and behaving as the electrician had behaved. Nothing violent happened in her, but a voice she had never heard forced the cry out of her: 'Ah! My hand on his back, and he not resisting . . .'

The curtain had risen, unveiling the floral choir, fifteen young women, young girls and little girls. She would have guessed it from the changed expression on her friend's face, from the pout of his lips, impudent rather than impure, with that impudence that coloured his whole life. 'He must have been wondering whether their hands trembled before they started singing. If he now felt about one of these women what I have felt about Bouchard, he would not hesitate for one second: he would take her off, give her a smacking kiss, and crudely ask her: yes or no. He feels he can do whatever he likes; anything whatsoever seems splendid once he has done it. With this insulting quality in him, will he get through life without trouble? How he must suffer from curbing his nature to bring it more or less on to terms with society! He plays far too many tricks on society to manage without its indulgence when, some day, he finds himself caught in one of its traps, and he worries himself sick at the thought of continually giving it power over him . . .'

Then she watched the women on the stage. 'Me, like them! Me!' Now she no longer laughed at the idea of being associated with this riff-raff. 'With them, it's bad; with me, it's good.' The drastic simplification simplified nothing now! When she had felt herself developing a taste for the men at the hospital, a few sophistries had been enough to reassure her; and gradually she had even come to enjoy contradicting her own principles. But now she rebelled; the things at stake were too deeply important. 'A girl in love . . . like them! Like every one of them!' When the curtain had risen a tremor had run through the hall. She twisted the meaning of this tremor, interpreting it as obscene. The gratitude which carried these poor wretches towards the messengers of the good life, the miracle of music which for an hour transformed these village school-mistresses, these convent orphans, these small-town shop assistants into enchanted instruments, all this meant nothing to her. She sullied them, she wanted them base and stupid; 'The more *musical* a woman is, the more stupid she is. I've noticed it time and again. The little goose who thinks she has a bit of talent and who makes music with her cousin and goes to Sunday concerts . . . and who is madly in love!' The horror of what she imagined pushed her far away from love, and she had almost recovered her self-possession when she saw Alban cutting through the crowd towards her. It was she who shook his hand and held it, felt the size of his hand, the moisture of his hand, full of blood and water. She felt strong.

'Thank you for coming here,' he said, 'on behalf of myself and the others. Did you see them watching you out of the corner of their eyes? They literally devour you with their eyes. And tomorrow they'll take you away with them, feed upon you for months . . .'

He had seen one of the boys staring at her with dreamy eyes; had felt him soften before all these promises of happiness, so weak in life's hands. The music was like the memory of past joys.

'But it's for you alone that I've come,' she said simply.

She regretted these words, wondering whether she would have said them when she was different. She no longer remembered what she could have been, what she could have thought or said when she was different. She could not feel her strength any more.

He asked about her new life. She answered cautiously. As she became aware how conspicuous they were talking together in the middle of this crowd – the two of them isolated even further by the faces turning towards them with angry whispers of 'ssh!' – she had started to weaken again. As for him, when he came close to her mouth it was as though he was approaching a flame; and he bent lower and lower still, to receive the odour of her mouth, for today her mouth smelt good (some days, there was no smell at all); and he made her repeat things, as though he were a little deaf, in order to smell it once more. And gradually – adorable mystery – he noticed that the air around her over a wide radius had become as it were the property of her mouth, had been permeated by it; for whereas at first he had been obliged to bend in order to catch its scent, now he received whiffs of it where he was, without having to move. And he was amazed, awestruck, wondering how, by what miracle, a human mouth that eats and drinks can yet have such an exquisite aroma. He remembered his mother saying when he was a little boy, that his mouth smelled of peaches; he remembered the smells of all the women he had desired or known, all different as faces are different and each one unique in the smell of the nape of the neck, which differed from that of the throat, which was unlike the smell of the back of the hands, which was not that of the palms, which again differed from that of the forehead. Such were his thoughts, none of them impure.

But now, near the door, there were whispers:

'It's hotting up, out there!'

'Hotting up?'

He opened the door a fraction.

'Ah!'

She slipped out behind him.

The *Trommelfeuer* was like a mountain chain of sound, without an instant of silence, without a break, uninterrupted. In their thousands, the separate sounds of the firing collided and clashed, suggesting to the young man thousands of levers being pulled and pushed back in a factory, their echoes welding them together, becoming continuous with them. This deadly rumble seemed to belong to the realm of silence, seemed to be a mode of silence. All around was the night.

She asked when the regiment was leaving.

'The day after tomorrow, maybe, in lorries. We're waiting for the order.'

'May fate be accomplished!'

'What!' he exclaimed, bristling because he had caught her out in a lack of intelligence, 'I am here at my own request, through my own resolution and obstinacy, and you call it fate! It is my own will which is fate,' he added with an attractive harshness which gave her a faint shiver of desire. 'Anyway, I shan't die, my passions hold me down to earth. But really, what a lot of fuss about death! Fancy being sad when one is going to join Plato and Marcus Aurelius! I have loved all that is noble; there is no pleasure I have not known; I have had happiness, too, real happiness . . . After all that, it doesn't appal me to have to end the game now. I have had my fill of living.'

He smiled, not without gravity.

'If by the grace of God I survive and some day, with the ideas they have at the rear, people should tell you that I hold cheap the lives of my fellow-men, you will be able to answer that I am one of those to whom it is permissible, since I held my own cheapest of all.'

Irritated by his 'grace of God', and thinking him a bit 'young', she did not reply. 'How can he speak to me about his pleasures? And tell me he has "had his fill of living . . ." ' Suddenly, she was reminded of an incident, long, long ago. One day she had noticed, on the fleshy part of his hand, three small scars forming an arc, indubitably the mark of teeth. 'What have you got there?' she had asked. 'Oh, nothing at all,' and he had withdrawn his hand. Now all at once she took in everything that was rumoured and everything she herself had half-guessed about the freedom and the violence of his life. But suddenly she thought: 'Yesterday, I would have been delighted at his frankness. To be able to talk about these things as equals was a sign of our solidarity . . .'

'Let's go in again,' she said with a vague, instinctive feeling that the women on the stage would fortify her as they had done before, would re-establish her by sheer contrast in the Doric order. Meanwhile Alban regretted his impatient outburst: 'What a lot of fuss about death!' for he had just been imagining Prinet's death, and he fled the thought, unmanned.

The music engulfed them, a new kind of music, shaken out by the orchestra alone this time, like some monstrous madness. They guessed it was Russian, or rather by a disciple of the Russians, for they could not recognize the music, and Dominique, who had thought to recover her composure in the barn, leant with sudden anguish over this gulf which drew her down as if in its depths there struggled some creature which knew her secrets and was about to call out her name.

The simple, melodious choruses had created a communion; the orchestra erected a barrier, speaking a hermetic language in which most of the audience heard nothing but a frantic and shameless emotionalism, others a mysterious annunciation whispered in their ear. There were sudden outbursts, then all the notes came tumbling, streaming down in disorder, like spilt liquid; and the women, who had come down among the audience, breathed heavily and straightened their busts, looking suddenly more beautiful in their uneasiness; and the little fifteen-year-olds looked away as if they had been told something improper. The musical swirl enveloped Alban like a deep sea surging, flowing round him, and from every visible and invisible point there came to him intimations of delight, born on the tide of this facility. The fluttering of the hands on the strings (did he not *hear* those hands?) the muscles running along the bare arm stroking the 'cello, and the straining of the head with that forced smile like a tired young oarsman – for him these details were less clear than the feelings which rose from the exposed depths of his being. Vows of eternal love, far-away countries, intimate bonds made and broken as easily as the groupings in a ballet, moments in which God had leapt at him as a dog does in greeting, and the sudden explosion of pleasure in a woman when you thought she

106

was going to remain passive – a wild outburst of life, a simultaneous memory of all the joys given and received, welled up inside him, choked him, set the nerves around his lips quivering with the effort to remain a man. 'O God! Spare the lives of these children who have yet so much to know. As for me, I have had everything. No doubt it would be sweeter to live; but truly I cannot find it unjust to be chosen to return to the shadows.'

He looked at Dominique. A soldier had slipped in between them, and according to whether he leaned forward or straightened up, the beauty and charm of her virginal face appeared or disappeared like a star between clouds. He looked long at her, thinking of what she would later become, with a feeling of peace and certainty. He had faith in her heart, in the seriousness and strength in her, the goodness and the delicacy, her sensitivity to greatness, her forward-looking nature. The soldier moved away a little. Alban was now too close to be able to look at her any more.

Suddenly, the music grew even more barbaric, the pupil outdid his masters, and Alban now guessed that the pupil was none other than the regimental bandleader who was now conducting the orchestra, a composer of the new school, well known to music-lovers. There came one wild moment when all the musicians were flailing their arms as if they were boxing, or as if they were engaged in a race and trying to overtake one another without moving, and as the women threw up their hands to pluck the strings of their violins, their bows, suddenly raised, looked like so many tapers, and all the musicians seemed to be the priests and celebrants of a new cult. The barrier erected by the music became high as a barricade. Amidst the soldiers and the officers, the spirit of Revolt rose up and flaunted its banner. The breaking of laws, the un-leashing of passions, the liberation of thought and life, the hope of a better world – all this was raised and loudly proclaimed in front of men who would die tomorrow for the established order. A tragic moment, for it was impossible to tell who heard this secret call and who did not.

Dominique leant forward, her eyes wide open as they might have

107

been in the act of love. And finding within herself no sign of protest against this music, she had a feeling of all kinds of inner fences being trampled and destroyed, her most precious possessions at the mercy of a horde of savage assailants. As the sleeping satyr who was caught by Sylla's troups and taken before the general for questioning by the interpreters, could only utter a horrible cry like the whinnying of a horse and the bleat of a goat, and Sylla, struck with horror, had him removed from his presence: so the phrygian mode was brought in and unleashed before the colonel and his men, and with unintelligible words it writhed and foamed at the mouth before their eyes. But the colonel, unlike Sylla, was not horrified. He sat in the front row, listening, an old nobleman of ancient lineage, the symbol of all things ancient, with his blue eyes paler than his blue-grey uniform, amused and placid. Alban would have liked to go up to him, shake his arm, shout at him: 'Can't you see that you're being betrayed, slapped in the face, that this music is undermining you, undermining your authority and your *raison d'être*? Ah! blind wretch, with your look of complicity!' He saw him sitting there, oblivious as a man who laughs while hidden murderers lie in wait for him, oblivious as a mother among her well-beloved children who, deep in their books, are far away from her, betraying her! Suddenly, in the middle of a phrase, the music stopped dead, cut off, suspended in mid-air. The audience waited, thinking it would start again after a pause. The conductor turned round, smiled at the misunderstanding he had hoped for, and bowed. The audience clapped.

'You're clapping?' said Alban to the girl with a kind of amazement, as if she had publicly condoned something obscene. It was indeed a whiff of impurity that he had just received from her, one of those signs that provoke desire, because they seem to attest a weakness which might make every acquiescence possible: a woman you notice cheating at cards, a woman who has a fit of coughing . . .

But the colonel had risen. He was saying that they would end up with the regimental song. He wanted everyone to sing it standing. His voice was the voice of a man. They all felt its beneficial impact.

Everyone rose. The music rose, itself like a rising crowd. The souls of all of them rose, too. God rose. The heavenly multitude rose. A feeling of brotherhood shivered down each spine. The song was ordinary enough, yet it had the power to bind this masculine body closer together. As they were singing:

The old 'uns of the Nth . . .
The old 'uns are still there!

Alban heard Prinet sing: *'the young 'uns of the Nth . . . '* – a childish, touching substitution which reflected the spirit of the whole battalion, and was enough to burst open his heart, releasing a flow of tenderness that washed over all these men. How remote, now, were the women's silly voices which earlier had held such power, had been such a wicked invitation to weakness and sentiment. An invisible church had risen in the barn. All were singing: Alban himself, the men who had been sniggering about the defeat, Prinet, like a still breeze, the colonel with the gentle blue eyes, whose voice could not be heard, and she too, his comrade. Alban saw her tensed features, the swelling of her nostrils, the strength of her neck, the lifting of her shoulders as she joined in the refrain, her eye-sockets ashen like those of the dead; he noticed the youthfulness of her teeth and her palate, the ample volume of air which was born within her and which shook her as it gushed forth. Through the mass of sound he took pleasure in picking out Dominique's voice and following it among all the others, and the fact that he could distinguish her voice was like a sign of an equally close intimacy with her soul. And in an impulse that was not impure, he felt he would have liked to take the song as it came out of her mouth, before it had gone cold, before it had lost its odour, and press it against him as though it were flesh. If only he could have heard the words she was saying instead of the miserable words of the anthem!

All her purities were ablaze in her singing; they burned, and melted as they burned, showing, like melted snow, the grimy earth and the mud underneath. 'I feel, I know, that this is good.

May I remain worthy of having sung their man's song with them!
May I truly remain the brother of these brave boys who are
going to their death! May I find in myself what I need to resist
temptation! But what? What? Ah! I must get away ... at once ...'

The voices broke away from the lips, flew off, were no more.
A hubbub arose. Everyone started talking, stepping over the
benches, rushing down from the galleries, jostling towards the
door. She said 'Excuse me ...' to her neighbours, who stood aside;
she heard Alban behind her saying 'Where are you going?' and
answered: 'The colonel is offering the ladies a glass of champagne'
(afterwards she did not remember having said this); and she went
straight towards the platform still saying 'Excuse me ... Excuse
me ...' and joined the group of ladies and officers. Only then,
furtively, did she turn her head.

She could not see him any more. She felt weak, felt her legs
going limp above the knees, as though this part of her was dead or
about to die. She was hurled to the highest point of anguish, like
an egg on top of a jet of water at a fairground shooting-stall. One
of the girls called to her. Then she talked about the evening, with
exaggeration, and this lie between her words and her thoughts
comforted her extremely.

'He must not follow me! He must not follow me! Let me be
spared the struggle! I could hide ... They may sound the recall and
he'll have to go. He'll think I was going to come back, that it was
bad luck ...' Then she saw him in the crowd, chatting to Prinet,
his hand resting charmingly on his friend's belt. Without another
word to the girl she crossed the room towards him, staring at him
as a tight-rope walker stares at the pole at the end of the rope in
order not to fall.

He said:

'You were there a long time! Come on, let's go outside.'

'Where?'

'Listen! Ah! Never before did God come down so near to me nor
offer me such great things!'

The bombardment was not so continuous now. There were

moments of silence, followed by earth-shattering convulsions similar to those huge sobs which children give after tears; then the frenzy of our guns, behind them, as though on turning round they would see a Presence, death knocking furiously at a closed door, shaking it, on the point of breaking it down and rushing in. He saw her uneasy expression.

'You look like a little girl about to be eaten by an ogre.'

'You think I'm afraid?' she said in a strangled voice, choking because she could not tell him that it was he who frightened her.

The moon, blurred and saffron-rimmed, glazed the fields with pinkish snow and gave a metallic sheen to the leaves of the trees. Rockets rose in the distance. Green rockets: 'Bring in the artillery.' Red rockets: 'Lengthen the range.' Up they went, reaching their zenith as in a spasm of acute pleasure, then falling suddenly as though some travelling shell had hit them. Tragic calls! Pathetic cries! Long tears streaming down from the sky! Who could have dared to make a wish in the time it took those shooting stars to fall? They called to mind the multitude of crouching men, the anguish, the coming of death, the murderous vigils, all the invisible suffering and brutality under that dark horizon, innocent as the most innocent countryside, from which the hideous hiccoughs rose into the divine night.

Fear! Fear! He was right: she trembled as she followed him, trembled like a little girl dragged off by an ogre. He noticed it, and said:

'Are you cold? Shall we go back? And what about that famous glass of champagne?'

'No . . . No, really . . .'

Just as earlier she had come back after having left him, now for the second time she clung to him when she had a chance of getting away, for the fact of their being here, in the middle of the night, terribly alone and almost compromising each other, seemed to her a burning of boats, a *ne plus ultra* which gave her a confused sense of freedom. And the awareness of her surrender was partly lulled by a vague feeling of need.

III

Now Alban was describing the sector. She felt he would have liked to talk about it at length. All these tales of war, of soldiers, were the symbol of his new life, his better self. But once again she felt that something had been torn open inside her, this time letting out everything that reflected the mind and soul of her friend, and she stumbled agonizingly against this emptiness as against a wall. Yes, it was true, she felt no interest in what he said, what he thought, what he was. What forced itself implacably on her at this moment was the memory of that other young man at whose side she had walked a few days before as she now walked beside this one. She relived the moment when she had put her arm behind his waist, slipped her hand under his jacket, and kept it there on his hip, feeling the play of the joints at each step he took . . . and she wondered whether the other, now gliding along beside her with the supple majesty of his long hero's strides, whether he, too, had that dear little thing there moving with each step.

Yet all this time, whilst she loved him so much more, she felt she was betraying him, as though she loved him less. Feeling him so close to her, believing her to be the same when in fact she was different, she felt she was deceiving him, that she was doing something shameful, and she was filled with a kind of pity for him. This pity, this feeling that she was doing wrong, powerfully nurtured her love.

She was thinking of all this when she saw, a discus-throw away, two soldiers walking on the road in front of them. One was holding the other round the waist in the way she was just imagining, then his hand went farther up and he was holding him under the arm, at the same time looking from side to side in a worried way. Dominique was intrigued, and a little embarrassed. But Alban:

'There's a fellow who isn't drunk only with Russian music. If he didn't have a good pal to look after him, you'd see him walking on all fours.'

'Is he drunk?' she asked naïvely.

'Can't you see!'

Then she thought about this gesture of putting an arm round another's body, to her a caress, to this man a brotherly support, and she reflected that *her* face showed anxiety lest they be caught in the act, whereas *his* showed anxiety lest his friend be punished. She was filled with self-disgust, but it was powerless.

They passed a spring, flowing through the nocturnal calm as though someone had forgotten to turn it off the night before. Further on, the water was still with the moon reflected in it, a little round thing projecting an infinite pillar of fire – just as a tiny word of one syllable can produce something infinite in the heart. On the horizon in front of them, caught at the bottom of the valley as in a crucible, the smoke from our guns gathered, violet- and rose-coloured, like a cloud fallen from the sky. And the long-drawn, musical voices of the shells called to them like the voices of the Valkyries.

She knitted her brows and shut her eyes tight in order to con-centrate and clarify her thoughts. 'We are alone. Another quarter of an hour and we shall be separated for an indefinite period. Tomorrow, perhaps, he will be dead. That's one thing . . .' (she had to make a tremendous effort simply to bring these propositions together) 'And on the other hand I have a desire, such a desire, to touch him, to . . . If I resist it, I remain intact in my pride, in everything that makes my strength, and in my power over him. If I succumb, I lose all this for one minute of pleasure; but I want that pleasure so much that it counter-balances everything, absolves everything; and who knows whether he also, later on . . . What shall I do? What shall I do? What is best for me?' From the moment she had felt herself going limp above the knees, and had crossed the barn staring at him, none of her resolutions remained firm. Every-thing was once more in the balance.

She felt blocked up on every side, incapable of deciding, incapable of speaking, her body unable to do anything but put one foot in front of the other as she walked, her eyes unable to look at any-thing else but the surface of the water, full of little ripples as if it were raining, though it was not. Behind them, the air was wounded

by the wailing of bugles, fragmentary as the cries of little boys overheard after lunch in the suburbs as they trail off to Sunday school.
Then a voice rose; a man on his way back to camp was humming
the refrain of a popular song they had heard that evening at the
show:

And if you don't like it,
Just tell us what you li-i-ike . . .

and a thrill ran down her spine at this intimation of bliss in the
deadly night; and it brought her closer to him. Ah, to think that
joy could be awakened by this crude, pathetic voice! One by one
she caught the smell of the grass, the smell of the water, the smell of
the earth, the smell of the night, the smell of the hay, each prevailing
in its turn. In a gesture as instinctive as that of laying a hand on a
bird escaping from its cage, she wanted to touch the man at her
side, merely to touch the material of his coat, even if she could not
feel his body underneath; and the wailing of the sirens, the fabulous
horizon, violet and blood-red, set this moment beyond life.

'Everything is permissible in a time like this,' she thought.
'What is the good of this immense upheaval in the world if we are
not allowed to behave exceptionally too? Is this epoch of extraordinary disorder to pass by without our ever being able to make
use of it? There are no more rules, good is no longer good, evil no
longer evil, conventions, illusions, all the old foundations are
overthrown, and I am here, alone, free, far from my people and
our laws, and yet tomorrow I must start again as before? Tomorrow?
But in five minutes! . . .' She saw herself in the bus, amidst the
gossiping women, when this minute would belong to the past,
the same past to which the minutes of ten years ago belonged; and
tomorrow in the strange room she would bend over her diary and
describe what she had not had, lifting her head from time to time
to shake off the feeling of oppression and suffocation; and she would
have to find the courage to try and remember the smallest details,
when it would be so good to be able to forget . . . Ah, the regret,
tomorrow! The remorse!

She heard him say 'Don't you think?' loudly, as though he were repeating it. She had not realized he was speaking. There was a moment of slight confusion. He had stopped, and she found herself a few steps ahead of him.

'Let's go back,' he said. 'I can hear one of your cars being started.'

She looked at him; while they had been walking side by side, she had not been able to look at him. In the darkness, his neck seemed strangely luminous, as though it had gathered every trace of light that lingered in the night, inaccessible yet close at hand like a mirage. And the effect of seeing him again was as if she had been given an injection of alcohol, while at the same time the act of looking back towards the rear, of losing sight of the flaming horizon and that impossible paradise, intensified her awareness of departure to the point where reality dissolves into music. She thought there was some desperate opportunity to be seized and used, some possibility which would never again arise on this earth. The idea of war as a time when everything is permitted and excused – like carnival-time in ancient Venice – took possession of her as do ideas which come not from our intellect but from the deepest layers of our carnal soil. She knew that she would not resist, that she no longer wanted to resist. Would he have resisted, he who had said 'I have never resisted except as an experiment'? And faced by the imminence of the act she had in mind, and the thought that it would have to be performed before they reached the cars which she could make out as a shadowy mass in the darkness, she tottered forward, really afraid she might faint.

'The moment we pass the barbed wire I shall reach up, I shall pull him to me, I shall kiss him. It will be the end or the beginning of everything.' She could no longer visualize any pleasure from the kiss, no more pleasure than she would have felt at kissing one of those tree-trunks; she saw it as an awkward duty, necessary to stop her trembling, a kind of formality which would introduce her into a new world. All her emotional life anaesthetized and inert, her sole concern was how the kiss was to be given. Would she first of all take Alban's arm? What would he do? On which precise area of his face would her mouth fall? In front of them, the barbed wire was drawing nearer; a long ribbon glittering through the dark countryside like a reflection of the Milky Way upon the earth.

The young man was saying:

'If you knew how happy I am at this moment. And why? Because you exist, and because you are as you are. Sometimes I may forget you, why not admit it? Sometimes I may spend several days without one single thought of you; but under this oblivion there is the knowledge that you go on existing; and if I try to imagine my life without this knowledge, suddenly – do you know? – everything collapses. Indeed, if I had not known you, there would rise in me now a terrible regret, a terrible revolt which would make me cry out and curse in my death agony, tomorrow perhaps . . . Soubrier, Soubrier, you cannot imagine my despair if what exists through you did not exist!'

'Why did he say that? Why? Why can't I believe any more that all his war experiences are far more important than I am to him? No, it's no longer possible for me to destroy . . . Ah, why has he wanted me to be like that? Why was I like that? Why aren't we like others, he and I?' – thus Dominique's thoughts sped like the wind, sped on with the noise of some terrible train. She wanted to speak, to say something, to make up for her earlier silence, but she could no more speak than if her tongue had been cut off, and she thought she had not answered at all, not realizing that she had muttered some childish phrase, absurd and hardly intelligible: 'I am as you think I am . . .' She could no longer see the barbed wire in front of her. They had gone past it.

Past! She remembered. Her eyes widened. She felt better, as one does after vomiting. It was as though the kiss had become materially impossible; as though really, once past the barbed wire, she no longer had to will, she only had to accept. Very well! She accepted. Henceforth she would live on pride alone. She would leave the hospital and all its sordid temptations. She would return to her former life, she would re-establish and maintain the style of life which was irreplaceably hers. Once more they would 'do something to improve the world' as her friend had once said. She would be heroic; she had missed that. The possibility of being heroic was like a grace that had been bestowed on her.

But from her left the voice came to her, and strength and gentleness were mingled in every phrase: 'That is why, when I have found myself blind, yes, blind amid chasms filled with music, I have been able to go on without stumbling as long as my hand rested on your shoulder for support, able to walk through the flames with the thought of your existence round me like an impenetrable armour . . .' She no longer heard, then heard once more: 'I had only to see your silhouette in the distance in order to feel an instantaneous desire for your happiness . . . this longing for your happiness tears my soul . . .' She heard no more, and then again: 'I have welded you to everything that is strongest in me. With you it is always my strength, always my strength!' She remembered something he had said:

'You must always imagine what I say to you as uttered in the midst of sublime music, Beethoven or Wagner or whoever you may find sublime, for what I say to you is born from just such music and can only be understood in that context.'

'Like lightning in the noise of a storm?' she had asked.

'Like birds, rather,' he had replied. 'I have blurted out my cries like great birds which will come back and wheel about in all your twilights.'

Then the immense choir of the soldiers rose and swelled and lifted her up to inhuman heights, among the marvellous winds. She saw the great black sky crack like a cup, a fountain of fire burst through the crevice, and another sky appear in which were the pure, men and women. 'Do not fear! Do not fear! I shall not be one whose body is forever offering or demanding. I shall remain hard in order to support you, and beyond reach, and impenetrable, and hostile, and barren, and without movement and without words, and with no other smile than the smile of the glaciers, dazzling and burning cold like me – this do I promise you tonight in this darkness, you alone beside me alone . . .'

They had arrived behind the barn, where the sound of voices could still be heard. On the other side, the cars were purring. They stopped.

'Dominique Soubrier,' he said, taking her hand, 'I say good-bye to you.' And then, with intense emotion, yet smiling, his eyelids a little lowered: 'Be good.' Still smiling, he went on to say, as to a child: 'I am very fond of you . . .'

She was before him, face to face with him. She looked at him, saw his smile, saw the innermost depths of his great soul descending towards her like a river. For three seconds she looked at him. Then everything melted, fainted within her. She bent her face over the hand which held hers. And she pressed her mouth to it, kept it there, her lips motionless, not kissing.

9

Argo

IN THE depths of the troop transport, which was like the vessel Argo, light shone only from the blue-glinting rifles, the metal gas-mask containers, the helmeted heads which emerged, face to face, through the windows like the heads of heroes through the portholes of a ship on a Greek bowl; it was a fine and warlike thing, rolling towards the battlefield through the silence of the ebbing night. The moon, which for a while had followed the lorries, had now been finally left behind, and had settled upon a rooftop to die. All around, the shadowy tree-masses began slowly to take shape, and one could make out the hay-stacks and the low, solitary hamlets; then suddenly the whole east burst into music. It was a mass of incandescence and lava, its colours intensifying from second to second, the bright ever brighter, the dark ever darker, conjuring up a vision of some titanic Acropolis, wars among the gods above new Iliads, fabulous Red Sea crossings, whilst in the background, behind these barbaric clouds, cities of orange trees sloped down. Then everything subsided, and the sun came out, white and distinct as a host or a pearl; it rolled along the road like an aircraft on a runway before taking off, and at last freed itself and rose. The first peasants appeared. Standing by the roadside, they watched the gallant soldiers on their way to the battlefield, and raised their hands in salute.

Sadness of the dawn. What would the day bring with it? It was so beautiful! What would it shine on, the sun whose birth they had witnessed and which, at this very moment, people were seeing over the Ranelagh gardens or in the Boulevard de Courcelles, low down between the houses like a street lamp not yet switched off? Everyone observed in silence the changing features of the passing countryside. In the midst of a deserted immensity full of the cawing of crows, over against the sinister horizon, were three or four airships which could 'see you' though you didn't know whether they were French or German; there were fresh shell-holes on each side of the road, and many a pair of eyes looked around for the nearest ditch. And then, as if to probe the wound, the convoy changed direction and turned back towards the rear; there were some, among the boys of the latest intake, who wondered (since after all, nothing definite had been said) if they weren't simply going down for a rest-period. But meanwhile they saw in the distance long trails of vapour which they took at first for early morning river mist until, as the wind rose, they saw that it was the dust raised by other convoys, other innumerable convoys all going in the same direction as their own, for the wind, whipping up the dust behind them, made it stand out in silhouetted clouds; and their hopes faded. They passed more identical villages, more identical fields; they passed flocks of sheep, and there were starlings perched on the sheep's backs, and the sheep looked almost black against the frosty ground; they saw ploughmen, and at intervals the blade of a plough glittered with dazzling brightness in this expanse of land as though man, cutting into mysterious matter, had struck stars from it. And from the backs of carts, from barges gliding by from doorsteps and from behind iron railings on which the hoar frost had woven a silver lattice-work, people raised their heads in salute.

It was an ever-rising benediction, gradually spreading like fire. The women and children blessed the gallant soldiers going off to battle. Once, when the convoy stopped, two old women ran to their gardens and cut down all their roses; another, even older, raised her hand without waving, and for the whole time it took the convoy to pass by she kept her hand there motionless, and sometimes it would weaken and she would quickly raise it even higher so that those boys might not think that they were loved less than the others; a young mother lifted up her infant in her arms; an old man gave a military salute; a little boy picked a pansy from in front of his house while the convoy was stationary, but at first he dared not offer it and then his mother pushed him, and as the lorries started up again he ran behind and, blushing, threw the little flower into one of them, and it was Alban who caught it, his heart stirred. And the gallant soldiers thought: 'We have seen this. We ourselves were peasants, clerks and suchlike and we never thought we could be so important. If we come back, we shall always remember this moment when we were loved so much. If we die, well, we know that we shall not die forsaken. We thank you all, men and women, for what you are giving us.' And on they went, catching fleeting glimpses on their way of home and happiness, of promises and avowals; and always, in an ever-renewed flowering, hands raised in salute and heads bared: hands that had tilled the soil, or spun wool, or held a rosary, or coaxed pleasure from the far reaches of the dawn, all were raised above bared heads, saluting as one salutes the dead.

10

Noctium Phantasmata

'MY DEAR Printet, how filthy you are!'

Alban saw the boy sitting in front of him on the threshold of the dug-out, his face grey and hollow with fatigue, soil in his ears, his hair, rough and discoloured like the coat of some small country animal, falling over his neck. 'We don't struggle any more. Gone are all the social trimmings! They are stripped bare now, our pathetic bodies and our pathetic little laws. And yet, divorced from the infirmities of the flesh and all the unlovely mysteries, our souls are intact and sound, with never a thought of betrayal.' And in this negation of appearances, their friendship took on a new stature.

July 19th! A sad day! Having alighted from the lorries near the Oise, for the past fortnight they had been wandering from village to village, billeting in each for a few days, and had finally taken up new positions last night, in the heart of this small wood, heavy with fragrant rain.

After supper, Printet had come and joined Alban, and was now sitting at the entrance of the narrow dug-out in the rain, as if he could not feel it. With his streaming helmet, his caked hands, that weird bit of oilcloth tied round him with bits of string, his leggings on which a fresh coat of wet mud showed above the dry one, he looked as though he had risen alive out of the age of the druids. A stray dog he had picked up stood in front of him, its muzzle on his lap, looking into his eyes with an expression of intense sadness.

Inside, squatting on a bed of bracken, Alban, his shoe in shreds, was trying to tie a couple of handkerchiefs round his foot to replace his filthy sock.

Sad day! Sad close of day! The great German attack which had been expected every day for a month had finally started on the 16th. It was said to have been less shattering than earlier ones. Even so, to Prinet and Alban, the fact that the enemy had crossed the Marne was disconcerting enough. Ever since March 21st, each German offensive had penetrated a little farther into the heart of France. Every time they wanted something, they had got it. On March 21st, they had reached Montdidier; on April 10th, Bailleul; on May 27th, Château-Thierry; on June 9th they had taken the Matz. And today they had achieved what has been through the centuries the most difficult manoeuvre, the crossing of a river, in just one night as though they had encountered no resistance whatever. They had even had time to build bridges! They were confident enough to fight the river itself! The two young men were numb with stupefaction and gloom.

Sad day! Sad close of day! Still, the rain had stopped. One could hear the rumbling of the guns, at regular intervals, like a man snoring. With the twilight, wave after wave of torpor descended on them. On the ground, level with their faces, they could see the gaping food-tins full of yellowish water, the bits of paper and the handfuls of grass that had been used to wipe the mess-tins smeared with congealed fat. And inside the dug-out, disappearing one by one in the thickening darkness, the confusion of miserable objects: a revolting mess-tin half-filled with food gone cold, on which the flies lay completely still, a hunk of bread dusted with earth which would crunch between the teeth, a mug with its coating of stale wine, a folded tent on which the dust crystals glittered, a small, soiled edition of Plutarch which Prinet had just returned to Alban, haversacks covered in grease and wax stains, a lot of miserable objects all patched and faded, a lot of miserable objects which you knock your head against at night, which come clattering down and make the earth trickle down your neck, which are so noisy when you're trying to hold your breath, which take up so much room when they are scattered around like this, and yet you will have sorted them out and strapped them up within five minutes, and you will carry them, pack and unpack them hundreds of times before this lousy life has finished with you. And over everything, over the food, over the blankets, over all the places where one might put one's face or one's mouth, and over one's body even (as though they wanted to make it quite clear just how much one belonged to them), were multitudes of dirty little animals – flies, cockroaches, mosquitoes, larvae – crawling out of the damp earth with the coming of evening, hatching out of the refuse with the heat, to settle and swarm and proclaim that tonight, in the silence, they would cover you as they cover the dead. And yet, for the two young men, because they were living it together, all this was good.

. . . From the depths of squalor, there rose the image of the girl . . .

See her now before him, Soubrier the beautiful, warm and golden as if she were always bathed in the light of sunset. She does not speak, the eternally silent one who is always the first to say goodbye on the telephone; she neither laughs nor smiles. But Alban knows about her gold tooth.

Relaxing after a race, she had opened her mouth to take in some air, and Alban had seen her gold tooth. She had seemed like a creature of nature bearing some inviolate nugget.

This gold was in harmony with everything that was dazzling and virginal about her. In whatever circumstances, at whatever hour one came upon her, she was always virginal and pure, and the handkerchief that wiped her face would remain immaculate. It seemed that nature had wanted to achieve in her a human masterpiece of the clear, firm style. She had never polished her nails, yet the light played on them; she never moistened her lips, yet her lips shone; the rims of her ears seemed to be varnished; the whites of her eyes were clear. Her hair had the faint glow of laurel leaves.

She did not use perfume but her clothes, at night, were folded between sachets of lavender, and its scent lingered until noon. From noon till evening, the smell of her skin prevailed. Her skin had its own smell, like fruit and plants, like the wood of trees; and this smell was like a hand kneading Alban's heart.

He saw her walking towards him with her determined gait which made her seem a little awkward when she walked without any particular aim. Her occiput and shoulder-blades were on the same plane. She held herself so erect and was yet so supple and relaxed that even in the street everyone sensed this spontaneity. Beneath her skirt, as she moved her leg forward, her thigh swelled a little, from the hip to the knee; a delicate curve, altogether divine. Her feet were as long as half the distance from her knee-cap to the ground.

She walks towards him, bends over his hand and kisses it.

A shiver runs through him. Pain explodes within him like a bursting water-pipe. He shakes his head to shake the vision off. 'What are you doing? What are you doing?'

'What is your dog called?' Alban asked.
'He is called Dog.'
'Dog, just like that?'
'Yes.'
'Dog . . . Jolly good! There's a name for you!'

Alban fingered the animal's coat, lifted its hindquarters by its tail, put his fingers between its jaws, twisted one of its paws, pulled its whiskers, turned its ear inside out, did everything a dog loves you to do to it. Dog uttered squeals, for form's sake, but was overjoyed at being fussed over.

'They say we're shelled every night here,' said Prinet. 'And incidentally, did you know we have a little graveyard in the wood? If I'm killed here, the people from home will come and see my grave. I wonder which station one has to get out at. But do you think they'll leave the bodies here?'

Alban shrugged; that was something that left him quite cold.

'I must confess I'm like the monk Joseph Bernier who, on his deathbed, asked for his body to be thrown on the garbage-heap.

Do we or do we not believe in the soul? If we do, then all this fuss about burial, wreaths . . . I must say I see it all as a dreadful victory of sentimentality over reason.'

He could feel he had shocked his companion. He in his turn was shocked by the lack of courage he found in him. 'He is moved by an *image*: he is revolted by the image of his body amid the refuse.' And when Prinet said: 'Me, if I were killed, I'd rather stay here with the boys,' Alban, although the words went to his heart, answered tartly: 'I'll tell your uncle that if the need arises,' so that Prinet said no more . . .

'Why am I so beastly to the poor chap?' Alban wondered a little remorsefully. But he had a deep wish to lead a blind soul straight to reality, like a horse led blindfold to the bull, then suddenly to put them face to face and leave the trembling soul there. At this game he did not spare those he loved best, and his excuse was that he did not spare himself. For which reason he sanctioned what he had said. Then the thought occurred to him that by staying here after nightfall, Prinet might be confessing to an obscure desire to be near him if they were shelled; and the thought displeased him, then touched him, then decidedly displeased him. Was he not losing some of his esteem for this person by supposing that this person needed him? Such was the nature of his disease.

'Will you be able to find your way back?' he asked cruelly. 'The night is so dark I can only make you out by the tip of your cigarette.'

'Don't worry.'

There was a long silence. Dog was probably asleep. The noise of the men could be heard no longer, nor that of the flies, nor that of the guns, nor that of the endless rain. No noise at all could be heard any more. Gradually, the night covered their faces. Thus it had been long ago, when in the winter twilight they used to cross the Luxembourg with their collars turned up: bands of schoolboys on the way home, loitering along the deserted pathways; a distant drum-roll came and went, evoking dreams of war among these children, many of whom would die; something feverish and a little sad rose from that old garden of culture in which, suddenly more resolute in the darkness that had fallen during the time it had taken them to cross from one gate to the other, they had felt glory walking at their side.

From an invisible mouth, from the mouth of the darkness, a voice came:

'Would you be distressed if we were beaten?'

It was like a voice from nowhere. For Alban could now discern nothing in the darkness.

'It's still you talking to me?'

'Who else!'

'How can you ask me that? Do you think I am one of those who only feel good when they hear the sound of bugles?'

Suddenly, France appeared to him as a dying person, and he was filled with remorse because of the wrongs he had done her.

'My poor country! I'm fond of her, you know. We're not very much alike . . . She likes smiles, she likes romance, she likes to give herself right and left . . . But I can't let her down. And after all, it's always better to do the right thing.'

'Yes, I too am glad I'm not a rotter,' said Prinet, and added: 'I've always done my duty.'

The slang and the slight pomposity, the little vows amid the cigarette-smoke, the little schoolboyish declarations of love – listen to them, listen to them! They are words murmured against a breast, and only silence can do them justice.

When Prinet took a puff at his cigarette, the tip burned brighter and lit up his face. For a second the long, dry hands emerged from the night, the handsome, severe, weak features, the tragic tiredness under the helmet, though less tragic than this morning when Alban had seen him, exhausted, sleeping in broad daylight. Was it Prinet whom Alban saw in front of the gaping hole of the dug-out, or was it, from the depths of the past, the younger of the centurions who warmed themselves at the door of the Tomb? O young centurions watching over France, you will not fall when you see her resurrected!

'I'll be on leave in three weeks' time,' said Prinet. Then, after a little while: 'Bah! I say that . . . And after four days I won't know what to do with myself . . .'

Another pause, then he asked:

'Do you ever think about death?'

'About mine, never.'

'If you had to take the tiny step which separates promises, intentions, words from the act which really means total sacrifice, the tiny step which separates those who agree to give a lot and those who agree to give all, would you take it?'

'I would.'

Alban panted a little, like the Pythoness at the start of her trance. The voice from the shadows played over him as the bow plays on the strings.

'I would, if I had to – I swear it by the sacraments I received yesterday morning! I do not know how useful my sacrifice would be, and when I get down to it I think I'm sacrificing myself to something which is nothing, to the kind of moonshine I loathe. And believing my sacrifice useless, perhaps even absurd, aloof, unobserved, renouncing life and the dear smell of its creatures, I must plunge headlong into the indifferent future simply for the pride of having been so free. In the Iliad, Diomedes hurls himself at Aeneas, although he knows that Apollo has made Aeneas invulnerable. Hector predicts the ruin of his country and his wife's captivity, before returning to fight as though he believed victory possible. When the prophetic horse announces to Achilles his impending death, "I know it," the hero answers, but instead of folding his arms and waiting for death to come, he flings himself once more into the fray and kills more men. Thus have I lived, knowing the vanity of all things but acting as though I were taken in by them, playing at being a man so as not to be rejected as a god. Yes, let my own indifference and that of the future perish within each other! After having feigned ambition without having any, after having pretended to fear death when I did not fear it, pretended to suffer when I have never suffered, pretended to wait when I awaited nothing, I shall die pretending that my death serves a purpose, but con-

vinced that it serves none and proclaiming that all is as it should
be.'

A long time elapsed without an answer from Prinet, as though
these words had killed him.

'Are you still there?' asked Alban.

'Yes, of course.'

'You're not saying anything.'

He heard the forlorn voice:

'I was thinking that you talk, you write, you proclaim all kinds
of noble and beautiful things, people follow you, rely on you and
then suddenly you slip away, you destroy everything, not only
what you seemed to be building, but everything solid that was
in you! I could count on one hand the more or less serious conversations we've had in which you haven't said things that made
my heart bleed.'

'Made your heart bleed . . . You're convinced that I'm unhappy!
You have to call it a "doctrine of despair"! But why did I speak
at all? Ah! Let the shell tear out my tongue, if it must take some
part of me! That they may at last take me for one of them! That
I may at last love without disenchantment, like everybody
else!'

Lying in the dug-out, sadness rolled over him as if he were lying
at the bottom of a river. His powerlessness, his generosity, his
doubts as to whether he could love completely those whom his
flesh did not love, his exhaustion at never being in harmony with
the greater number, even the notion of death which had dazzled
him a short while ago and had now grown dim because the boy
did not admire it, and a lot of other things, a lot of other reasons for
being alone and comfortless, wove a sad net which crushed him
down against the earth, his arms spread out as on a cross.

The voice reappeared like a star coming out of the clouds:

'Do you know the oath of the young Athenians? I've just read
it in your Plutarch.'

'No,' he said in a blank voice.

' "I will not profane these sacred arms. I will fight for my home

129

and for my gods, alone or with a friend . . ." ' (he paused a moment) ' "I shall never desert my companion in the fight . . ." '

Alban divined the veiled entreaty, the hope, perhaps the reproach, the unexpected boldness in the night which emboldens the weak. 'No, no,' he thought, 'I shall not desert you, my companion in the fight! If only you knew how easy I should find it to give my life for you! And yet I would make this supreme sacrifice for a friendship which I sometimes doubt! Poor old chap! My incoherence "makes your heart bleed", but you should thank me for not being more logical, because then I might desert you . . .'

He was about to speak when the whistling started. In a flash of intuition, he knew that they were in the direct line of its trajectory. Hardly had he pushed the blanket off his legs when a lurid glow lit up the dug-out as if some spirit had just entered. The air was shattered. The earthen ceiling seemed to collapse upon them.

'Out!' yelled Alban. 'Where is the shelter? Can you find the way?'

'No, no, let's stay here, I can't see a thing . . .'

Alban flattened himself against one of the walls to lessen the surface of exposed flesh. He heard his friend's voice:

'It's the first time we're catching it together.'

'Where are you? I can't see a thing. I can't even see the entrance to the dug-out.'

'Look out!'

The sound was curving down, swelling and gurgling, coming straight at them now. Terrible, the noise of a huge train rushing through space, swooping down on you . . . God!

He felt it had happened, the horror, the crushing, the splitting of his body at the loins, the earth in his mouth and his nostrils, choking him, his brain full of earth: death. Mechanically he rose like a thing shot through with an electric current, blindly he knocked his head against something solid, staggered a few steps forward, moaning 'Aaah! Aaah!'; then he realized he was standing, but he did not know whether he was dead or alive, he did not know whether his body existed, whether his limbs were not scattered about. As he was once again taking his breath to cry out 'Aaah,' something coming from his brain must have clicked and intervened, for he did not cry out. Then he realized he was alive.

Without having noticed the noise of the train, he heard a new explosion nearby, saw the flash of light streaked by the shafts of the trees, and did not even lower his head when the splinters, the lumps of earth, the broken branches rained about him.

In the darkness, Prinet's voice, jerking out:

'I . . . I . . . I can't . . . I can't talk any more . . .'

He did not answer, as though he had not understood.

'Alban!'

He did not answer. Little leaves torn from the trees dropped on to his face, light as a woman's fingers. A suffocating smell of burning poisoned the air.

'Alban!'

The voice was horrible, the soul really issuing from the throat, spat out of the body in supplication.

'Prinet!' shouted Alban, himself once more.

'I am wounded.'

'Are you going to die?'

(He probably did not realize what he was saying).

'I don't know,' came the voice, pitiable and very low, pressed against the ground.

Again the whistling. Another one. Another. Flashes all around as in a storm. Then they stopped, the range lengthening, the shells falling farther away. The whole nocturnal space was full of hideous cats, like cats that have been walled up alive and whose twisted bodies have left their imprint on the stone. They came hurtling through the air, mewing and shrieking, swooping on men's necks to devour them.

'Where are you?'

'I'm here.'

'I can't see you! I can't see anything! Where are you wounded?'

'In the thigh, perhaps in the stomach, I don't know.'

'I can hear your voice all round me.'

He touched him, ran his hand along the other's arm.

'Take me to the first-aid post. I can't move.'

'But it's impossible! I can't see a thing. Not a thing. I'm touching you, but I can't see you.'

'I can't stay here! I can't stay here! I may have a piece of shrapnel in my stomach! I may peg out in a minute if nothing's done for me.'

'It's impossible! I'll get some matches and we'll see what's the matter with you . . .'

'You'll get us spotted with your matches . . . Ah! Enough of all that! Enough! Enough!'

Frowning hard, opening his eyes wide with a splendid virile effort, Alban tried to control the confusion of his mind. He stretched out his hands, feeling for the matchbox, no longer recognized anything, wondered whether they had been flung several yards, yelled 'Filthy brute!' as he stumbled over Dog, and quickly realized that there was no hope of any light.

'Have you got your first-aid kit?'

'No. What about you?'

'No.'

Again he stretched his hands out, thinking he was feeling everywhere when in fact his hands, trembling at the end of his arms, kept coming back to the same places, and all his will power could not control them.

'Can't you find any?'

He kept stumbling against hard objects and hurting himself, kept putting his hands in the mud, his mind adrift again, sinking, sinking, as things do in nightmares. And the shells, whistling and arching above their heads, imprisoned them beneath a web of sound.

'Can't you find any?'

He felt a haversack, plunged his hand into it, felt his razor, his soap, a wallet full of papers which scattered all over the place, and other, indefinable things which he flung away right and left.

'I can't find a thing! I can't find a thing!' he cried, almost weeping with impotence. Then, absurdly:

132

'I'll go and fetch someone,'

'No! Alban! I beg you, don't go!'

Ah! these words, the theatrical phrase uttered in real life, next door to him, by someone who might be dying. He felt like shouting: 'Don't die! Don't die!' as if the other needed convincing.

'But I can call!' he exclaimed, suddenly illuminated with this simple idea, which should have been their first.

He called out, did not recognize his own voice, got no answer, called out again. All around them, the invisible sky was filled with the long-drawn wails of the shells, like wails of infants; it was as if the whole sky were some living thing lamenting. Not a soul answered, although there must have been hundreds there.

He came back.

'Is it bleeding much?'

'How do you expect me to know when I can't see a thing. I can't feel the wound . . . I feel where it hurts, though . . . I can't smell any blood on my fingers.'

'Perhaps it's only a small piece of shrapnel.' (Hope was rising again). 'And your stomach?'

'I can't feel anything there. But didn't Lieutenant Guillou get some shrapnel in his thigh, which moved up and perforated his intestine?'

'That's what they said, but . . .'

Wasn't it true? Hadn't everybody said that? Anguish gripped him again. Then his foot crushed something with a dry little noise . . .

'The matches!'

He struck one which didn't light, counted five more in the box, struck the second match with infinite trepidation. The flame sprang up. For a moment he saw the body, the face. The match went out.

'Where's the box?'

He could no longer find it. He groped, felt it fall, moved his hand along the ground, came across a tin mug, dipped his fingers in, and felt the matchbox swimming in liquid; in the disorder of the dug-out, his half-filled mug of wine had remained intact and the matchbox had fallen into it. He struck all four matches. Not one of them lit.

133

He leaned back against the wall and turned his eyes with their burning rims towards the gulf of the night. He thought of nature's vast indifference, protecting and torturing them in turns, and his intellect welcomed it, finding it meet and proper. Above their common turmoil nature and he came together, the least accessible parts of both were joined. He reached for the mug and greedily drank the rest of the wine.

'I wonder what time it is?' asked Prinet.

'Not very late. About eleven, I should think.'

'Eleven!'

Another four hours to go before dawn.

'You're not feeling too bad?'

'I'm not in pain, but the whole of my right side is paralysed.'

'Perhaps you were only hit by some wood or earth.'

'And you? You're not hurt?'

He smiled. At last, some concern on his account! He said no, without a trace of bitterness. Then:

'You know, you ought to try and sleep.'

'Ah! Sleep!'

'Are you cold?'

'A little.'

Noiselessly, so that Prinet would not guess what he was doing, he took off his greatcoat and arranged it over the young cadet, thinking that he would have covered him up like this had he been dead.

'Go on, sleep. If there was anything really wrong, Dog would whine. Dogs have presentiments, you know; they know a lot of things . . . But you see, he's quiet. He's asleep already.'

He sat down. He put his hand on Prinet's shoulder, and once more turned his eyes towards the invisible sky. Just as a distant meadow seems at first just a greenish mass and then, after a few seconds, the little spots of the flowers appear, he gradually discovered stars in the sky, seemingly imprisoned in the network of foliage. No noise could now be heard, except for a half-severed branch which would crack, pause and then fall in a long rustle of leaves, unless its fall was cut short, halted by other branches. In the east, far off, behind thousands of trees which silhouetted themselves against it, a reddish glow would rise, here and there, then sink, then shoot up even brighter, as if, in this great silence, things were crackling and burning.

Now he could feel light, regular breathing beside him. And almost at the same moment, something alive and warm touched the back of his hand as it rested on his friend's shoulder. It was the sleeping face.

And all at once hope rose from the abyss, hope and the vague certainty that nothing evil was possible now. The trance was broken, the fear of death dispelled, the spirits of darkness fled in anger because of this pathetic earthbound sweetness; his heart opened and spread out like a great fan of wings which swept beyond the boundaries of the night; and mysteriously he knew everything he had failed all his life to understand, through having steeled himself against human tenderness.

The face was heavy on his hand, yet his hand could more easily have freed itself from a vice, and he who was awake stirred less than he who slept. On this hand, the other day, Dominique's lips had moved; the place of her kiss was the very same on which the soldier's cheek now rested. The touch of one was as wholesome as that of the sacred elements on the altar; the other was a defeat of what is best, and the promise of a worse degradation. One came from a soft and quivering flesh, the other from a hard bone which almost hurt the fingers, from a hard thing which, if it could have been detached and thrown, might have killed a man. Two kinds of life met in this small arena, one to be crushed by the other.

'I'm afraid! I'm afraid!'

'It's all right, old chap, it's all right.'

'Did you hear the crowd going by, singing, playing the fiddle and the mandolin?'

Alban shivered.

'You're dreaming.'

'I can hear Trivier snoring. His wife hits him on the nose with her evening gloves: "Have you finished snoring? I want some sleep."'

'Go to sleep, go to sleep. There's nothing to be afraid of.'

'Am I awake, or am I dreaming?'

'Anyway, you're talking nonsense.'

'Have I only just gone to sleep, or is it almost dawn?'

'It must be about midnight.'

'Oh lord!'

He remembered the passage in Plutarch, which the cadet must have read some time that day, and from which his hallucination had come. In the middle of the night preceding the decisive battle between Antony and Octavius, while Alexandria awaited events with silent dread, suddenly a barbaric harmony of instruments of every kind, mixed with the cries and dances of satyrs, could be heard in the distance, growing louder and louder still, then receding and vanishing, without anyone having seen anything . . .

The image sprang up in his mind, and fell back like a fountain, drenching and chilling him. Once again, at the opportune moment, the spirit of the ancient world had sent its exiled son the little sign he needed to create more beauty or strength; the great tomb opened a little, and out flew an owl or an eagle to bring him the omens. Thus, then, the same dream had passed through this dear head whose warmth he felt on his hand, in this anguished night of the great war, as it had passed, two thousand years before, through the anguished night of an ancient people, on the eve of the battle which had given birth, with Octavius's victory, to the Roman order and the fortune of the world! O signs and portents! Surely the fabulous coincidence would continue to the end! Surely the coming day could not be like all the other days!

As the cold grew keener, he guessed that dawn was near: they had reached the second part of the night, which is endless to the man who must stay awake. In the east, far beyond the trees, the strange glow still came and went. Much more familiar with the antique world than with his own, and moreover disposed by the

tensions of the night to accept anything uncritically, Alban thought
he was watching the wonders described by the historians and the
poets. Rivers of blood and overflowing lava might indeed be
surging through these deep glades; and did not these silent lightning
flashes in a clear sky exactly resemble those which had presaged
Caesar's death? Something Prinet had said came back to him: 'It
says in your Plutarch that important battles are always preceded
by torrential rains.' These great phenomena of nature seemed
familiar to him; he was at ease with them. The ancient world and
the modern world, the realm of phantasmagoria and the realm of
things, mingled to create a strange universe in which he no longer
felt threatened. All night the earth had been in agony, but it was
labouring for a new age. The morning which was about to be born
was the third morning of the world, similar to the morning which
rose after the Flood.

Something stirred beside him. He could no longer feel the contact
on his hand, which the cold covered at once. A few empty inches
separated them as would have miles of darkness.

'Are you there?' asked Prinet.

'You know I am. What about you? How do you feel? I'm sure
you're better.'

'It's not hurting very much. There's just one spot which feels
somehow twisted, and then all around it's sort of stiff, dead; but I
can move a lot better now.'

The young man sat up, leaning on Alban's shoulder. Having
woken up, Dog rubbed himself against them.

'You don't think you might only have strained a nerve or a
muscle while you were jumping to shelter?'

'Of course not!' the voice said, reproachfully.

'They say one is fooled all the time, that sometimes one doesn't
even know one has been hit by shrapnel, sometimes one thinks one
has just got a bruise. It's quite possible that a badly strained nerve
might feel like a foreign body in a muscle . . .'

'You must have heard that from one of the Staff clerks.'

Feeling mortified, no doubt, Prinet did not say any more. And his friend began to have a strong presentiment that there was nothing wrong with Prinet. And the misapprehension, the slight veil of absurdity over the danger and anxiety which were only too real, gave him a feeling of tenderness and pity, as though he had been watching over a frightened child.

Suddenly he rose:

'Daylight!'

'Where can you see daylight?'

'I don't know. But I feel it coming.'

'In twelve hours' time, there'll be another night like this one.'

'The end of it all is near.'

'It will never end.'

'While you were asleep, the night was full of wonders.'

'Ah!'

How sceptical this 'Ah!' as who should say: 'You're telling tall stories again.'

'Tomorrow, we'll sum it all up with some such remark as "Ah, yes! things were pretty tough at the time." And there you are!'

'Oh!'

'What's the matter?'

'The star, it's gone out!'

'And another!'

They could make out the tree-trunks.

'I shall soon be able to see you.'

A bird called for them alone, sang for them alone. Then the voice:

'Listen, I must tell you . . . But it's queer, I hardly feel anything now . . . I'm wondering . . .'

Everything was beginning to appear. It seemed as if the light was rising from the ground, like mist.

Alban:

'I can see you!'

He was smiling. A desire to laugh was rising from his belly.

'You're no more dishevelled than before . . .'

Then the boy uncovered his thigh. They bent over it. There was not a drop of blood.

In the pallid twilight, the colour of a spider's web, Alban saw the young face rise at last like a human dawn, the eyes red-rimmed and heavy with sleep, the hair full of earth, and on the cheek, not yet effaced, the three red marks left by the knuckles. Then, without thinking how cruel he was being, he burst out laughing. It was not only because of his friend's slightly crestfallen look, it was because of the pleasure of having demonstrated his superiority once more, because of the need to relax, to take a deep breath, because of the sun bursting within him as it was about to burst over the world. He was overcome with a desire to mock the young cadet, to make savage fun of him. And all the muscles of his face went into action in his savage and wounding mimicry of his friend. And he laughed like a shameless faun, made half-divine by the extravagance of his amusement and his childish lack of charity.

But his eyes grew suddenly grave. The darkness had receded, and now they could see. The dug-out had disappeared; even its site was no longer recognizable. A few yards away, a crater yawned, and all around was devastation: the trees cut off at man-height, their fall broken by the neighbouring branches, the grass mown by fire, fragments of boards, some nondescript objects which must have belonged to Alban, all charred and blackened. Beyond this, the living trees had stumps for branches, gashed trunks, leaves scorched and wrinkled as the leaves remaining on the burning bush must have been after God had appeared. And at intervals all around, half-buried in the ground, as motionless as if the apparitions of fire had ravished them in an endless dream, as if they had been there all night, ash-coloured men stood staring, stupefied, with wide-open, unseeing eyes.

The young man said not a word, but the elder's laughter had ceased. And they both remembered.

Then, from the east, before the sun was yet visible, broke a tide of gold which did not leave the ground, bathing the men up to the waist until they began to move as if touched by a magic wand. As the tide rose, the tall tree-trunks, upright and naked under the still nocturnal vault, seemed like jets of light springing from the ground, through which one's hand might have passed, or else like long diaphanous candles offered up to the unknown god. The primrose-coloured horizon gently lit the piece of blue sky they could see. From branch to branch, with a high-pitched clamour, the birds' annunciation soared.

But from the thickets a man emerged, full of night. Jumping from one excavation to another, he turned in passing towards the two friends and said with a broad smile:

'Hey there, boys! We've got 'em! Report from the colonel: we've attacked all along the front, the Boche are on the run, we've recrossed the Marne, taken ten thousand prisoners and two hundred guns.'

PART TWO

II

My Comrade . . .

My comrade, was it by your wish?
I am Roland, he who loves you so.
THE SONG OF ROLAND

THE PLAIN in front of the forest of C . . . stretched as far as the eye could see, like an ocean of which the edge of the forest might be the cliffs. It was July 23rd, 1918. The heat was stifling. It was noon. The cloudless sky was not blue, but greyish, as though, like a red-hot iron, it had grown paler with heat; the light was livid and the shadows were weak, as though an eclipse were about to occur. To the west, the horizon, invisible in the dust, was filled by a continuous rattle of machine-guns. In this direction, all unknowing, went the road, white as ivory or milk. In the distance, along the edge of that same road, three, four shells burst. The smoke from the last one could be seen hovering motionless for a long time before breaking up, black as ink, so thick and so clear-cut that it might have been taken for a great solitary tree on the plain.

Along the road, preceded by Dog, went Prinet, Alban and the telephonist Riffard, on their way back to their units. Alban could have set off at nightfall, when the heat had died down, but he preferred to travel with his friend. Let it also be said that his nature inclined him to such extremes. He might not deliberately choose the cruellest hour of the day for such an exertion, but if the necessity arose, he was liable to find satisfaction and fulfilment in an excess

143

of fatigue. The bird of the storm, suspended on its wings, rests among the warring elements . . .

The heat was stunning. Its motionless rage was as wild as the wind's. In peace-time, one would no more have gone through a small strip of this sunlight than through a river; even hens would avoid it. For a few yards, a hedge provided a narrow ribbon of shade. They stopped, leaned against the bank and removed their helmets. Prinet, so correct in civilian life, had uncovered his chest down to the pit of his stomach.

'Do you know what it is they're shelling over there?' he asked, holding up his map. 'It's a farm. Look, in 62–80.'

Alban looked. After a moment:

'I think you're wrong. It's the bridge we're going to cross.'

'Of course not!'

Prinet pored over the map again. He frowned.

'Yes, it's true . . . I'd got mixed up. We're here, then?'

Alban longed for Riffard not to have heard. After all, supposing the cadet had been leading his platoon!

'So we're going to have to cross it!' said Prinet in a muffled voice.

'It's going to be great fun! We'll have to be careful not to miss our chance.' Alban thought of the Greek gymnasts who killed themselves if they failed to take off in unison. He had always wanted to go through a barrage, tacking about, calculating where and when the shells would fall: the same sensation, he thought, as one has when crossing the crowded boulevards during the rush hour.

Implacable sky! At first, their helmets protected them best but gradually became so hot that they could bear them no longer. Then they put on their forage-caps – Prinet his beret – with their handkerchiefs (filthy) as neck-flaps. And after a while they put their helmets on again, then changed over once more. The dust, crunching between their teeth, made the air unbreathable. The grass and the leaves by the roadside were coated with it. It was like flour on their lashes, their eyebrows, Riffard's moustache. Prinet walked in front. So slender and lanky with his long legs, he looked more like a boy cadet in training than a chief, a leader of men, marching to the savage battle. Alban knew he was not very strong: how could he survive this heat? His lips were shut tight. Alban noticed that his eyes were hardly visible, they had sunk so deep. There were drops of sweat on his nose, that looked as though they had been placed there. Sweat also bathed his chest, which was fresh as the heart of a new loaf.

They came to a rise and immediately saw the bridge, around which the air was dark with smoke, still hanging thick as after a fire.

'Clumsy fools!' said Riffard. 'It's still intact.'

'So far,' said, Prinet sombrely.

'Let's wait for the next burst. As soon as it's landed, we'll pass easily.'

'And what happens if it blocks the bridge?'

'What an idea, sir!'

The tone of this 'What an idea'! These Frenchmen, really! You would have thought that, in four years of war, the Boche (that trash) had never managed to cause the slightest damage to anything French. But Alban was struck mainly by the respectful address, by the 'sir'. He looked at his friend, and realized that he would have much more confidence in Riffard than in this youngster. He felt there was something monstrous in the fact that the former was under the latter's command, that he might be shot for disobeying his orders. And yet at the same time, Prinet's authority, the ridiculous long stripes all over the sleeve – too short of course! – made him more touching. He would have liked him less as a private.

They had decided to wait for the next burst, and had stopped a hundred yards or so from the bridge. Strange sensation, strange spectacle: the deceptively innocent bridge upon which, at any second, death would pounce. Alban looked at Prinet. How beautiful, he thought, how beautiful emotion is on a man's face! As for Riffard, he was as pleased as punch. Dog was eating his fleas, and you could hear the little rasping noise of his teeth.

'Just look at the river, getting to hell out of it!'

It was true that the river was fleeing helter-skelter towards the rear. It was comic to watch it. But Prinet was whistling softly.

'Stop whistling like that, will you,' said Alban, who had recognized the sort of whistling one hears from little boys when they are scared, at night, of the bogyman at the bottom of the garden.

The shell was heralded by a noise like the drone of a giant bumble-bee. Alban strained his eyes to try and see it in its trajectory. Why could one not see it? Could it be going as fast as that, despite its weary throbbing? It was all very strange. It fell at last, but did not explode. Another one, too far. Another, in the river. O lily of foam after the peonies of fire!

'Come on!' shouted Prinet.

Alban saw him run, holding his packs in his arms so that they did not bump against him. Behind him, he heard Riffard's voice: 'Not yet!' Nevertheless he sprang forward. He had just reached the bridge when the air hissed, he flattened himself on the ground, and the shell landed twenty-five yards away. He got up and ran for all he was worth.

'You started too soon!' he shouted reproachfully to Prinet.

'Well! You shouldn't have followed me.'

How pale he was, the young cadet! How wounded he was, bleeding all over, not in his flesh, but in his soul! Twice in half an hour he had been wrong, he had failed. And for a second Alban saw his eyes – literally – swimming. For a second he recognized a trapped look he had seen before . . . where? Ah! yes; on the face of Captain Véran's batman, a valet in civilian life, who was afraid.

Around them, dust was falling like drizzle from the trees shaken by the blast of the shell. Then along came Riffard with his cheerful, laughing face. Scowling, he threatened Dog: 'Ah! bloody animal, bloody animal!' He explained:

'If I may give you a piece of advice, sir, get rid of your dog. You were in front, so you didn't see, but as I was crossing the bridge he was under my blooming feet, he had me over good and proper. I tell you, they were clobbering us, it might have been nasty. I quite like a tyke myself at the rear; there's nothing wrong with a dog . . . But here, the way it's going to be, when one second can cost you your life, it's hard enough looking after yourself without having to bother about dogs.'

'He's absolutely right,' said Alban. 'I've been thinking exactly the same thing for some time.'

'But what do you want me to do with him? If one of you would look after him for me . . .'

'What! I didn't think any of us was going back to the rear.'

'Well then? You don't think I'm going to throw him in the river?'

'That's exactly what you should do, though.'

They said no more about it.

The sun was terrible. The inside of their bodies was as dry as if hot air had been pumped into them with a blowpipe. Prinet, drinking from his water-bottle, poured some of the rusty yellow water over his face and his temples, from which it ran down via his open collar on to his chest without cooling him in the slightest. Then:

'There's still some left. Do you want it?'

Alban was longing for it; his own water-bottle was empty. But he glanced at his friend's face and guessed that the kind offer had cost him a good deal.

'No, I'm not very thirsty; keep it for yourself.'

'Here you are,' Riffard said to Alban. 'Take what you want, it's full.'

And he handed him his own water-bottle. The simple peasant had understood it all.

Obscure general post of altruism: first Prinet, then Alban, then Riffard, each, one after the other, denying himself. The secret tenderness of war, redeeming all the rest. . . .

But, as he raised the water-bottle to his lips, Alban felt something on his forearm, the material sticking to the skin.

'I bet I've got a piece of shrapnel.'

They gathered round him. Nothing to be seen on the greatcoat, but on the jacket a small brown stain. He took off his coat, rolled up his shirt-sleeve. And he felt a surge of love for his own blood.

A gash, wet, shining, incarnadine! And at the bottom of it, the small chip of metal. Riffard stretched the wound with his fingers. Alban picked out the splinter, the size of a small coin, and threw it away.

'You're not keeping it as a souvenir?' Prinet asked.

Alban shrugged at this girlish idea. But later he thought: 'It's true. I haven't sent anything home, not a souvenir, not an enemy trophy, not a shell splinter. One day my little boy, if I ever have one, won't even know I was in the war.'

But now Riffard was leaving them, taking a short-cut towards his company. They shook hands: 'Good-bye, old fellow, good luck.'

Off he went, and Alban reflected that his wife, the farmer's wife, would never know how brave he was. She would call him a lazy good-for-nothing, think herself his superior.

Scarcely had they lost sight of him when they saw a heavy German aeroplane heading towards them from behind the enemy lines; only fifty yards up, it grew bigger and bigger, aiming straight at them, and even Alban was impressed. 'Watch out for machine-gunning,' he thought. The cadet had already slipped into the ditch, bordered at this spot by a thick hedge, and had concealed himself as best he could under the branches. Alban did the same. But in the middle of the road, excited by their strange appearance, Dog was looking at them and barking. A dog standing barking in the middle of a deserted plain must surely arouse suspicion.

'Your stinking dog will get us killed,' grumbled Alban.

They felt the monstrous insect swoop over them, drowning the little brute's barks with its roar. For a few seconds the suspense was almost more painful than shellfire; there was a terrifying zenith; then the plane had passed, and flew steadily on towards the horizon.

'This only confirms what Riffard was saying,' said Alban, getting

148

up. 'A little more care on the part of the observer, and your dog would have given us away.'

Then, harshly, his nerves still taut:

'Will you please be good enough to kill this animal, if you don't want it to kill you or your comrades.'

'Kill Dog! An animal who has shared all our misfortunes, who was our companion in the shelter! If I have to do it, I will, but only as a last resort.'

'Would you have done it when the plane was coming straight at us? Come, stop being so childish, what you're saying is not worthy of a grown man. I tell you again that, as far as my own life is concerned, I don't care about the dog, since I'm leaving you both. But he is a danger to your life and the lives of your comrades. If it were only yours, it would be your own business. But to risk other people's lives for a dog, no!'

Anger was rising in him, he was beginning to bite his lip: one of those dreadful fits of rage he used to have as an adolescent, when he would shout at those who tried to bring him to his senses: 'No! No! Let me be angry! I don't want to control myself!'

'And if you haven't the courage to get rid of it yourself, *I* shall do it,' he concluded, his brain like a blood-soaked sponge.

'I'd like to see that,' said Prinet, in a jerky voice, his pupils growing paler.

'Well, what would you do? Kill me?' the other jeered, a nasty expression about his mouth.

He could face stoically the resistance of things, but people's resistance drove him mad. And then he was disgusted by this sentimentality, as some people are disgusted by snakes.

He opened the holster of his Browning.

'Alban, if you do that . . .'

The bullet must have broken something in the hind-quarters, for the animal sat down and remained sitting, gazing at its killer with eyes of unbelievable sadness. He heard the voice behind him: 'Brute! Savage! Filthy brute!' and waited for the blows, but received none other than the animal's imploring look, more human

149

than the eyes of men. He put the barrel under its ear and shot again. The animal sank slowly, as a page of an open book lifted by a breeze sinks back when the breeze drops.

He lifted his head and looked at his friend. He saw him, choking with emotion, make as if to start speaking; but he said nothing, turned round and set off across the fields towards the track which led to the lines. Then, having first made sure that the dog was really dead, he too set off again.

Out of pride, lest Prinet should catch him out in this weakness, he did not once look in his direction. 'Of the two of us, am I the one who *needs* the other?' He walked on for a while, expecting Prinet to stop and call to him. He remembered similar sulking walks on the way to and from school, six years ago yet as vivid as if it were yesterday. But today, at such a serious moment! 'Is he going off to fight like that, without a word? Was it for this that we went through so much together? It's impossible.'

He heard nothing, and each step he took tore his heart. Then, very simply, he stopped, and looked at the slim retreating figure in the fields, already a hundred yards away. He had an impulse to call, to run after him, but the picture: 'Me, running after Prinet' filled him with shame and nailed him to the ground.

He stood there motionless, his eyes fixed upon that minute living thing in the expanse of fields, smaller than a tree-stump, but with its heart, its complexities, its choice of yes or no, its monstrous power to hurt. 'He won't even turn round!' The very moment this reproach came bursting from him, he saw the boy turn towards him, his face screwed up against the sun, but without stopping, without stopping. He did not move, his face was expressionless, yet his very attitude seemed to declare: 'Yes, I expected more from you.' For another second they were face to face, not heart to heart; then the cadet turned away. And Alban was never to see his face again.

Fiercely he turned and walked on. Something was bursting in his chest, and he thought it was anger still. His eyes fixed furiously on the dusty ground, he said to himself: 'I shan't turn round again until he has had time to disappear.' He did turn round after a while, and saw only the dry, hot countryside, shimmering away to infinity.

From that precise moment, from the moment he realized that the tiny speck of life had disappeared, leaving him alone in the middle of the deceitful desert, he felt, very sharply, the sensation of a cripple whose stick has just been snatched away by some vicious hand. He threw a glance all round him, as though in search of help. He was afraid.

12

So Much Suffering!

'Is it my fault?' reflected Alban, sitting in the dark, his arm in a sling, among the lorries and the horses of the Service Corps. 'Kids like that shouldn't be sent on a man's job. It knocks them sideways, and no wonder. He is most certainly in the wrong. Even at the height of my anger, if I had had to give my life in order to save his, I would have done it, I swear I would!'

But his uneasiness had abated, for the following reasons.

Earlier that evening the Medical Officer, while examining his wound, had said:

'Ah! there's a splendid wound if ever I saw one! And just on the eve of an attack!'

'That will do!' Alban had said, horrified by this man as by a leper; and, snatching the bandage from his hands, he had walked away. After twenty yards, he was caught by an orderly:

'The mo orders you to come back. And he's not fooling either.'

'Tell your mo that he can go to hell.'

Nevertheless he had gone back.

'Here's your evacuation form.'

'I don't want to be evacuated.'

'What do you want?'

'I just want to go up like the others.'

'Good god! Well, I'll tell you this: I prefer a chap who sticks his foot under a lorry so as to be able to get away to a chap who feels like going up. Do you hear that? Right! You'll spend a couple of days here at the depot and then you can do what you like.'

'I don't want to stay . . .'

'You say one more word and you'll be in trouble, I'll bloody well have you inside . . .' He choked with exasperation. And Alban, taking pity on him, had stopped tormenting him.

So that now here he was, condemned to spend two days of battle with the old men of the Service Corps, humiliated, deprived of his pleasure and of the chance of winning glory. What would he do? Would he stay? The regiment was due to pass in a few minutes; why not simply take his place once more? But doubtless the MO was watching him and would raise the roof – and such open and direct disobedience was a serious offence . . .

In fact, however, his predominant thought was that, as the regiment went by, he would be able to spot Prinet, talk to him, accompany him for a couple of hundred yards along the road; and all the shadows between them would be swept away. Already a vast tramping of feet could be heard on the right. Then the first men emerged from the darkness, and the Fourth Battalion began to march past.

Not a word could be heard, nothing but the noise of feet and the dragging of sticks on the ground. But a rough, warm smell assailed the nostrils, stronger than the smell of horses. Silent as they were, they might have been an army of shadows. Even the little glowing tips of their cigarettes and pipes seemed ghostly. In spite of the moonlight, it was difficult to make out the faces.

The cars of the machine-gun company heralded the end of the battalion. But they went past in such numbers that Alban, surprised, questioned one of the drivers:

'Which battalion is this?'

'Fourth.'

'What? Not finished yet?'

'We're leading.'

'What about the fifth?'

'Up ahead.'

'They can't be! What are you talking about?'
A voice said:
'Here are some blokes from the fifth.'
'Do you know the cadet, Prinet?'
'Never heard of him.'
'Tall, thin chap, in a chasseur's uniform.'

No answer. An officer on horseback forced him back. The men went on marching past. He recognized one from the Fourth Battalion, then one from the headquarters company. Utterly ignorant about military matters, he became more and more confused as he tried to establish some kind of order in this crowd. He had a sudden foreboding that he would not find his friend.

'You from the Nineteenth?'
'Not on your life! Those sods!'
'You haven't seen Prinet, the cadet?'
'No, no! From the Nineteenth? They're not coming this way.'
'What?'

The man had disappeared into the mass. On it flowed, like a human river, with Alban on its banks. He recognized men from his own company, had to listen to their bantering remarks and answer them: 'Wounded? You lucky bastard!' 'All right for some!' 'Shirker!' Alongside the river, men who had relieved themselves by the roadside were running back to rejoin their platoons. Moonlight glimmered on the helmets and on the metal of the rifles, and the glowing tips of the cigarettes moved on and on like evil spells.

Suddenly he saw Prinet in front of him, easily recognizable from behind, so tall and slender with his long, springy stride. It was over in a flash. The shape disappeared in the darkness. He rushed after it.

'Prinet! Prinet!'
'What's he looking for?'
'Prinet, the cadet.'
'He was in front with the officers.'
'No, no, he's over there somewhere. The young chasseur.'
'We haven't seen him. He's not with us.'

Alban walked back along the column. He hadn't the heart to go on running. He felt certain he would not find him now, and although he went on inquiring, the discouragement in his voice discouraged answers. From the new silhouettes – cyclists, men without haversacks, wearing forage-caps – he guessed it was the end of the regiment. Soon he found himself alone on the road. As before, he felt that each second took him a little farther away from his comrade. He sat on the bank, sad at heart.

Now he could hear in the distance the clip-clop of horses, nothing else, as if it were cavalry approaching; then, a little later, the rolling of wagons. It was the Regimental Maintenance and the Front Line Maintenance. Having shown his pass, Alban climbed up beside one of the drivers. The sinister forest closed around them.

They drove on for a long time. The darkness was intense. One could tell there was a wagon in front only by the sparks under the horse's hooves. Then, on the horizon of the road, between the trees, they made out a moonlit clearing, and as they advanced towards it, it was as though they were approaching an enchanted lake. 'If a plane comes along as we're going through the clearing . . .' thought Alban.

And immediately he gave a start. Since when did he have such fears? Was the dissatisfaction in his heart causing him to see everything black? Never, during these past three months, never had it occurred to him that he might be afraid of an aeroplane . . .

The head of the convoy reached the clearing. After the utter darkness, it was like being in broad daylight. A whistle blew, and then from the head of the column came a 'Whoa!' which was passed on from cart to cart:' 'Whoa! – Whoa! – Whoa! – ' They stopped.

'There we are,' thought Alban, 'stopped in the open, and at a crossroads.' Despite himself he looked up at the icy sky, expecting a threat. They set off again. They had covered no more than fifty yards when a familiar whining began above the forest. They heard the distant explosion up in front, and Alban ducked. The convoy was still advancing.

'It might be the regiment getting it.'

'Maybe,' the driver agreed.

He was exasperated by the man's phlegm. Then, at about the same distance, the same whining, then a third and a fourth. There were eight in all. Then it stopped.

Alban felt oppressed and on edge. Physical anguish abolished the pain in his heart. Suddenly he felt the cold and put his helmet on again to warm his head ... Why didn't they stop, instead of making this moving pattern along the road, visible to any observer in the sky? Yes, but then the march might not be completed before dawn; they would have to manoeuvre in full view, in broad daylight. He had a foreboding that the night would not be over without upheavals. 'In no time the shells will be falling here. We must be about three hundred men. Is there even an assistant MO? What shall I do? I'll jump down from the wagon and get away from the road, but on which side? Usually they end up by lengthening the range; so I'll run the other way, towards the Boche. But then I'll be getting close to their lines ... Where are they? How far?' He pictured himself running through the copses, getting entangled, knocking against trees, perhaps even disappearing into a pond.

'I'm mad,' he thought, 'I'm mad. Even this afternoon I wasn't afraid. Yet Prinet can hardly represent one of those "clouds" which in the Iliad come down over the beloved hero, that he may walk unharmed in the midst of the battle! After all, it was with him that I was wounded! It really is ridiculous.' He clenched his teeth and bit his lip in an effort to regain his self-control.

They were on their way again. Why? Nobody had whistled. Who had given the order? In fact, who did give the orders here? Ah, to think that he was in the hands of these Service Corps people, these good-for-nothings from the rear! To think that he, who knew all about fighting, should have to go into the very jaws of death, simply because this fat Admin. Lieutenant had given the order, this bespectacled pen-pusher perched precariously on his hack! And then these idiots who kept switching on their torches. Another one! Another! Wasn't there a single leader here to sentence these murderers to a fortnight's jail? Of course not, they'd sooner risk death than make a decision.

Now he noticed a strange gleam on their left, a sheet of white light behind the trees, which stood out in silhouette against it. It would have been impossible to say whether it was several miles away or within range of a grenade. He asked his neighbour, the driver:

'Isn't that light over there?'

'Light? No, it's the fields.'

'Brute!' he thought. He stared anxiously at the chalky expanse stretching on and on. Was it, perhaps, the beam of a searchlight? But then the others would have noticed it . . .

Noticed! What could these brutes notice anyway? Had death been there, they would have led you on to it with the same unconcern.

However, by dint of straining his eyes, he realized that the mass of trees on his left was diminishing in depth, becoming ever thinner. Soon there was no possible mistake; they were indeed fields stretching out beyond. The forest was coming to an end, thrusting a narrow wedge along the road until it became a mere row of trees. The clearing opened, pale under the moon. There were shouts of 'Whoa! Whoa!'

'I was sure of it! They're stopping right in the open!' Alban, his will-power shaken by a gust of panic, jumped down from his seat at the risk of hurting himself – the horses, backing, were at right angles to the wagon – so as to be freer to move in case of an alert.

There they bivouacked. Within a few moments, sleep overcame Alban, conquering his fear.

They set off again at daybreak. Soon they reached a farm which had been transformed into a main dressing-station.

The farmyard was a cemetery of living men. Side by side, as they would be that night in their graves, extraordinarily alike on their identical stretchers, under the great sun which devoured their distinctive features, all at the same level, no higher in the air than the green grass as it lies under a clement sky, all alike and side by side, Frenchmen and Germans were completing at last their great expiation of uncommitted sins. All was silence on this terrace of death, as if these innocent men had nothing to say. But amid the silence and the stillness, in these faces of lead and earth, the eyes looked, turned, followed you everywhere. These eyes, which had never rested but on the most insignificant things of the world, had become filled with a supernatural beauty; the whole soul had taken refuge in them, driven from the putrefying body; and they shone like those fleeting stars – window-pane, metal, slate on a roof – which gleam the more brightly in the dusk as the light around them ebbs away. And it was a soul filled with suffering, and the whole face was lit up by this suffering as by a lamp, and each took on a ghastly pallor, like a lamp lit in this sunlight. And yet an infinite nobility had come over these men, who were now safe from laughter, safe from words, a profound mystery surrounded these poor creatures, yesterday coarse or nondescript, today the tabernacles of a formidable secret, who were silent only because they had heard, whispered in their ear, 'the secret words that none may utter'. Above this charnel-house, trembling in the misty aura created by the souls as they took wing with their unsatisfied desires, their fruitless plans, their hollow dreams, with all their potentialities cut down and trampled before they could flower, letters of fire spelt out the Apostle's words: 'Behold they whose names are written in the book of life.'

From time to time Alban, his heart aching, tore himself away from the spectacle and went into the farmhouse where the 'walking wounded' were being hastily bandaged. Through the door, as through the open doors of the field ambulances, there came a stale whiff of organic matter and overheated blood. Had anyone seen Prinet? No, no one had seen him. And anyway, as he questioned the men, he met no one from the Nineteenth company. So, standing in front of the courtyard porch, he watched the men arriving along the road. Those who could walk caused him no uncertainty, but those who were either carried, or pushed on trolleys, and whose outline he could not see, filled him with choking apprehension. But soon, despite his desire to be there to recognize his friend at once if it became necessary, despite his fear of seeming impelled by some obscene curiosity endlessly to contemplate these dying men, he went back to the group of badly wounded, lugubriously drawn towards the presence of death.

The French had just been taken away in small carts, and there remained only the Germans, who were to go last, naturally enough.

They had been there for two hours. Once, their stretchers had been shifted, to shelter them from the sun. Then the sun had caught up with them, and for a long time now they had endured this torture by fire, and no one dared take the initiative to move them, or rather no one took it into his head to do so. There they remained, gnawed by the gangrene which crept up higher every second, feeling it creep up, feeling that there was still time but that in another five minutes it would be too late, and seeing the Assistant MO pacing to and fro in front of them; he could have given them an injection half an hour ago, but it was his turn to rest.

What were they thinking? What could they be thinking? Alban noticed a few NCOs among them, less badly wounded: smooth-faced young men, a little emaciated, with fine intellectual heads. He discovered similarities between their faces and his own. He pictured himself there in their midst, the flat cap over one ear, and one of our men pointing him out and saying: 'He's got a real Boche face, that one.' 'At this moment,' he thought, 'I might be discussing Hesiod with them.' When he looked at them, he hardened his expression because he felt he might be about to smile at them. But around them were the usual poor wan faces, made even paler, under the oil-coloured hair, by the purple band of the forage-caps, or green as the *feldgrau* itself from which they emerged, green as the faces of Byzantine Christs; and clustered thus around those three or four who were not marked by death, it seemed that they must destroy them by their mere contact, as ten rotten fruits will pollute a healthy one if they encircle it in a dish. There were some who did not look much more than sixteen; one of them lifted his bare arm to reveal the smooth armpit of a child. Since most of them were covered up to the chin by their great-coats, one could not tell what kind of unspeakable affliction had turned them into living corpses, and this uncertainty raised a new question mark above these sphinxes of suffering.

Around them, a few men in French horizon-blue stood looking on: handsome beards from the mechanized transport corps, territorials employed in the roads department, old carcasses adorned haphazardly with Italian medal ribbons, all the ignoble faces of men who have not been under fire. Some of them were clowning: 'Pariss! Pariss! Victory for Wilhelm!' Others crowded sympathetically round one of the Germans, a minor casualty who spoke a little French and said that Boche morale (he said Boche) was low. He at least might get himself looked after.

Going to relieve himself for a moment on the deserted side of the farm, he met a young German, who had probably come for the same reason and who had the look of a trapped beast when he saw him, his pink cheeks turning grey: 'He thought I was going to cut his throat here,' thought Alban.

No sooner was he back than he noticed a new casualty, probably only just brought in, and his eyes riveted themselves upon him, he could no longer look away. Alone amid this crowd of prostrate men, this one was sitting up on his stretcher. His torso was bare, enveloped from breast to stomach by a wide dressing, and on his back the ring of fresh blood soaking through the bandage indicated clearly why they had not been able to lay him down like the others. Every visible part of his flesh was irrevocably marked by death: the flat, slightly hollow chest, the jutting shoulder-blades, the slender hands, all were mottled and deathly pale. But the face, Alban would never forget the face; it became imprinted in his heart like Jesus' face in Veronica's handkerchief; years and years of sufferings, joys, hatreds and loves would pass over this face as over all the other memories of the war, and all these other memories, the names of comrades, the great décor of azure and ochre, the horror of such and such a place, would be erased save one, this face, which would never be erased. Very German-looking, with small eyes, an aquiline nose, a slightly receding chin, a forehead which one guessed must be receding too, although it was completely hidden under the scarlet-striped forage-cap worn right over the eyebrows, this beardless adolescent's face seemed cruel, shifty and viperine; and this combination of malice and youth and impending death touched Alban in his most secret depths. Already the nostrils were pinched, as were also the lips, which were indistinguishable from the rest of the face; for the whole was tinged with a uniform grey that was the very colour of ashes. And perched above the thirty recumbent forms, alone amid this horizontal fraternity, the boy contemplated what he himself would soon become, the living image of the Spirit of Death.

He saw. He knew. The mystery of his silence was unbearable. Alban could not tear his eyes away from him. And he covered him with his pity, as though it might have sheltered him from the sun. 'What question is he asking himself? Whom does he blame? But does he blame anyone? What does he regret? He is in this air I am breathing now, six yards away from me. If I came near enough to be able to touch him with my hand, even then I wouldn't know his thoughts. I can read nothing on his face. I too would be as inscrutable as he, if I were in his place.' Suddenly the sunken eyes swept round, came to rest on Alban, stopped there. Alban held them for four seconds, then turned away, hanging his head like a buffalo that a man masters by the horns, turned his body and moved away.

Everything vacillated inside him, everything had come adrift: 'I know, I know. Some day Germany will start again. Each man whose life we now spare will kill one of us; this one, if he lives, will perhaps kill my son. It is *my* victory if his back gapes open and his flesh decomposes. Yes, my body would shudder, yet my reason could not but approve if, as they passed through the door, their throats were slit discreetly on the other side. We are not playing this war like a game of football with both teams stopping and drinking together when the whistle goes; we're starting a war that will last a century and any means of destroying one more German must be fair. Moreover, do I not realize that in Germany our casualties are treated in the same way as we treat theirs? So, what then? What is it that shocks me?

'My reason tells me to be hard, yet pity corrodes me like a cancer. Ah, what a terrible thing it is to care about people! No, no, I didn't suck the she-wolf's milk; I am the son of a woman; these insensitive doctors are the strong men, not I. The spirit is willing but the flesh is weak. And yet, only yesterday, wasn't the flesh itself implacable? I too have killed men like this one, and my flesh did not tremble at the sight of their corpses. If I myself had scorched these men with a flame-thrower, would I now be contentedly whinnying before them?'

Ah! It was time he recognized himself for what he was: the modern man after all, the obscene muddle, the monster shaped from all the instincts, all the ideals of the world over twenty-five centuries, the most ill-matched, the most contradictory, adding up, super-imposing themselves without ever excluding one another. Something in him cried out: 'Not only are we fighting a just war, but we are defending ourselves with ridiculously fair weapons, and we are in fact destined to be beaten, even after an apparent victory, for the simple reason that we undervalue force'; and a voice answered with one word, just one, an absurd word that was nevertheless offered in reply, ceaselessly, to everything that was said: 'Murder . . . murder . . .' – as though to destroy the invader was murder! Something in him shouted that this predatory life suited his nature, that tomorrow he would be happier fighting – unjustly this time – a few Arabs, that he would never be happy in the town, and a voice answered: 'What is happening here is abominable. Nothing can excuse the futile hecatomb.' And each of these voices prevailed in turn, or else they all shouted together like quarrelling people. The two thoughts fought each other like two eagles at the summit of space, wheeling round and uttering terrible cries, and the black feathers fell, and they loved each other as they fought.

Suddenly, as he walked along the road, he saw a stretcher being wheeled towards him, and the legs sticking out under the blue greatcoat were wrapped in black puttees. Black puttees! Prinet's chasseur's uniform! As happened whenever a shell exploded in his vicinity, a wave of blood rushed from the centre of his body towards the skin. He was pierced with a foreboding as sharp as a surgeon's scalpel. But after another few steps, he recognized the homely, plebeian face of Lieutenant Le Hagre.

'Ah, lieutenant. Not too bad, I hope?'

'A bullet in the calf. And tonight, I'm for hospital.'

What a pleasure it was for Alban to talk to this little mechanic promoted to subaltern, whose charm consisted in the fact that it was hard to imagine him as an officer, but irresistibly easy to see him as a private! There was a kind of release in seeing him thus, in his posture very like the half-dead men next door, but very much alive, with a pink complexion, a smile on his lips, 'and tonight he's for hospital'!

'Which is your company?'

'The Twentieth.'

'You wouldn't by any chance have seen the cadet Prinet?'

'Yes.'

'Yes . . . ? When?'

'This morning at dawn, before the attack. The Nineteenth only attacked at noon.'

A slight hesitation, then:

'And . . . What was he doing?'

'Having a nose-bleed.'

Alban did not understand, imagined this meant a wound.

'Wounded?'

'No, no, he blew his nose too hard, it made his nose bleed. And he was worried sick, you know, because it didn't look good on his handkerchief, and the captain was there. D'you know him?'

'Yes. And you didn't see him afterwards?'

'Ah! Afterwards, no.'

'Was it bad, where they were?'

'We only had machine-guns. But the Nineteenth, they caught the

163

big stuff. We don't even know where it came from. Might have been our own guns.'

The big stuff . . . But no, Alban was more at ease. He had been seen! His nose was bleeding! This childish blood, compared to the horrible blood here, made Prinet a trifle ridiculous; it was in exactly the same vein as the enormous agony in the shelter ending up as a bruised tendon. One day Alban would tease him about it. Moreover, they had only attacked at noon; they had risked their lives for five hours less than the others. And then, how could one trust one's presentiments? He had had a presentiment in the shelter, and it had proved wrong. He had had a presentiment just now, on the road, when he saw Le Hagre's black puttees, and that had proved wrong too . . .

'Cigarette, lieutenant?'

Yes, Prinet would come back. And a new thought struck him: 'We'll try to get him somewhere safe.' It seemed to him that his whole war effort had just been given a precise aim. Only, since he, Alban, had to stay, would he have to stay alone? He remembered the feeling of abandonment he had had the day before on the road . . . Ah well, never mind. He would pull strings all the same to get the cadet away. But would Prinet consent? Ah! How terrible to be always in the dark . . .

He found he had come back, beside the stretcher, to the cluster of Germans. He would have guessed it with his eyes closed, from the thick smell coming from the bodies, the hot clothes, blood, leather and cooled sweat, above which, quite distinct, floated the stench of decay: a dense and sickly mixture, that thickened the air as though compressed beneath some invisible cloche, or like some monstrous dunghill. The boy was still propped up above the others, but Alban's eyes avoided him: he was afraid that if their eyes met the German might make a sign to him or call him over; anything seemed possible now. And what would he do then? What would need more courage: to answer his appeal and go to him, or to pretend not to understand, and look away?

And still that sun! Still that sun! Ah! It was indeed the panic

164

hour. From time to time, he guessed that one of them had just died, without at first knowing which one; a god would move away, somewhere, so as not to be profaned by seeing the dead body. Once an orderly came quite close to him, holding a piece of tent-cloth with which he covered up a face. He was about to move away when the wounded man next to the body became agitated, turning towards the dead man as if to draw the onlookers' attention to him. Eventually they gathered that he wanted the cloth pulled back. Out of curiosity, a sergeant lifted it.

'He isn't dead,' he said calmly. 'He looked at me.'

And, instead of removing the cloth, he only pulled it down to the chin. The face appeared, livid, contracted and wet (with sweat) like a discarded piece of chewing-gum, with terrified, imploring eyes like the eyes of Dog on the road. 'Perhaps at this moment Prinet is just like this man, with flies in his mouth and his eyes.' The faint breeze of hope which had risen in him at the sight of the young lieutenant now dropped stone-dead. And, as it always did whenever his reason strayed, the power of Christianity began to take control of him.

'Ah,' he thought, 'how like he is to the children of the Gentiles, for whom no prayers are said. In our colleges, when a child is on the danger list, they write to every monastery and every seminary to ask them to pray and say masses for him; step by step, a net of prayers is woven in order to protect him. But *he* isn't loved. As a child, when he was sweating with fever, whose cool hands soothed him? And now, who will pray for him? Can I alone make up for all those who will not pray for him?' Just as he did not fear death for himself, but feared it for his friend, so, though too proud to pray for the preservation of his own life, he felt no shame at all in praying for the preservation of his friend's. And in doing so he was filled with a sort of sweet satisfaction because this ease of self-forgetfulness for the sake of others reunited him, over a long period of drought and emptiness, with that golden age of selflessness his college years had been for him. The pain of his six-years' exile from that togetherness in suffering he had been granted in the winter corridors was now

165

suspended. Beneath a dry, harsh landscape, two living streams had met.

At that moment, from one of the cars which had come to take the wounded away, the driver, an 'ally', got out and approached the dying Germans. The woman accompanying him, her forage-cap over one ear, had pulled out a camera and was moving among the poor creatures with the same slightly glazed look, in her excitement, that we get in France under the influence of drink. Her companion pointed out the best subjects to her: the men who were most picturesque in their death-throes, those whose wounds were most clearly visible, those who had the most characteristic features. Having used up her roll of film, she put the camera back in its case and produced a dainty pair of scissors. She leaned over the men, cutting off their shoulder-straps and buttons. They looked at her with vacant eyes, no feeling left. They even helped her, tugging at their badges. On the other side of the yard, standing apart, not mixing with anyone, two drivers from another 'allied' nation watched the ignoble scene in silence, an unforgettable hint of disgust at the corner of their mouths.

'Will no one take a revolver and shoot them?' wondered Alban. 'Will none of these dying men rise up before he dies and kill these people who have made themselves the tempters of poor creatures in their extremity? Must it be me who avenges their honour?' The desire to kill the driver and the woman swept over him, frightening as sexual desire or thirst. Fortunately, they went away.

The dying men shrivelled up like fried fish under the heat. When it was all over for one of them, someone would say: 'There's one, over there'; and they would look and see a gaping mouth, stretched beyond measure, showing all its teeth like a dead horse. Often, the man had hardly expired before the flies had settled on him, in his mouth, in his eye-sockets, on each bloodstain, huddled so close together that they looked like some sort of sea-moss or black sponge, so drunk that one could have picked some of them off with one's fingers without disturbing the others, precisely, in fact, as if they themselves were dead. One of the men had died pressing a photograph to his lips; it had been sucked in by his last gasp and lay half-buried in the now gaping mouth: the void left by a soul has such powers as this . . . Another one moaned every time someone went past him, and stopped when they had gone away, and with each moan his naked stomach hollowed like the stomachs of wild beasts when they roar. Another was so badly placed on his stretcher that his head stuck out and hung backwards without support. As he found himself near him, Alban slipped under his neck a rolled-up blanket which happened to be there, among a pile of helmets, masks and bloodstained shoes.

Then he noticed that one of the orderlies who until then had done nothing – literally *nothing* – was now, having seen his action, arranging a little comfort under the head of another condemned man. 'Have I induced some pity in him?' he wondered.

But now, with a great effort, the man he had helped was trying to remove one of his rings. 'He wants to give me a ring in sign of gratitude,' thought Alban, backing away, trying to disappear. The man was holding the ring out to him now, repeating one word, always the same, which Alban did not understand. 'Treatment,' said a French soldier who had been watching the scene behind him. 'He says: treatment. He wants to be treated.' Alban turned away horrified, feeling the distressed look of the man upon him, with his rejected offering, with the outstretched hand and the pathetic ring . . . From that moment, Alban acted with a kind of automatism, as if in a trance: an artificial kind of will-power had taken hold of him and carried him away.

He walked over to the farmhouse. The Chief Medical Officer passed by the door. He stopped in front of him, stood to attention, and saluted:

'What do you want?'

'Sir, I'm not sure whether you know . . .' (his voice was harsh, staccato) 'but there are some Boches over there, and there would still be time to save them with an injection; but in half an hour it may be too late. An injection doesn't take long. It would be all over in five minutes . . .'

The man looked at him for a moment as though he did not understand. Then he burst out laughing. At first, his laughter came pouring out spontaneously; then it became forced. Alban watched him with a kind of horror, and it was only with a great effort of will that he managed to stay at such close quarters to him . . . At last the doctor said:

'What do you think I care?'

'Even some of our chaps over there are saying it's going a bit far.'

'Well, they can say what they like. And as for you, you can mind your own business. Get out.'

Alban spun round and walked back towards the Germans.

He walked like someone with a definite purpose. In a few seconds, very distinctly, as though his mind were lit by a flash of lightning, he pictured to himself all the disapprobations that his action would earn him, all the suspicions of the armchair soldiers. He pushed his way through the men who were standing round the wounded, penetrated among the stretchers, thrust his face into the heavily-laden atmosphere as into something palpable which stuck to his cheeks, felt rather than saw all the eyes turn towards him without a single body moving. Once he was well into this ground-level humanity, in the narrow path between two rows of bodies, so narrow that he seemed to be treading on them, he was afraid. But he went on walking towards the young man who was looking at him, galvanized in his heart as cataleptics are in their flesh, but trembling more than the dying men.

When he had reached him, he knelt one knee to the ground. And to see him so near made him breathe heavily.

He asked, in German:

'Can I do anything for you?'

'No. I'm going to die.'

'Are your parents still alive?'

'My mother is.'

'Give me your name and address, and I shall let your mother know, one day, that I was near you.'

The words were a little obscure, yet very clear to both of them. The other looked at him and, as before, Alban exerted all his strength to keep his head from turning away under his gaze. For a moment the German looked at him in silence, then he said:

'I'll give you my wallet. Send it to her when you can.'

He ran his hand through the jumble of green cloth over his knees and in the effort he made, pain took hold of him, twisted his colourless lips at the corner of the mouth, baring a sharp, very white tooth.

'Ah!' he said. 'They've taken it from me.'

'Give me your mother's name.'

'My mother is Maria Ertle, in Bremen, Rheinstrasse, 19.'

Alban hesitated:

'And you, what is your name?'

'My name is Conrad.'

At that moment, someone tapped Alban on the shoulder. There was a sergeant behind him:

'Come along, you're not allowed to talk to the prisoners. What are you doing here?'

'I am a priest,' he said, 'and this man called me.'

'Hurry up then.'

He turned to the boy again:

'I'll write to your mother.'

'When I appear before God, I shall testify that you had pity on me.'

'I didn't do it for that,' said Alban, his teeth rattling in his mouth. 'Well, good-bye.'

He took the greyish hand, dry and icy cold, like the skin of a snake. He held it a moment, firmly, repeating: 'Good-bye, take courage,' and he poured all of his being into this act of self-giving. But when he tried to withdraw his hand, he felt the man clinging to it. 'Let me go,' he said, standing up, but held by this long hand which was covered in dried blood like a coat of flaking paint, 'Let me go, you know I must go away.' Then the other whispered:

'*Verlasse mich nicht!*' (Do not abandon me!)

He repeated the faint supplication several times, while Alban began to lose his head, kept saying ever louder: 'Let me go! Let me go!' and this ever louder plea mingled with the other ever weakening one. At last Alban, exasperated, unfastened with his free hand the fingers which held him as one unfastens the gripping fingers of a corpse. And without another look, without looking at anything except the wall of the farmhouse glittering in the sun, he walked away, his eyes wide as though someone were holding them open with their fingers.

When he had reached the dressing-station, he turned round. The boy was still sitting up, with his back towards him. But the bowed head and the shaking shoulders told him that he was crying. 'So that is what I have done,' he said to himself.

As he was turning his eyes away, he caught sight of the orderly in whom he thought he had induced some pity. With a mug in his hand, he was offering a drink of water to the Germans who called him, at the risk of rendering fatal any stomach wound which might yet have been treated! Then Alban reflected that he himself was the source of this murderous pity. And he was troubled in his mind, not knowing what was good or what was bad.

But the sergeant who had tapped him on the shoulder when he was amongst the wounded came up to him.

'You told me just now that you were a priest. I've just heard the truth from this man, who knows you. You're not a priest at all.'

'No.'

'All right. You'll hear more of this.'

Once the sergeant had gone, the other wailed:

'If only I'd known . . . I've got you in a mess.'

But Alban simply asked:

'Which company are you in?'

'The Eighteenth.'

'You don't know Prinet, the cadet of the Nineteenth?'

'Yes I do.'

'Ah! Did you see him this morning?'

'I saw him at Morainville, before the attack, not since.'

'If I wanted to go and see him at once, what should I do?'

'You take the main road. You know the main road, don't you? Can't go wrong. You get to some poplars. That is, if you haven't already stopped one in the mug! But I can't tell you about that, can I? I'm just telling you what you've got to do . . .'

'Go on, go on. When I've got to the poplars, what do I do then?'

'You go left.'

'You're pointing to the right!'

'You're not trying to tell me I don't know my left from my right, are you?'

But already Alban had gone. He collected, from a corner of the farmyard, his rifle, his packs, his rolled blanket which he slung over his shoulder, and set out along the road, almost calm.

13

Ares

THE ROAD was carrying countless wounded towards the rear, and from the fact that he alone was travelling upstream, he alone was going away from life towards death, amidst men who, one after the other, stared at him as he passed, Alban drew a naïve pride and his face took on a sterner expression. Two hundred yards beyond the village, on the roadside, a cigarette between his lips, the Chief Medical Officer was directing the evacuation of casualties. The gravely wounded and the obvious malingerers who pretended to have been gassed, infantrymen, gunners, negroes, territorials, fresh-faced lads from the engineers who showed no sign of any ill effects – all were evacuated, filing smartly past this kind of check-point where pink or white tabs were being distributed; and, as people who hear that they have been decorated cannot bear the thought of remaining for a few more hours with an empty button-hole and rush off to the Palais-Royal, so these men stopped, clutter-ing up the road, to tie their tabs on their chests. 'Indeed,' thought Alban, 'now more than ever those who stay must be doing so because they really want to, or else because they are the most forsaken of helots,' and the tale which ran through the regiment came back to him: 'The divisional general is fed up. The order is to evacuate as many men as possible so that the division can be relieved.' And he asked himself, not knowing what the answer was, so little did he know about his friend: 'Would Prinet want that?'

Neat piles of new shells abandoned by the enemy lined the road on both sides. They rolled under-foot, their detonators intact; it was a mystery that nothing exploded. In the sun-streaked coverts nearby, helmets, placards in German, fresh tracks of horses and wheels, told of the hasty retreat. The men crowded round a German post-orderly's bag which had been left open, each carrying away a letter which they would never be able to read. The first corpses appeared. A dead horse was doing the splits, its neck gracefully inclined, and in this classic posture of a galloping horse it resembled a figure in some half-mythical monument brought down from its high pedestal. In front, beyond the line of poplars, smoke from the time-shells was hanging in the luminous sky, black and compact like blobs of catarrhal phlegm in a basin of water.

A limping artilleryman signalled to him as though he had something important to tell him. When Alban came up: 'Look at old J. C. directing the traffic up there,' whispered the man, pointing towards a hillock on top of which a statue of the Sacred Heart stretched out its arms in the traditional gesture. And Alban roared with laughter, and went on laughing even when he saw another wounded man, on a comrade's shoulders, his face lolling against the carrier's head and inundating it with vomited blood (he seemed to be devouring his skull, as in Dante's poem). Now the wounded were thinning out, arriving from the right through the fields where, no doubt, the fighting had most recently flared up. Alban now found himself alone, without that slight excitement he had felt at being watched with a kind of respect by the men coming back. Five hundred yards in front of him, at every other moment, a black or white flower would blossom from space, seemingly giving the lie to the Homeric expression: the barren air. He was thinking: 'I was perfectly safe, and here I am deliberately going to where the killing is. It's a queer idea, really. A very queer idea.' But it did not disturb him, obsessed as he was by the thought that he might find the cadet and fight beside him. 'He'll see what I can do when I take enough trouble. Tonight I shall get a bar to my *Croix de Guerre*, or rather I shall be killed, but I don't care.' Last night, separated from his comrade, he had trembled shamefully at the thought of dying in the rear among the shirkers he despised, yet now he felt, equally strongly, a wild indifference to being killed, and even, in flashes, a real desire to die, if it were to happen under Prinet's eyes and after some exceptional deed.

And through it all, the thought that at this moment he ought officially to have been with his maintenance unit, and that anything he might do was thus to some extent 'for his own amusement', the thought that he could go right, or left, or even run away if he felt so inclined, without being any more at fault than he had been as soon as he had left his billet behind him, satisfied his inborn taste for independence. Everything seemed easy, as during those college days when he was always on his own, in the yard during prep, doing his prep during break, at choir-practice while the others were out walking, in the library during Benediction, never in line with the others and yet never punished, not once in seven years. And now in the same way, knowing full well that he had in fact abandoned his post, still he had not once envisaged that he might be punished.

There came a moment, however, when he noticed that, over on his left, green leaves were falling from trees bordering the road. A faint, soft noise, another, then another: the air was swept by the trajectories of bullets as by the teeth of some great invisible rake. Casually, he half lay down, leaning on his elbows. Reason told him to lie down in the ditch, but that would have made him feel ridiculous and a little ashamed; having so far experienced only shells and grenades, his head did not contain the images necessary to convince him physically, as it were in the flesh, that bullets kill. So, after a minute, since anyway the hissing of the bullets was growing less frequent, he got up and started to walk along the ditch, simply hunching his shoulders like a frightened little boy afraid of being hit by a ball lobbed high in the air, and making sure that his blanket, slung over his shoulder, was covering his heart.

The shrapnel shells were bursting very close now, and at each one of them he turned this way or that, as if slow-moving trains were passing through the air around him. On the left, in the direction of the farm, heavy shells were coming down. There were no more bullets, save an occasional spent one or stray one, which flicked along the road, raising a minute crest of dust, or else into the grass, quick as a tiny lizard that has gone before you see it. In this way he arrived within sixty yards of the poplars.

He straightened up and ran across the road. A bullet screamed past. Close by, a voice made him start:

'What's that half-wit up to?'

From a crater, a head emerged. With a running jump he landed in the hole. There were three men in it.

'Where were you off to like that? You must be in a hurry to say Kamerad!'

'But,' he said, 'I was going towards the lines . . .'

'Towards the Boche lines, you mean, and just as if you were going for a stroll.'

'What! Aren't there any more Frenchmen over there?' he mumbled hesitantly as though he was afraid of saying something silly.

They were laughing: 'He's got it bad!' Alban finally understood that there was nothing now between the Germans and himself. And moreover he could now make out, above a mound of earth, the quick flashes of the Mausers darting out almost before you could see them, like reptiles' tongues.

He told them he was on liaison duty, taking a message to the cadet Prinet, of the Nineteenth.

'Ah! so that's it. Why didn't you say so? You shouldn't be afraid, you've got a tongue in your head, haven't you?'

He asked where the Nineteenth was.

'You see those houses over there . . .'

A ·77 was coming at them. They flung themselves flat, became one with the earth, realized they were safe, saw the lumps of earth flying above their heads.

'Good-bye.'

'You're in a hurry, aren't you?'

Forgetting that he had told them he was on liaison duty, he replied ingenuously:

'Yes, I am, he's my pal.'

'Otherwise, you might have stayed here, nice and cosy. *We* don't intend to go and pinch the Fritzes' flag, I can tell you.'

Without seeing anything wrong in their words, he simply said:

'No, no.' The ·77 had at last given him a foretaste of death, and if he had to die, he did not want it to happen among men he did not know and with whom he had nothing in common: a wasted death.

He asked for directions. The Nineteenth had been holding the hamlet a kilometre away. One could get there without too much difficulty by taking cover below the bank of the stream which ran alongside the poplars. In any case he would come across some of our fellows who were posted there. He slipped out, reached the brook without mishap and, after pausing for a minute, began to crawl, glad not to be afraid.

On he went, dragging himself through the mud. A dozen shells came over, without seriously worrying him. Was he not half-hidden by the hedge, a powerful protection against shells? Bullets flew above him without giving him the feeling that they were aimed at him. He had pushed back his haversacks, and took care that they stayed there, to protect his back. Beneath him, insects settled on the stagnant water, ants crawled helter-skelter along the poplar-roots, dried-up twigs from last winter crackled: a tiny, indifferent world of its own, the same as he would have seen had he been crawling on all fours in the Bois de Boulogne. In front, hidden behind the same bank, he caught sight of some horizon-blue great-coats. There was a squad of them. He recognized some men from the Eighteenth.

'Liaison. Is the Nineteenth over there?'

'Yes.'

'Is the cadet Prinet with them?'

'Don't know. Very likely.'

'Everything all right?'

'Getting along nicely.'

176

He went off again.

Suddenly, on his left, a crackle of rifle fire and the quick rattling of a machine-gun broke out together. Instinctively he looked up.

In the distance, French soldiers rose from the ground and ran forward. They were springing up from everywhere. Some of them fell as though they had stumbled on something. Farther off, behind the trees, green greatcoats were moving too, and falling. It was difficult to understand the actions of all these men. Sometimes they would all converge on the same spot, sometimes whole files would start, break off, then come together again, like sections of some vast snake, and then disappear, sucked in by the earth, one knew not where. 'It might be a film,' he thought; it might equally well have been God knows what frivolous thing – manoeuvres, a child's game, or a football match such as one sees in the Bagatelle gardens when, from the polo-ground, one looks over the whole plain.

Only then did he see that in front of him some Germans were getting up and running away. 'Kill! Kill!' He aimed and fired. Was not the man he was killing a brother to the one for whom his heart had bled a little while ago, in the courtyard of the farm? He did not even think about it. 'Kill! Kill!' A Frenchman coming up behind him passed practically over his head, turned round, shouted 'Out you come, you there' as though in reproach, then crossed his legs in a funny way, sidestepping like a groggy boxer who makes the audience laugh because he seems to be pondering whether to fall or not. He fell, and his helmet rolled on the ground; he held up one arm like a gladiator asking for mercy, but nobody reprieved him, for he moved no more, submitting to his fate. Alban, who had lowered his rifle in order to watch, fired again, once, twice. The kick, knocking against his shoulder, echoed in his wound, and his dressing irked him so much when he bent his arm that he stopped firing. He saw a soldier near him, bareheaded, empty-handed.

'You want my rifle?'

The man took two steps towards him, stretching out his arms, then, with his feet and legs together, sideways, all of a piece, like a diver showing off, he flopped into the stream. Slapped full in the face by the mud, Alban gave a shriek, whereas, the day before, he had been hit by a piece of shrapnel without noticing it.

He was in the act of wiping his face with the back of his sleeve when the blast from a ·77 bowled him over on to the ground, his hands clasped to the back of his neck; the explosion cracked inside his brain so that he thought his face would split apart, and he felt a violent blow in the back, the kidneys, the legs, as of an avalanche crashing down on him from a great height. He picked himself up, reeling and bewildered, found he could not stand, fell on his knees, felt sure he was dying because he was choking, began to cough violently, felt certain that his chest had burst, that he was going to vomit blood through his mouth and nose. He vomited earth, coughed, coughed again, vomited more earth. He dragged himself back to the river-bank, not daring to look at himself for fear of seeing blood all over him. His left arm was hurting. Staring across the landscape with eyes dilated as after a sleepless night and filled with a sort of ethereal wonder, with his right hand he began to feel along his arm from the shoulder downwards: 'Ah! Here's a bit that's left . . . This bit is still there at any rate,' and he was so afraid of putting his fingers in something soggy that, once he had got to the end, ridiculously, from sheer joy, he shook hands with himself . . . Alive! Relief flooded over him.

And now, once more, what was he to do? Judging from the direction, it must have been men of the Nineteenth he had seen attacking. Now, they had scattered far and wide. Where could he find Prinet in such a mêlée? Ah! All this just for the sake of finding the dear old brute, all the same . . .

Suddenly he was struck by the sound of a voice, which perhaps had been calling for some while, but which he now noticed for the first time. Behind him, quite nearby, someone was shouting feebly:

'Help, two twenty-six! Help, two twenty-six!'

He already felt touched by this way of calling one's regiment as someone else might call 'Mummy!' when he realized that he knew the voice well. Wherever had he heard it before? He knew it was the voice of someone he liked. Guided by the sound, he went towards an enormous shell-hole.

Lying at the bottom of the crater was Bellerey, a youth of the 1918 class who had just been promoted corporal and whom Alban knew well. He tried to get down beside him.

'Move over a bit so I can get down.'

'I can't. It's all coming out . . .'

'What?'

He saw him take his hands away from his stomach, saw the gaping wound from which the intestines were hanging, saw the eyes stare, then turn away; and he, too, shuddered.

'Could you give me your first-aid outfit?' Bellerey asked, using the second person plural. The boy never used the familiar form of address to him, not even now that he was a corporal. Ah, how polite he was!

'Stupid, you don't have to talk to me like that,' said Alban to this boy, who in ten minutes' time wouldn't have to talk to anyone again.

His first-aid kit? He had used it up yesterday for his arm. He had not thought of asking for another.

'Haven't you got yours?'

'I handed it over to a pal of mine.'

He had scarcely any breath left, yet he said 'handed over' when it would have been so much simpler to say 'I gave.'

'I can do nothing for him,' thought Alban, 'nothing at all except not leave him. I can do nothing – and yet, perhaps I can do a great deal . . . Ah, don't others deserve what I am about to give him just as much as he?'

He wiped the boy's forehead, under the dry hair, cut straight at the front as the Gracchi's hair must have been. He took off his tie, loosened his collar, performed in advance these rites for the dead. He settled the boy's head in the hollow of his shoulder and put his arm around him. Then he sat still. Whereupon the boy, like someone who has suffered too much, said these frightening words:

'I'd had enough.'

179

After that, he said no more.

A percussion-fuse shell landed quite near; Alban did not move. He did not mind dying here, now. Horror and sweetness mingled in his soul in a unique balm, and he no longer had any desire to move, no, now he would not move even in order to escape black death. He thought: 'I am giving him what I can. I am doing what I had to do. All those who know assert that, out of all my possible duties, I have done well in choosing this one.' And he felt that even if the boy's dying went on for ever, he would stay with him until death, that even if night should come, even if the guns should select this precise spot for total destruction, he would not move, he would not go away. Ah, had he not heard the same call twice already? 'Do not leave me,' Prinet had entreated him in the shelter, and the German: '*Verlasse mich nicht!*' And at this hour, on this plain and farther away, thousands of men were calling on others not to abandon them, struggling against indifference, realizing at last that one cannot be alone, and falling back alone, struggling alone, dying alone. 'But my disobedience has allowed me this good deed. Had I been on duty, I should have gone to the attack with the others, I should have seen him, perhaps, and heard him, and I should have had to go on with the others. Being free, I had the right to stop. Bellerey owes this poor comfort to the cadet.'

Memories came flooding back to him. Several times in their quarters, Prinet and he had invited Bellerey to their little supper-parties: two bottles of 'vintage' wine at three francs each, some grapes and raw summer tomatoes, the whole served on a grenade-case. Then he would see the eyes of the little country lad, who used the second person plural and never offered his hand first, fill with surprise and pleasure because the young gentleman was such a decent chap, so like himself, although so different. And he was over-whelmed with an extraordinary certainty that both of these two would have given their lives for him, as he would have done for them, and this without their seeing much of one another, without their really knowing one another, without their being the only ones to benefit from that privilege: a simple and miraculous promise to which nobody had ever alluded, either by word or action, but which they had read, once only, perhaps, for a second, and perhaps even then without quite recognizing it, in the gravity of their eyes.

Then came other memories. In Granrupt three weeks ago, Bellerey had pulled a scrap of paper out of his pocket and had held it out to him, a look of mischievous pride in his hazel eyes. And Alban had read, in the childish handwriting, reeking of forgery: *I, the undersigned, Chief Medical Officer Dubrulle, certify that Private Bellerey (Alexandre), of the Eighteenth company, is suffering from orkitis (sic), which prevents him from, etc. . . .*

'With this, you see, if the racket starts tomorrow . . .' Alban had begged him to abandon the idiotic scheme, which was anyhow transparent even if the spelling mistake did not give it away, and which could have led him to a court-martial. 'Of course not!' he had replied. '*Orchitis* with *ch*! *Ch* is pronounced as in *chop* and they don't call it *ortchitis*.' He would not be dissuaded; the quartermaster-sergeant himself had failed to convince him, and it was only with the greatest misgivings that he had at last given in to their arguments. Then, by little words and little silences, by such a clumsy bit of manoeuvring, he had asked Alban to write him a new certificate in a fine hand; and Alban had had to refuse, had had to disappoint him, and could almost read his secret thoughts; 'He seemed nice and friendly and all that, but as soon as it's a question of giving some definite proof, he's just like the others. I expect he'd have scarpered just like that if things ever got nasty . . .' How remote it all was! What had become of the wretched scrap of paper which was to save him from the 'racket'? Perhaps at this very moment, he was holding Alban responsible for his death.

As he was thinking of this, the boy started to moan: 'Ah la la . . . Ah la la . . .' Always the same, on three notes. With his left hand, which was underneath the boy's arm, Alban took him by the wrist and firmly squeezed the hand on which a copper ring had stained a finger blue. Then the moan lengthened, modulated; yes, there was no mistaking it, he was humming; what started as a moan had developed into a sort of chant which kept him occupied, did him good, eased his pain a little by expressing it. Then, listening to this mild lament like that of a dreaming baby, feeling so sad at not being able to do anything for him, and also because they were so close to each other, he kissed him tenderly.

The rustle of bullets could no longer be heard. The shells no longer burst above them, but further on and less often; the battle had shifted and was probably settling down. From time to time, from the shattered walls of the crater, a lump of earth would fall and a little softer earth would trickle down like blood from a wound. Once, with one of these lumps of earth, a small purple flower fell on the boy's shoulder. 'Now you're in bloom,' Alban nearly said to him; but he refrained, thinking of the flowers on graves. Another time, when some earth had fallen on the rough hand without provoking any reaction, Alban thought he was dead and looked at him. The face had taken on a wizened look. The groove under the nose had lengthened a little; two wrinkles stretched towards the mouth; the eyes, turned up to the sky, no longer blinked although they still moved. Alban increased his pressure on the wrist, squeezed it so hard that it became an effort. Until the first second of darkness, the sinking man would feel comforted.

A short time elapsed. No more shells could be heard, nothing but sporadic bursts of shooting, at wide intervals. Above his head, a slow cloud crossed the disc of sky; the sky was losing its strength; he sensed the end of the day. He turned once more to the boy lying on his left, on the side where his own heart was beating. An infinite calm stupor inhabited the face which had found peace. Youth had surfaced again, the eyes no longer glittered, the mouth was half open as if about to issue an oracle. He undid two buttons on the coat, slipped his hand inside the shirt, warm as freshly-ironed linen. Nothing beat against his fingers. Bellerey belonged to the earth.

He withdrew his hand, but did not try to free himself. He was not afraid of his distant comrade. Thoughts glided through his mind like sails on a peaceful sea. 'If I had wanted to, I would now be eating with the Service Corps or even in Paris, at the Ministry. I have held in my arms the son of a small farmer, I have kissed him. This thing that lies beside me is a dead man; I am still holding his wrist. I do not want to go away. And yet I must go and find the other one. I do not know where he is, nor whether he is alive or dead. Night is falling. How strange it all is!' Yet, in spite of this last assertion, it all seemed to him, on the contrary, very simple and very ordinary. He lay there for a moment. Was he alone? Were there two of them? The falling lumps of earth were more suggestive of a presence than this body which had been the crown of life.

And then he freed himself. He took the wallet and the copper ring, tried to stretch out the corpse's legs a little more decently, covered the forlorn face with his scarf. When he could think of nothing more to do, and told himself that it only remained for him to get out of this tomb, he felt embarrassed, almost distressed, as if he had forgotten something of the utmost importance, and as if to go away like this was a sacrilegious desertion. Standing on the crater's edge, he had a brief attack of dizziness. Then he took a last look at his comrade, and saw that he was already like so many others, although to him he had been so very different. Like the thousands of men who, faced with a dead comrade whom they must leave to rot alone, had had to lie to themselves and had promised: 'I shall come back,' like the thousands of men who had never come back, he made that promise in his heart, and then turned towards the sad fields – himself heavy as a corpse.

Not a sound could now be heard. Over where the sun was setting, the sky was purplish, like an immense wound. In the distance two farms were burning; the two columns of smoke rose straight up and vanished without a single bend; it was as though the air, pierced and pierced so many times, had been killed at last, together with everything else. Alban was reminded of an old and well-loved image, 'Rome in flames', and found that it too was dead: the Empire, the whole of history, all thought, all knowledge since the beginnings of the world, were as nothing compared with Bellerey dying. A short distance away, the three houses making up the hamlet, though still intact, had been shaken and battered by the shell-blast, and drooped sideways, telescoped, like three subsiding Chinese lanterns: a bizarre spectacle it was, these human dwellings going in all directions, as if turned to stone in the middle of a fit of convulsive laughter, or during the leaps and contortions of some monstrous jig. Night was falling. Under the pallid twilight, the whole field from which proud battle had retired was like a thing that has served its purpose, a set after a play that will not be performed again, or a float after a carnival. Here and there, bodies were lying around, and in this uncertain light it was difficult to distinguish their uniforms, as though they all belonged to the same country and it was through some ghastly mistake that they had slaughtered each other. Suddenly, as if at the click of a switch, the forearm of a corpse shot up and remained erect. Everything around seemed more inert. Like a tiny lamp above these prostrate forms, growing more and more indistinct, an identity disc flashed on the wrist.

Alban went towards the farms which had been the centre of operations of the Nineteenth company. Yes, yes, yes, it was indeed the Nineteenth, he recognized it now, by the dead. Here was Chuquet, Marcel, the little drummer: his bloodless fingers stiff in the air, he looked as though he were using sign-language for deaf-mutes. Here was Sergeant Ridel, who used to say in a noble guardsman's voice: 'I have no soldier's honour.' Here was Bruchon, nearly a yard of his bowels hanging out like paint out of a flattened tube and clinging to the ground like a monstrous umbilical cord linking him to Mother Earth. The outbuildings of one of the farms had been burnt down. He thought he had trodden on a little black thing like the charred carcass of a dog; he looked closer: it was a man, the size of a three-year-old child. 'Perhaps it's Prinet,' he thought, stupefied by the excess of horror. A dead man was squatting with his back against a wall, a bandage wound round his head revealing only the eyes. There must have been a first-aid post here, before the Nineteenth had taken up position. Suddenly, it seemed to him that the eyes were moving. Was it an hallucination? The regiment was full of tales of soldiers who, after dark, had seen the dead move. He went nearer (it seemed as though his nerves had been cut

184

to shreds). The man turned his head towards him, quite alive. And, amidst so many corpses, this spared life was as touching as the advent of shadow or water after hours and hours of bright sun.

Standing beside the man, he saw that the bandage had reddened over the mouth. The eyes, the only visible things amid all this white, like the eyes of oriental women, were watching him as one watches something never seen before.

He asked:

'Are you from the Nineteenth company?'

The eyelids nodded assent. Alban knelt down. The mysterious face was right up against his, only the eyes visible, not the features, nor the age, nor the voice:

'Do you know the cadet Prinet?'

Again the 'Yes' sign.

'Have you seen him today?'

No sign. But anguish flitted across the eyes as in the eyes of frightened cats, the eyebrows puckered, the head fell backwards. The young man bent a little lower:

'Was he in the attack with the other lads here?'

The eyes had closed, refused to speak any more. Alban loomed over him.

'Eh? Was he in that last attack? Answer me, will you!'

He felt in his hands an urge to shake and brutalize this tortured flesh. Suddenly the eyes opened, and the long brownish hand, covered with minute splashes of blood like flies' excrement on a mirror-frame, gestured vaguely. Alban sensed the muscles contracting under the bandage, the straining to speak, the grunt from what was no longer a mouth. A little pinkish saliva stained the cloth around the old crust of dried blood. Then the head moved a little, meaning 'no'.

'Is he wounded?'

A very definite nod: 'yes'.

'Seriously?'

The same sign, and then the hoarse, unintelligible sound, issuing

185

from the throat only, in the absence of lips. And then exhaustion after the effort, head falling, eyes closed.

Alban rose, removed his helmet, wiped the sweat off his forehead with the fleshy part of his hand. The odour of fresh blood, sickly-sweet, like the scent of the flowers of certain trees, turned his stomach, though he had breathed it many a time in the *arrastraderos* of the bullring. Why was he going away? Were there not other questions to be asked? But he felt a weakness inside him.

Darkness was nearly complete. The day, man's friend, was accomplishing its destiny. Far away a light shone, like a star fallen from the sky; three telegraph posts on a hill suggested gallows or the three crosses. On an evening when, over hundreds of kilometres, the whole army must be on the move, not a sound could be heard; no, not a single sound on an evening when the whole army must be on the move. But from time to time the horizon glowed, for a fraction of a second, like a flash of summer lightning.

Now the moment of impotence had come. Why had he moved away? Why had he asked no more questions? He had been afraid, he had lacked strength. Ever since leaving the maintenance depot he had been strong and blind to everything, because then there was something to will; but now, what was there to will? It was the hour of impotence. There was no hand-rail on the staircase he was on now, it was very very dark, this staircase, very dark and very empty, and there was nothing to lean on. Ah, there was nothing for it, he must lean upon the divine! A cry burst forth in his soul, the ancient cry of those who were the first to bear his name: 'Faith in miracles!' Why should he deny himself these crazy means? At boxing, he was known as an 'infighter'; in life, too, he was an infighter; everything that could be tried must be tried. And so he crossed the threshold, into the realm of the absurd.

Mary receives more than Martha, the labourers who work one hour receive as much as those who work twelve; he who saves his life, loses it; St John falls at the feet of the young brigand chief and kisses his hand. This kingdom is not of this world; there is nothing therein that is not contrary to man's customs, an object of scandal and a stumbling-block. '*Am I not allowed to dispose of my wealth as I please?*' Here, once more, Alban found unlimited powers. And this is what he proposed: to offer himself in the other's place. He announced the offer aloud, so that He who hears should hear. Let Him take him, Alban, in exchange! Suddenly, a scruple came to him: he realized that this offer of his life would cost him nothing and that therefore the deal was invalid. However much he pictured himself lying on the ground among the dead, with the corpse-like face he remembered in the photograph taken of him at the end of a cross-country run, the image remained harmless. Whichever way he handled the thought of his death, it remained for him like an unloaded revolver; you could press it against your temple, or your throat, and pull the trigger again and again, and it would still be powerless to harm you. What could be the value of a sacrifice which cost you nothing? And so he looked for what would cost him dear. All the vows that filled his boyhood were instantly rejected: gifts to the poor, distant pilgrimages, proud humiliations. Let the Gentiles jeer! For this was what he thought up, a lunatic proposal beyond the bounds of human understanding: if Prinet lived, he would renounce, for a long period of time – three years, for example – the exercise of his intellect; would not read, would not express himself; when a thought occurred to him, he would not jot it down; he would let his brain lie fallow. He, who had pushed the fear of wasted time to the point of neurosis, who always carried a book in his pocket so that five empty minutes might not remain unused, had hit upon the perfect sacrifice, to sacrifice intellectually three years, to amputate three years from his brief life. He promised this, he swore it by St Michael and by those he loved. This vow once made, he had truly reached the bottom of what was within his power. He felt better. He went back to the farm. He had recovered his courage. He would question and know the truth.

He was back once more beside the body, and he bent over it once more:

'I am the man who was talking to you about Prinet a little while ago. Do you remember?'

'Yes,' from the head.

Then he bent even lower, right against the pathetic face, as though no one must hear what he was about to say, as though he wanted to speak so quietly that he might not even hear himself.

'Was he killed?'

A big 'yes' from the head, and again 'yes', energetically, as though something had been found at last, and a kind of pleasure, as if now all had been said, as if now it was all over and he would be left in peace, and again: 'Yes. Yes. You have found out. You know what you wanted to know. Now leave me in peace.'

14

Alone and Afraid

ALL THE gods and the helmeted warriors kept watch in the solemn night. Wounded flowing back from the front, hospital units occupying positions won, had repeopled the hamlet. Among the wounded were several men from the Nineteenth. Alban went from one to the other. They told him: 'We were waiting to attack. We were due to start in a few minutes. The shell must have landed straight on top of him, and exploded as it hit him. When we picked ourselves up, he wasn't there any more. There was a crater just where he'd been. Cornut had disappeared too.' A few details apart, three of the men told the same story. 'Perhaps if we'd been able to look, we might have found bits of him, but it wasn't possible to go back and see . . .'

With no sign of effort or strain Alban questioned them, lucid and dry as if he had been drawing up a report for the colonel's secretary or the CSM of the Twenty-third. An odd reflection made him pause: 'He used to complain that no one saluted him. At least he would have been saluted in his grave. But he won't have a grave.' A host of minor feelings occupied him. He was surprised at not finding in these men any bitterness towards him, although he had left them for the rear on the eve of battle; he was grateful to them for showing, by the dignity of their words, that they recognized his friendship for the cadet, knew all that had been silently undone; he noticed nevertheless that nobody expressed a personal regret, something stronger than the soldier's resigned melancholy: 'Yes, that's how it goes . . .' – 'Another one gone . . .' – 'Ah, it's not much fun . . .' He seized upon all these details, which did him neither good nor harm. At the same time, his detachment did not fool him. 'It's going to be horrible later on.'

Quickly attended to, for the arrivals had become less frequent, the wounded soon left. As soon as the last one had been driven off and Alban found himself alone, abandoned by faces and words, grief was upon him in a flash, lassooing him, pulling his legs from under him, sitting him down on a milestone.

His hands joined on his lap, his lips drawn in, almost disappearing – so fiercely were they clamped together – he sat through the silent outburst. It was like the struggle of a raging wind in a chimney, now rising to a fury, now dying down, yet always dull, muffled, without a sound. There was not a tear in his eyes, nor any desire for tears, nor the possibility of tears. But the roof of his mouth was suddenly laid bare by a painful sore, like the frightening preliminary symptom of some shameful disease.

The idea of praying for this soul, the thought of where it might be, the hope of meeting it again one day, were as remote from his mind as if faith in an after-life had never existed on earth. Had any comfort been offered, he would have rejected it with contumely, as though, extreme calling forth extreme, it was only in his consciousness of a total lack of hope that he found the strength to remain upright.

Then he buried himself in memory, and his soul's foundations shook. He called up each memory in turn, to test his courage on it. They rose within him, lacerating him, and then, as though they had knocked against his tightly-closed lips, they trembled and fizzled out without having delivered themselves of their burden, exactly like a shell that fails to explode. Some he looked for, yet could not find. He realized, for instance, that he had already forgotten certain expressions on his friend's face. But he could still see his freckles.

He longed to drink some wine. It seemed to him that it would cure him at once, as a headache disappears with aspirin.

He was still sitting on the milestone, his face a mask of suffering. Upright, motionless, he waited for the worst of the storm to abate; just as, in the old days, when his nose was bleeding, he used to sit still, saying nothing, his head thrown back a little, with people fussing round him whom he would not answer. Although the milestone was at the foot of a wall, he did not lean back, but sat rigid and inscrutable, like some well-trained flunkey on his seat. Yet, from his face, anyone who looked at him would have thought he was in a rage.

The sky changed, became yet darker. A new star appeared, poised itself like a tear, sister of his own which would not flow. He felt himself carried away, suffering, into the midst of these unsuffering things; he thought that too much is forgiven those who suffer: 'Ridiculous effusions about *the indifference of nature*! What do people expect? That the trees should dry up every time a mortal dies?' At the thought of all the silliness, the absurd sentimentalism and hollow grandiloquence that have been wrapped around the natural dignity of the world, he shrank back as sharply as a snail bumping into an obstacle and withdrawing into its shell.

The sky changed, turned indigo-blue; and the stars were like villages in the sky. A modulation flowed through this immensity, making it even vaster, then another, and another, from each of the eight whirling heavens heard by Scipio long ago. In his present trouble, these old dreams, these ancient illusions of a world which had died some twenty centuries back, came to the young man like familiar companions, the substance of his daily life, full of heart-healing powers, capable of modifying thought, of inspiring action. He felt indeed that thousands of beliefs, thousands of experiences had been necessary for his soul to bring forth what it was begetting in this solemn hour; he felt that, from the thousands of dead mourned every day, not one was mourned with the kind of regret which was his; and these considerations carried him to a height where the power of suffering to make him suffer was as if blinded, where his suffering lost its emotional overtones and any quality which distinguished it from joy. At this height, Prinet's death aroused neither questioning nor disquiet, but appeared in a sense a perfect act. All the manifold powers of life were incapable of restraining his secret acquiescence in his friend's death. Just as, during the night in the dug-out, having put the utmost effort into helping one whom he thought in danger, Alban had leaned on the parapet, and himself and nature, like two streams uniting, had mingled in obscure complicity, so now, when all was accomplished, a phrase came to his lips, one which had already been uttered by a man, but which sprang from him so spontaneously that it was as if recreated: 'O world, what thou willest, that I will. What is, must be.'

He had almost uttered these sublime words when the modulations issuing from the sky became so distinct, so powerful, that reality tore him from his dreams. 'German planes!' At the same moment, he heard an explosion in the distance, then another . . .

Alban leapt to his feet. Within a second, as one lantern slide replaces another, Prinet had disappeared and he now saw nothing but himself.

In five minutes, the planes would be overhead. This place, which was used both for billeting and transit, had no doubt been spotted. What then? Was he going to be killed? He, killed, among these indifferent men! A word sprang forth, blocking his mind, blinding him like the midday sun: No! No! No! No!

No, not that! No, not that! Enough of all that! He did not want to be killed. His death would be useless now, wasted. The anguish in his flesh at this moment was too keen for him to realize why his death seemed to him futile, wasted, why all his possible feats of arms, all the projects with which he had flattered himself had gone stale: without reason, purpose or reward. None of this did he ask himself. But suddenly it was revealed to him.

This time, he rebelled. How absurd! The idea that Prinet could be the corner-stone of his existence and that everything must collapse when he had gone! Come, come, he was a nice chap, of course, but after all . . . Memories came flooding back to him: so many moments apart which they might have spent together, so many moments together which were equally empty, so many times when conversation petered out . . . Was it not simply that his nerves had been stripped bare by today's ordeals? Then he remembered that first sensation of fear, when he had found himself alone on the road and the boy was disappearing, and that other sensation of fear, last night, on the wagon . . .

Another explosion, over there. And another. Fear, fear, a sensation genuinely new, something really never felt before. Not the fleeting fear which explodes like a shell under death itself, then vanishes, the shudder of the flesh, the uncontrollable reflex; but chronic fear, the state of fear, the deliberate refusal to die, to take a risk or even to face up to reality, the flight before the future, the fear of tomorrow's fear and the day after's, fear in the shape of cowardice. Yes, this was indeed the sort of fear that gripped him in its claws as he stood there in front of the farmhouse in the moonlight. He looked to right and left. No shelter. Where could he go? Into the cellar of the farm? Laughable. Into the little wood? They always aimed at little woods, which were a natural shelter for troops. No, in the middle of the fields; that was the least likely target. Then a new fear. A man alone at night in the middle of the fields . . . What if a sentry were to shoot him? What if he were recognized – the shame of it! What was he to do? What was he to do?

The rumbling drew nearer. He guessed there must be a whole squadron. A heavy, staccato purr, now muffled, now throbbing in the night air. You could feel them panting and labouring, swollen with their deadly cargo. And on they came!

Alban walked round the farm, keeping close to the walls, as though by straying a yard or two from them he would expose himself to that pitiless eye watching him from the sky as in the times of the legendary dealers of justice. Here was the entrance to the cellar, fitted out like a shelter with sandbags and splinter-proof shields. As he entered, he heard a short, harsh rending noise as of linen being torn, followed by an explosion, very close, and the crash of falling tiles, while at the same moment a bag of icy water seemed to burst in his chest, and now he was steeped in it. This was it. They were over the village.

'Anyone in here?'

Arms outstretched, he groped his way through the darkness of the cellar which he realized was full of men. But, as if the mere fact of raising one's voice would be enough to attract attention, only one of them, the nearest, against whom Alban had stumbled, answered in a whisper:

'Get in there and keep quiet.'

This time, they hardly noticed the whistle before there was another explosion. The house shook. Then again, a little farther away.

The sky was rumbling on all sides, was now one huge drone. Alban could 'see' them circling, circling over the village like hawks above their prey. From the loudness of the engines he took them to be very low indeed, 500 feet or so. It struck him that if he took three steps out on to the road, one of them would swoop on him and riddle him with machine-gun fire. He had visions of Dantesque demons pouncing on souls. It seemed to him that this farm, with its situation at a cross-roads, its importance as a depot, the lorries and stretchers around it, must be regarded by the enemy as a major target. He remembered that he had no helmet, no blanket to roll up over his stomach (taking care to leave his legs free so as to be able to run). His whole being was like a wet cloth wrung by two hands. The droning went on. From time to time a man could be heard letting out a long breath which he had held in out of nervous tension. The jangling of a curb-chain could be heard outside, and the noise of a horse snorting as though it, too, were ill at ease. And a tiny sound could be heard that was very familiar to Alban: he guessed that there was a cat in the cellar washing itself, and this was a faint solace. Indeed, if only he could have felt that warm little body beneath his fingers, everything would have seemed less trying . . .

And then, the droning receded. If it were true, if only it could be true! Already he breathed more freely.

He thought he could still hear them long after they had gone. At last he really felt the silence, weighed it, measured it rapturously as one plunges a lead into the ocean. Silence! Then he began to tremble, uncontrollably.

He trembled in the darkness, trembled as he never suspected

194

it was possible to tremble. Lying on a kind of wood and wire frame on which they had gradually made room for him, he shook and tossed like the convulsionaries stretched on Pâris's grave, and hearing the springs creaking beneath him, he was terrified that the noise and the movement might be noticed by the others. He managed to clench his teeth so that they stopped chattering, but however hard he tensed his muscles, clenched his fists until the nails dug into the flesh, or gripped the wooden struts, he could not prevent himself from shaking with such convulsive violence that a photograph would have reproduced ten of him instead of one . . .

And then it subsided, and with it the deadening of thought that had been an unconscious solace. Now he began to think. Tomorrow they would be leaving, moving off, *up front*: the words filled him with nausea; the day after tomorrow, perhaps, he would be back with his company, up front, right up front, alone, utterly alone. He felt his body itself shrink back, such was the reluctance of his whole being. An ignoble wish flashed through his mind: if only there were heavy losses and the division was relieved. Like the 'no!' he had uttered earlier on from the depths of his being another cry arose: Enough! Enough! Enough!

Everything became more confused. A voice (but where?) said: 'Each man will be cured by his own particular remedy.' A voice said: 'All that is tied will be untied.' A voice said: 'The Ranelagh Gardens,' like a place one might be going to any minute.

And suddenly, again! God! Back again! Of course! They had gone to reload and now they were back. He wanted to ask: 'Aren't there any other shelters apart from this one?' but he did not dare. It seemed to him that he was the only one there who was afraid. He frowned hard in an effort to imagine that Prinet was there, beside him, as he had been the other day. He tried to remember what his state of mind had been then. He had to admit once more that the fear he felt tonight was shameful while the other was not. He twisted round, trying to find the position in which his body would be least exposed, and finally curled up like a dog as though a small part of himself would thus be half-protected. He was pleased when one of the men, more inquisitive, poked his head and shoulders out of the shelter to look, for this body would receive the main impact instead of his own if a bomb exploded nearby. And then he felt his life oozing away from him through his legs, felt that he was receding, taking leave of himself, falling into an abyss as one does in nightmares. He thought he was about to faint; he sat up, shook his head, opened his eyes wide. 'Disperse, O fearful shadows! Let not another night descend upon the earth! O God! O God! I am dying as I await my death!'

Nearer and nearer came the intermittent droning. The noise mingled with Alban's *misereres*, which were interspersed with endless vows: he would have Masses said, he would give donations to religious orders . . . Judging by the celestial rhythm, Alban guessed that the planes were even more heavily loaded this time: they had stocked up with bombs, all destined for the hamlet. He moistened his lips. His heart beat against his ribs like a beast dying inside him. Then the overwhelming desire which up to then had been prowling, struggling, shrieking in the depths of his being, suddenly crystallized. The decision presented itself to his mind, clear, perfect, viable, as a faultless child emerges at long last from the mother's labour pains. In his impetuous, high-strung way, dominated by overwhelming visions which now plunged him into terror as earlier they had roused him to valour, once again he drove a casual impulse to extreme and superhuman lengths. Tomorrow morning, as early as possible, he would get himself evacuated.

He was so engrossed in the idea that he had not heard the whistling. But the bomb exploded. There was a noise of things collapsing, hesitating, then collapsing once more. Then another explosion, further off. Alban redoubled his supplications in the void: 'Let me live until morning! Let me not be killed four hours before I leave these shores of hell forever, forever!'

Bombs were falling all around. Yet somehow he was no longer afraid. As a martyr, rapt in his ideal, hardly feels the torture, so the thought of his departure absorbed him so intensely that danger no longer had any power over him.

196

Now there were no more explosions, and the droning of engines had died down. One of the men, invisible, said: 'They got the church.' And this first human thought, which was also a statement of fact, brought it home to him, tangibly as it were, that the second alert was over. And Alban repeated: 'Tomorrow morning . . . Tomorrow morning . . . Another three hours, and then never again.' He was no longer a human will, but a raving element; he no longer had aims, but one single aim. And to achieve this aim he would do anything. He would put his foot under a passing car, he would lie, he would kill, yes, he would kill one, two, ten men: terror gave him the strength of a gorilla. Tomorrow perhaps, in a few hours, he would be in a Ford; each minute would take him half a mile farther from the place where death lurked. Ah! Joy! Joy! Spasm of joy!

Sleep overwhelmed him.

He had a little dream about Louis XV knick-knacks.

Dawn. They went outside. He was afraid that everyone would read his shame on his face. While they yawned and stretched, he thought to himself: 'I'm leaving them. It's disgusting. But that's the way it is.'

They recognized the steeple of the church, decapitated, resembling, in this pallid half-light, the wreck of a ship, some horrible thing at the bottom of the sea, seen through layers of water. 'I'm abandoning the poor church, which only had to ring its bell in order to frighten evil spirits away! I'm abandoning my comrades. I'm abandoning the remains of my only friend. I'm abandoning everything I had vowed to defend. Oh, how foul it is! But there you are, that's the way it is.'

The men washed in the cattle-trough. He merely wet his face, on which the water dried at once, so hot was his skin, and moistened his parched lips, which were stuck down at the corners by a greenish crust of saliva. The men were talking:

'There were some officers killed.'

'Guichard, from the Thirteenth.'

197

'He was a good chap, you know. He understood what life was about.'

'De Marolles, from the Thirteenth.'

'Don't know him.'

'Prinet, the officer-cadet from the Nineteenth. A real stinker, he was.'

'He wasn't a stinker, really. Only, you see, an officer with a face you don't fancy, there's nothing for it: he's just got to leave the regiment.'

'Le Hagre was wounded. Ah! he's a one . . .'

Alban moved away, filled with a sense of something silent that had entered into him forever.

The raw network of his nerves made his skin sore, and it quivered very slightly, as if it were seething with maggots. There was pain around his eyes, at the back of his head, behind his ears. Every time he sniffed, he felt a sharp stab behind his right ear. His jaw hung open a little. He was numb with fatigue. Sometimes, after a long day spent caressing a girl without the natural conclusion, he had felt the same exhaustion in the evening.

On the steps of the cellar were a cat and her kitten: it must have been them he had heard licking each other in the cellar during the night. Skeleton-like, with terrifying eyes, they were devouring some excrement with a hunted look, like flayed beasts resuscitated from a butcher's stall. Alban watched them and thought of himself. What else were they doing, both he and they, but fighting death, half-mad and trembling with passion?

The sun was rising in a cloudless sky. A sergeant told him: 'Your maintenance unit will be here in a moment. Then we all leave at noon.' Alban looked at these men with an odd feeling. What did it matter to him that they were leaving at noon. He too would be leaving, but it would be before noon, and not in the same direction. Oh, no! Not in the same direction! Blasphemous jokes, a ghastly jubilation, relaxed his features. 'My lovely little escape-routes! An escape-route . . . An escape-route . . .' He repeated the words indefinitely, and they tasted good in his mouth, recalling the divine beauty of great, cold, juicy pears in August. He looked at them again, at these young French peasants with whom he had shared so much, his companions, his comrades. One of them smiled at him. He wanted to go up to him and say: 'No, no, I can't deceive you ... I must tell you ... Don't smile at me, for I'm deserting you.' Well then, why not stay? But it was impossible. His body dragged his reason away as a spider drags away a dead fly. He walked through the hamlet on to the road, and he knew where he was going.

In the little garden of a house, the assistant MO was doing up his puttees. Alban stopped in front of him. The officer straightened up. Without a word, Alban took off his tunic, removed the bandage from his arm, and revealed the small wound.

'Can I stay behind with this?'

The assistant MO parted the lips of the wound slightly, revealing the new part of the flesh, a luminous, shiny red, like that of sucked barley-sugar. The man asked for an explanation, which Alban gave him.

'I'll write out your evacuation-form. You'll get on the first Ford going back.'

There was not a quiver on Alban's face, which wore an angry look. But while an orderly was preparing to put a fresh bandage on his arm, Alban looked at this arm, hard and polished and golden like some beautiful object of Imperial ivory. Then, for a second, the idea flashed through his mind that with such a body it was impossible to do wrong, that he must be mistaken in thinking that he was doing wrong ... And in a trembling, wild impulse, as if he were reassuring a loved one, he murmured: 'No, my body, you shall not die.'

15

Chewing-Gum

AFTER A week in the divisional field hospital, two miles from the little town of Verberie-sur-l'Oise and twenty miles from the front, Alban's one passion was unchanged. He wanted to go back to the rear, for ever.

For him, the war was dead. Dead because Stanislas Prinet was dead. He saw everything very clearly now. He had believed that the hub of the war was alternately his pleasure, or his desire for freedom, or his patriotism, or his need for repose; it was nothing of the sort; Prinet was the hub of his war, Prinet the cause of his reckless buoyancy. 'That night when I was sheltering from the aeroplanes, if I had been going to see him again the next day, would I have run away?' The answer exploded like a rocket: 'No! No! No!' – a rocket that illuminated everything.

And then, he was afraid. Afraid now that the boy was no longer in the regiment. Afraid of death, no doubt, and he could look *that* fear in the face. Afraid, above all, of an obscure and meaningless death: the 'wasted' death, the 'spoiled' death which he had already rejected on the day of the battle, beside those three indifferent men, while at the same moment he accepted, he almost desired the other death, the one he would embrace under the eyes of his friend.

For he had consented, he had wished to die in his presence. To think that it had been capable of that, their easy-going friendship, so direct and unhysterical, sometimes even negligent, free of intro-

200

spection! To think that affection alone, like a slender lever, had sufficed to lift such a weight! Ah, had he not known for a long time that his moral consciousness was founded on people – Dominique, for instance – that for him in the last resort it was always people that mattered. But now he wondered whether reality existed at all in the absence of such people, since the war appeared so utterly different to him according to whether or not the eight-hundred-thousandth part of the French army called Prinet participated in it. The essential question was not: 'What shall I do?' It was: 'With whom shall I do it?' And especially in battle. First choose a leader, then a comrade. These two choices once made, no more obstacles remained.

There had been something within him, supporting him like an armature. This was now collapsing, and he with it. Empty, too, was the front, empty, or full of a vast futility. Nothing in it escaped degradation. The cigarette he smoked, the mug of wine he drank, were henceforth diminished. The sufferings that were bearable yesterday, because the other was sharing them with him, had become hateful. There was no longer any sweetness in suffering. Gone was the silent esteem, warm as a hand-clasp. Gone, the remote presence, at the other end of the battalion, remote but certain. Gone, the soundbox that could make a given moment reverberate far and wide. Gone, the reason for action, and its reward. Instead, there was duty, harsh and naked, and death at the end, and in front of it Alban, who looked at it awhile, then shivered, and shook his head. God forgive him!

Such were the reflections that had been tormenting him for the past week, and that tormented him this morning as he sat watching the Oise flow past the bottom of the park where the field-hospital had been set up. Shortly before, the MO had examined his wound and had not liked the look of it. What would the outcome be? He wanted to leave the front, but could no longer bring himself to do so: blood tells. In his hour of panic, he had pictured himself writing letter after letter to influential relations. Today, shame held him back. He lacked both the courage to be brave and the courage to be a coward.

The river flowed on in front of him beneath low branches. Mossy stone steps led down to it, into that liquid kingdom where all things must be gentler. He could see the steps continuing under water, alive with a mysterious life. He gave a sudden start. Dominique was coming towards him.

'You here!'

Even before he had time to reflect that love alone could make her stick to his tracks in this way, he had, alas, recognized it on her face. Her face oozed with a love she could not hide. From the thousands of hours of the past, one alone remained – the hour which had seen her, in the night, prostrate upon a man's hand. That hour alone was true. All hope of future good was destroyed.

She asked about his wound. He whistled softly.

She asked whether anything else had happened. He did not mention Prinet's name. He would have had a feeling of sacrilege in speaking of his death before a woman in love.

As she explained how, learning of Alban's arrival at the divisional field-hospital, she had managed to get herself posted as a supernumerary to the 'sorting' hospital at Verberie, 'her knowledge of English being useful with American casualties', Alban felt an intense sorrow welling up inside him. Whereas the sorrow that had sprung from him for the dead Prinet was simple, pure, inexpressible because of its very simplicity, this new sorrow, complex, blurred by the intellect, demanded words. He spoke, therefore, in a very straightforward fashion, partly from a wish to be freed from this uncertainty, partly from contempt for the trickeries of the heart.

'My dear Dominique,' he began, with so strong a note of affection in his voice that he himself was struck, perhaps even surprised, by it, 'dearest friend, we must speak bravely to each other.'

And as her lips moved to interrupt him, he went on with a half-smile:

'You have guessed. Yes, in Granrupt when we parted, there was that gesture of yours . . . And now today . . . Listen, Dominique,

202

you must tell me, so that I may know: have you fallen in love with me?'

She had anticipated the question, but shrouded by a veil of pretences. She was taken by surprise. She replied blindly, her most sensible intentions abandoned:

'But I don't need to answer that. You can see it.' (yet without raising her eyelids). Then, as he said nothing, she added: 'It isn't my fault,' in a faint voice.

He saw her now as a baleful presence, like a disease.

He already knew what she was telling him. He had too long avoided any thought of it not to know it. The masterpiece of fourteen months was utterly destroyed, the noble flower cut down that had been their unique splendour. Absence had undone what presence had built up. A door that they had forced open upon one of the paths of greatness, was rolling back and closing. And both war and peace were alike corrupted.

'Something vast has been destroyed,' he said slowly, 'and you are going to suffer badly. It is hard to be impaled on one's love, to know and yet to go on giving it, to go on giving it to the man who cries out to you that your love is a burden to him, to go on giving it without being able to stop that love any more than the blood pouring from a wound. I beg of you, if it is not too late, do not bestow upon me this gift which diminishes us both.'

'It is too late,' she said, her eyes staring.

But the young man's emotion, the spontaneous impulse with which he had pitied his friend before pitying himself, made her suffering a little easier to bear. The whole of Alban's error was lodged in his brain; she knew this only too well, having deluded herself with him for so long. And, certain that she was right, she spoke, spoke with her woman's voice, low-pitched, a little clouded:

'What magic spell will ever free you? At the word love, you recoil, you suffer physically, like one possessed at the name of God. But you know nothing of love, as I knew nothing of it until yesterday. You are nauseated by the sight of loving couples, with their romance, their linked fingers, the man walking with ridiculously small steps to keep pace with the woman on his arm. But even they, the mediocrities of love, if you had but experienced one minute of what they feel, you would fall on your knees before them. Alas, you must always be exceptional, aloof, with never a moment's respite . . .'

'I can still hear you, at Palestra, on the first day we ever spoke with real trust: "Naturally, I beg of you, there must be no question of our loving each other." And I answered: "I should think not!", already reaching out impulsively towards our high estate!'

'Ah, how can you dare to use against me words belonging to a time when I was foolish and unaware? And how can you be so perverted as to revel in my frail friendship, when you reject this infinite thing which I have culled for you from the depths of my heart?'

'Perverted, because I appreciate purity?'

'In the excitement which my purity and my apparent indifference aroused in you, there was something almost morbid . . .'

'The virtues we lack, we call defects. To a man who has white corpuscles, a man with red corpuscles is a degenerate.'

'I was a delight for your mind; I satisfied a particular ideal of young womanhood you had formed for yourself; you saw me in a certain framework and you contemplated me therein without stopping to ask yourself whether it was a normal one, by what efforts I maintained myself in it, or whether I would break my back if I lost it. God, what a part I played!"

'Be careful,' he said with his lips alone, without unclenching his teeth. 'You have failed; you are excused. But you are not excusable when you try to throw doubt upon what was the best of you and of us both.'

'The best of us, this phantom, this caricature of perfection and happiness! Here, look at this!'

She took a photograph from her bag and held it out to him. Alban recognized a snapshot taken some time ago by a friend of theirs. But on the fading print there were greenish blotches, probably caused by a faulty developing process. A hidden agent of decomposition lived within this shining paper, and now the images of the two young people were smudged about the edges, showing an ear missing, a hole in the mouth, faces of half-decayed corpses. Either it was of no importance, or it was an appalling portent.

'Us! That's us! Look at us, eaten away by this leprosy! Well, when I look back, I see those fourteen months corroded by just such a disease, so virulent that even on the days when you had a real desire for gentleness, I still needed courage . . . The best of us! This sterile relationship, this nameless thing which continually transcended friendship and which you tortured so that it should not become love, which could not progress, could not improve, which was blocked and thwarted! "Something new": how much hope, how much longing have I put into those banal words! Something new, no matter what, even if it were only an increase of harshness! Did you never feel sick when you looked at the calendar and saw the weeks passing, passing forever without a change, and us moving towards the time when this thing would be over, this thing that would never have been? Did you never notice that I was tired, tired of us, sick of us, of you, of these eternal conversations from which one emerged exactly the same as when one started? Every time we met I had the crushing sensation of something to be taken up again, to be recharged, to be started again endlessly as though, during our absences, each of us undid separately what we had so laboriously woven together. Oh, yes, my words, my ways remained the same; those conversations simulated movement; the empty words kept us afloat as air-filled water-wings keep a child above water. You noticed nothing, I told you nothing, and between us something was dead. It was as though I had had a dead child by you, and you, to fool yourself, stroked him saying: "Isn't he beautiful!" You built our relationship on the principle of contradicting nature, and in this you found – admit it – your sole pleasure, a pride in exerting your strength to steer to the left something whose spontaneous movement was to the right. And I have been no more than the testing-ground for your monstrous experiments.'

Around them reverberated the wild concert of the flies. The river languished beneath its foliage like some glittering divinity.

Alban answered:

'You have been the instrument of my virtue, if one calls virtue the act of plunging deep into nature in order to resist it or to correct it. Yes, I forced us to walk straight, like a trainer with wild animals, and it is true that they sometimes roar. You have been my preoccupation, my wonderful partiality, and I was so happy to be nice to you, to be able to be nice! For it is true that, for fourteen months, I bathed in the astonishment of not having to despise you. I have taught you with love, I utter the word at last, with love, that is to say with utter sincerity. I felt for you a deep intellectual solicitude, a manly solicitude in which my tenderness was enclosed, directing everything without ever expressing itself, so closely united to my smallest action that you were incapable of recognizing it and still doubt it today, wretched girl! If ever I acquired anything of importance during the course of this year, I could not wait for you to have it in your turn. I remember the joy I felt when you told me that you knew Greek: everything suddenly enriched, orchestrated . . . I remember once when I was walking and thought I had found the observation post from which the whole of Antiquity stretched out before my eyes, and all that day I was restless, miserable, because I was prevented from telling you about it. It seemed to me that our whole friendship would be erased if you did not share in my discovery . . .'

He paused, for his words were faltering, his voice was jerky and proceeded now like a horse on the wrong leg.

'The next day I waited for you, in the dripping morning, on the path which took you to the stadium. You saw my feverish intensity. And when you understood, you were not surprised, you were not disappointed, but thanked me wordlessly for offering you, instead of a silly lover's scruple, this fruit of my knowledge, this perfect sweetness which became bitter to me if you did not bite into it with me. All this existed. You were my brother and my son. I cannot say more: this gravity of love is my essential gift. I took a chance on you as on a youth, as on a being whose nature, quite naturally, without his even willing it, sustains you while you strive to do what is best for him. I wagered and lost, since now you have fallen back. What you stumbled on, I do not know . . .'

'You don't know? As if I hadn't always stumbled on everything, when I pretended happiness so that you wouldn't stop being happy yourself, when I tightened my lips as I struggled under your selfishness and pride, to force myself into this coldness from which you drew such horrible pleasure!'

She hung her head, brimming over with sobs.

One day when she was competing in the finals of a high-jump championship, the bar was at 4 foot 4 inches, and twice she had failed. At the third attempt, when a failure must put her out of the competition altogether, she hit the bar again and rolled on to the sand, where she remained inert. People had run to her, thinking she was hurt, for she was as lifeless as if she were dead. But when they lifted her up, they found her unhurt: it was her sudden disgrace that had broken and crushed her. Meanwhile as he leant over her, Alban had seen the tears in her eyes; and he had responded to these tears with an extraordinary transport of friendship and esteem. But the tears which now flowed because of him only gave him a sense of the ridiculous, and of an impropriety bordering on the absurd.

He was about to cry out to her that she was lying, that the idea of such a sacrifice had never entered her head; but the words froze on his lips. This cheap theatrical lie, this doubt cast upon the high quality of their relationship, this collapse, these tears, in one second it all broke over him. Emerging from under the wave, he cried: 'Do I still love her?' just as, after the explosion of the shell, he had cried: 'Am I still alive?' It was as though he saw the woman striking him, striking the affection he gave her, and he thought: 'Will my affection survive?'

She wept, and he looked at her without a word. In this void a people of shadows, born out of the air behind the grieving woman, began to file past in silence. It was the soldiers. They appeared and vanished, then others came; all this in silence. Bellerey passed by. Ertle passed by. Nothing could be read on their blank faces. Beneath them the woman wept, in vain.

The only one of them Alban had seen in tears wept because he felt he was dying. When the cadet had died, Alban had not wept. They passed by. Prinet passed by with his face averted. Below, the woman wept. In the hierarchy of tears, what place did her tears occupy? She was the flower of her kind and, within her kind, she was right. Yet all that was born, all that would be born of her was invalidated in advance. He saw her striving far away from him, in vain.

Then he knew that he would go back to the front of his own will, as he had done before; and immediately he realized that it was over, that he had really left his friend, for it was in order to be consistent with the harsh treatment he inflicted upon her that he took this decision against which his flesh rebelled. His affection lived on, but all that was noble in him drew away from the girl, overridden by a stronger disapproval. Her red eyes, her crumpled handkerchief, her hands convulsively clasping and unclasping, everything in her attitude that brought her down to the level of the crippled multitude even though her square shoulders, her Palladian neck, the magnificent swelling of her thigh belied and controverted it – all this nourished his painful anger and he felt a growing desire to hurt her. Like a cat refusing to come near its dying mother, like a tiger pouncing on its fallen trainer, like a flock of hens pecking at one of their number because she is bleeding, so his animosity augmented with her grief. She took away the hand she had raised in front of her eyes and suddenly, seeing her so ugly in her tears, he desired her.

Desire! The raised pennon signifying the end of the battle! So now, all was accomplished. The age-old substitution had taken place. In the void left by the collapse of the soul's love, the love of the body found its place and burst through without further hindrance. The last of the dykes erected by his friendship and his respect was now breached, and a wave of lust, held back for fourteen months, broke over the oblivious woman. His eyes were terrible upon her; it struck him that, during this month of absence, her hands had grown larger; he had a physical perception of her weariness, her headache, everything that made her defenceless; he wondered with passionate curiosity how her face would look if she yielded: he could not imagine it. And the strangeness, the un-expectedness of his desire, after a relationship the essential quality of which had been to anaesthetize desire, a strangeness so immense that it made his desire appear like some extraordinary transgression, the supreme joy and the artless vanity he always brought to his excesses, the bitter-sweet flavour that was added to his lust by the animosity he felt for her at the same time, and finally his natural genius for avoiding sadness and regret, made him feel suddenly that all was well, and that after all it was triumphantly right, now that this great monument had fallen, that it should be replaced forthwith.

She raised her head:

'Perhaps, when I told you, just now . . . Would you forgive me if it was just a fit of temper?'

He did not answer. His sensuality mingled with the pleasure of making her suffer. His heart rejoiced at the thought that he could exert his power over her simply by remaining silent.

It was then that Dominique saw him take out of his pocket a little flat packet from which he carefully removed the paper; it was a piece of chewing-gum, which he put in his mouth.

'You don't want to talk to me any more?'

No, even had he wanted to, he *could not* talk to her any more. It was as if the muscles round his mouth were no longer capable of anything but this chewing tic, as if they had lost the power to make him utter any sound save Prinet's stammer that night in the shelter: 'I . . . I . . . I can't . . . I can't talk any more,' as if, with an almost hallucinatory intensity, he felt himself turned to stone. And a thousand things fell into this silence, went on falling, yet did not fill it.

'Tell me, is this what you've thought of? Do you think I'm going to go on questioning you like this? Is this the torture you've invented?'

'The torture! What a way to express herself! We shall see her getting more and more tied up,' he thought with satisfaction. He looked at her, how she was made, she who spoke of torture yet

209

had never suffered in her flesh. A score of little scornful expressions came to his lips, like bubbles on the lips of a baby: 'Getting all worked up ... Playing the heroine ... As good as a novel ...' From time to time, his eyes half-closed like a huge, self-satisfied lion, he felt like devouring her face; he felt like squeezing her as one squeezes a tube of toothpaste, to make her vomit out her soul, her innermost being, to force into his mouth a part of her as yet absolutely intact, which had never yet seen the light of day, the very depths of life.

'I'd better go, then,' she said without moving, letting fall these words which were her own downfall.

On the other side of the Oise, on a telegraph wire, a swallow was polishing its feathers, lifting its wings in a near-human gesture. 'Does it suffer at times?' she wondered. 'What does it feel when it suffers?' She turned her eyes away from it, back to face her persecutor. His lips were as if eaten away, so tightly were they pressed together, and with his chewing-gum stuck inside his left cheek, his pupils paler, almost pure green, his close-cropped hair baring his head and the nape of his neck, his whole face thinner, very closely shaven and with a sort of patina (yet less tragic under the wear and tear of war than under that of peace), he seemed to her like a snake, reared up motionless, so motionless that you might think it stuffed, though the bird is as paralysed under its gaze as though it had been bitten. And in the same way, though she had just said she was going, she felt unable to move a limb. But she managed to turn her eyes away: the swallow had just flown off: the wire was still quivering. She watched it go on quivering for a long while. Suddenly she no longer saw it, no longer saw any of the wires.

Hideous telegraph wires! Suddenly, in the same place where a second before she had seen only the blue sky, they reappeared, like a materialization of light-waves, so piercing that she nearly screamed. Then they disappeared, absorbed by the sky. Then they blinded her once more, hurting her eyes, twisting the nerves at the top of her skull.

Beyond, in the summer countryside, an inexhaustible Creator

poured forth his riches. Her eyes blinked, her soul blinked, the deserted sun-drenched fields were hateful to her, with their terrifying silence, their sly animality. She pictured more and more of them, all exactly the same, stretching out to infinity. She was oppressed to the point of physical anguish by the monotony, the sadness and the stupidity of high summer. She was certain that, with the same cause for misery, she would have been far less miserable had it been winter or autumn. She saw the two-mile stretch of road which she would have to cover soon – no, now! – under the sun, in the dust, her chest crushed by this abominable pain . . .

'Alban,' she said, 'I beg you not to let me go away like this. I have to go back along the road, I don't know how I'll do it . . . Please, I beg you, say something to me.'

She tried these words as she might have tried others, at random, like different keys in a door, at random.

'Ah! How shall I ever be sufficiently happy to make up for what I am suffering now because of you!'

Her words fell here and there like leaves from the trees; were lost, scattered in the open air. Between four walls, she thought, they might perhaps have been gathered in. A hammock hung close by, reminding her of the curious fact that when she was carefree she could swing, but if she was sad it made her feel sick. Thinking that she might at this moment have been swinging there made her stomach turn. She thought all this vaguely, in the kind of dazed stupor one feels when one has laughed a lot. Her head was full of a buzzing emptiness, as if there were a hole in each of her temples through which a violent draught was blowing.

'Alban,' she said again, 'I beg you not to let me go like this, when . . .'

Then she stopped, gave up, did not go on.

She looked away from the distant, staring face, cold and ghostly like the halo of the moon, but still chewing, biting at the gum, ceaselessly writhing with destructive movement as though it were her, Dominique's, flesh that he was tearing to pieces; and yet at the same time, she saw in this chewing something childish, or rather *kid-like*, with that persistent kid-like quality which, far from rendering Alban harmless, was precisely what made him dangerous. Her attention was caught by an ambulance-boat gliding gently, so gently down the river; the white forms of the nurses on the deck gave it the appearance of a convent carried away by the flood; and an effort was needed to realize that there was something other than happiness aboard. The vision had disappeared behind the trees, but the wash still quivered. She imagined him on that deck, badly wounded, afraid to die, needing her.

Now she could not take her eyes away from the water. From the quivering wash, images rose and blended with her sadness. The roots of her hair above the nape of her neck were painful, and she had the feeling that he had gripped her there for hours, held her under in order to drown her, while she struggled and fought. She slipped a finger under her head-band to get some air, just as she used to do in the stadium. She had a headache, and felt like someone on the verge of fever, as if all these ghastly words had penetrated her to the bone, like the October twilight when one is sitting under the dying sky; and she was cold, afraid and hurt. And yet, in spite of all this, she felt, in the depths of her heart, her love flowing, ceaselessly flowing, flowing more strongly each time she looked at him. As Alban had stifled with pride his horror at Prinet's death, so she stifled her own a little by the sweetness that came to her from still loving him. And she sheltered, as in a crystal tower, in this pure, lost separateness which she erected in the midst of summer.

'I love you, my dear,' she said, 'and neither you nor I have the power to prevent me from loving you. I love you, and the good I do myself in loving you destroys the harm you are doing me . . .'

She spoke, and her heart floated away on the open sea of love eternal. Her tenderness rose, reconstructing the world, annihilating war and death. But he, seeing her equanimity apparently restored: 'So I was right in thinking that their tears, which they prize so highly, cost them nothing. They give their eyes a little dab, and hey presto! it's all over. Another great grief followed by a slice of cake.'

As each reason for respecting her collapsed, desire, which had been lying in ambush, rushed into the breach. And in his thoughts he rolled the woman over and over as the tide rolls a pebble; he frolicked and splashed about in her, barking with glee; yes, raging and biting with strangled barks, like a frenzied dog. He desired her with a vigour and intensity and completeness that were beyond possession. And it seemed to him impossible, unimaginable, that there should be any cause to regret the reversal which made this desire permissible. When he had believed her to have a mind, he had treated her like a man, had desired only her mind. This had been beautiful while it lasted, but it was now over. Now that she was mere flesh, he treated her like a woman, he desired her flesh, and this desire too, like the other, was beautiful. And all the frenzy which was in him at this moment vented itself in the wild convulsions of his jaws and lips around the piece of chewing-gum; a triumphant lasciviousness radiated from that voracious mouth over his whole face, a lofty bestiality restored its whole benevolence to his soul. And in both the visible and the invisible parts of him, in all that was himself and all that made him himself at this moment, there was nothing that was not admirable.

She saw this change in him and misunderstood it. Accustomed as she was to his changeability, his childishness, the mobility of mind that made him into two people, one of whom ran wild while the other watched with a smile, accustomed as she was to his passion for certain 'exercises' (pretending to be impassive, coming down from the heights of anger with a burst of laughter, etc.), she thought he had persisted in his silence for no other reason than to amuse himself by making her suffer. She found this quite natural, excusing everything as long as he wasn't angry, disposed already to accept humiliations, even, perhaps, to wallow in them. Suddenly relaxed, she felt a burst of tenderness for him, moved nearer to him, and was about to put her hand on his arm, which was leaning on the table. On the verge of the act she hesitated and, in an odd, rather touching way, leaving her hand beside the young man's, she placed her little finger only over it.

213

She saw him shiver, as if this minute contact (which must have given him the sensation of a drop of warm wax falling on his skin) had established a current between them. Before she could move, he was on her lips, pulling back her head, smothering her face with his mouth. She felt him heavy on her lips as if she were carrying the weight of the globe, motionless, paralysed with horror. Then she was free again. He was walking away along the bright pathway, and the pools of sunlight slid over him. She was just in time to notice, from the movement of his jaws, that he had kept the chewing-gum in his mouth.

She did not move, did not rise. It was really over now. She had offered him her heart and all that it contained; she had given him everything, easily, as one does in dreams. And he had rejected it all. To remove any doubt on her part, he had given her this unequivocal kiss, had communicated to her mouth what distinguishes impurity from tenderness. He had walked away serenely, like a cockerel after covering a hen; he left her more debased than if he had held her down on the gravel and raped her. It was all over. She had no feeling.

16

Summer Sickness

DOMINIQUE SOUBRIER made her way back through the baleful summer landscape. The sun bore down upon her. There was not a single tree along the road on which she trudged towards the town (for, after all that had happened, she could still put one foot before the other, she could still stand, still walk). She walked with her head bowed; she needed to make an effort of will, to say 'Come on!' to herself simply in order to lift her eyes, and sometimes she even closed them altogether, filled with nausea. A miracle that she was not knocked over a dozen times, since she walked no faster when the lorries hooted behind her. Had a lorry run over her, she would not have uttered a sound. Nor did she bother to move when the clouds of dust enveloped her, and the revolting hot smell of petrol and oil. But she stumbled with distress, now really ready to scream, as if she had a shell splinter in her heart and each step were tearing her apart.

Never had she suffered as she suffered now; it was much worse than anything she had ever imagined. For there was neither dignity, discipline nor imagination in her suffering. Sinking down into the depths of grief, even though she knew she would surface again if she kicked when she touched bottom, she also knew that she would never have the strength to do so. Her grief was that of an animal.

The chateau of Apremont, on the outskirts of Verberie, had been used for a week as a 'sorting' hospital. The wounded from three divisions poured into it, only hastily bandaged, and set off again for

215

the rear within a few hours. It was there that Dominique was going, certain that as soon as she arrived she would plunge into sleep, and hailing this oblivion as her sole remedy.

She walked on, zigzagging in the middle of the road, blinded by a veil of tears, or perhaps only by the fumes of her grief. A small girl, swinging between the shafts of a hand-cart, stared at her and giggled. She could still find in herself a tiny unwounded place to receive this wound. 'I must look ridiculous.' She imagined her earth-coloured complexion, chewed at the bitterness of her mouth as at a sponge, felt her whole face sore as if it had just been dipped into some chemical, or rather as if it were decomposing. Her lowered eyes saw her white shoes now soiled from dragging in the dust. She looked at her hands, the nails a little dirty, felt that her sweat must have soaked through the band on her forehead, thought of time's ravages, of things tainted, tending to fall apart, of the necessity for struggle; and a host of gadflies pursued her as though her body were as acrid as that of a horse. She looked at herself in her small mirror: 'Here is a suffering human being,' she thought. Yet she did not look more tragic than usual. She tried to remember how she looked when she was not suffering. She could find no point of reference. What was she like when she had nothing to forgive him? She remembered, without being able to imagine how it felt, a time when she used to say: 'I must live, no matter how much I suffer!' And now she cried: 'Let me not suffer! Let me not suffer!' fleeing from life as from some wild beast.

Having reached the chateau, she went straight to the kitchen, drank five glasses of the liquorice water prepared for the wounded and then, without supper, without inquiring about her duties – in any case very flexible – she went up to the room in which the three nurses slept and, fully dressed except for her bonnet, she sank into oblivion.

She was woken up in the middle of the night by a voice behind the door asking her to come down. For the rest of the night she wandered among the bleeding men in the dim light (because of the aeroplanes) as in a nightmare.

216

The disproportionate importance she gave to her own grief caused her to look upon these men's sufferings with a certain detachment, and indeed she almost envied them. Since she was falling, it helped her to see the whole world fall. But when, having been called to help a young Arab with leg-wounds to walk to the ambulance which was to take him away, she felt him leaning heavily upon her, when she felt his arm tighten round her neck in a muscular embrace, when she felt the velvety hand brush against her cheek, then all the good she had derived from the hospital came back to her in flesh and spirit. And she knew where her heart's cure was to be found.

Once again, the eternal act was performed: a fleeting touch lightened the soul's worst distress. She now had a single aim to pursue until dawn: as an exhausted swimmer goes from buoy to buoy, Dominique went from man to man. Her grief vanished. She was filled with pleasure whenever her senses were fired by a touch – holding a hand, laying her own hand on a bare shoulder, clasping a torso to help a man up. Even the time spent in seeking and provoking such occasions drugged her grief.

But what is the good of enumerating these stagnant joys, these dark rushes of blood? There is no pleasure in recounting how easy she found it to take advantage of the circumstances: the darkness of the night, without any precise duties or supervision, in the midst of a jumble of wretched creatures dazed with exhaustion and pain and more or less naked. In this unparalleled promiscuity, none of the poor wretches who saw this virgin of consolation bending over them guessed that she was consoling herself first.

A bitter picture, though. I see her, I see this Persephone in her nocturnal kingdom. And at this very moment, in other hospitals, and in the trenches, the canteens, the railway-stations throughout the whole vast international empire of disorder, thousands of other beings were trying to console their misery with similar moments of purple and shadow. They would find the next war less horrible when they woke up next day.

Secretive, taciturn, a bad mixer, Dominique – as one would expect – kept a diary. Since her duties kept her busy in the evening, it was usually on the following morning that she noted things down. The one-night perspective gave an effect of sobriety.

She knew that she was awake from the blinding distress which exploded in her soul. One by one, with the speed of bubbles rising and bursting on the surface of the water, reasons for grief rose and burst in her consciousness: grief of every kind, from the latent grief in her heart to the problem of having to write a 'difficult letter'. It was the infinitely cowardly hour, when the weariness of not being happy made certain unavowable pleasures appear very simple to her; it is – alas! most certainly the best hour of the day. Through the gaps in the shutters no daylight could yet be seen. Feeling the sweat on the backs of her knees, slipping her legs between the sheet and the edge of the mattress for coolness, tossing from side to side with her arms outstretched like a swimmer doing the back-stroke, with a physical sensation of suffocation, she imagined her shiny nose, her teeth not yet clean, her hair undone, and thought in a kind of stupefaction: 'In three hours' time I shall be with him, all my faculties alert, and in four hours' time it will be over, I shall know. I shall know . . . What? Well, whether he has been nasty or nice.'

Then her lips began to form an 'Mmm . . .' for something like 'My dear, dear Alban . . .' (burying her face in the pillow), but nothing came but a groan. She moaned; her overflow of love poured out in moans, like the overflow of suffering in hospital beds. Everything that within an hour, on the road, would seem monstrously unattainable, now seemed easy to achieve. She thought and thought, she was aching all over with her thoughts; she was drenched in her own moisture and at the same time dried up like a fish abandoned on the sand. From the courtyard there rose the heavy rhythm of men marching: the stretcher-bearers, undertakers of the living. She got up at last, and the water she dabbed over her tired face only made things worse; her features remained blurred and misted over like window-panes; she rose from the depths of her delectation as from the bottom of a well.

At this hour, only three months before, leaving the curtains drawn lest her father come in and tease her, she would poke one leg out of bed and rub it with embrocation.

The following passage was written the day after the high drama on the banks of the Oise.

August 5th, 1918. Go to wait for him this morning at the gate of his hospital, from 8 to 9.15. As the time passes, I begin to feel some relief. I am so afraid that I almost hope he will not come. He comes out and I am about to run away. I don't know what it is like for a soldier to have to cross a field under machine-gun fire to the enemy trench, but for me, having to cross this road under his eyes is something appalling. I do not know what expression to assume. His face has none, neither pleasure nor annoyance.

I give a little nod as though I were there by chance (a pathetic game, this, and whom does it fool?). I had noted down nine things to say to him on the back of a visiting card: I meant to glance at it surreptitiously, but he started off so naturally, as if the whole thing was quite unimportant, that the phrases which last night sprang burning from my heart now refuse to come. I feel they no longer match my present feelings, and yet I know very well that my feelings haven't changed. It seems to me that, had I not prepared and learned these phrases more or less by heart, I would not know what to say to him, because at this moment *I have no feelings at all.* Here, in front of the hospital, among these men who are concerned with life and death, they seem so out of place, they seem so very remote and artificial and strange. That I should be here now, and with this end in view! That I should have come back for this, at 8 o'clock in the morning – the time when I used to go to the stadium – back to stir up all this! I feel that there is something abnormal, pitiful and slightly grotesque about it all, that it is I, among all these wounded men, who am the unhealthy one, the sick one – yes, and he is my sickness.

How many of his words might have given me an opening! Yet I did not take them up. I derived a kind of intoxication from not taking advantage, not pressing, letting things go. For twenty minutes we walked side by side, apparently no different from what we had been in other days, whereas in fact nothing was the same; and I had an odd feeling of dishonesty towards the passers-by, who thought us plainly happy. For twenty minutes we walked side by side, without one word being said that contained anything of

219

ourselves. But it seemed quite natural and right that I should not suffer from this. If there had been a complete silence, a long silence of several minutes, then a supreme moment would have been reached, and we could not have parted without having things out; but neither of us wanted to have things out, so that there could be no question of drama. At last I saw the massage huts draw near. I do not know whether I hated having so little time left, or whether I was pleased because at last all the bridges were burnt.

I was the first to hold out my hand; I was the first to cut our meeting short. Then he said these extraordinary words: 'When shall I see you?' (without looking at me). And I, who would have loved to say: 'In a minute, of course. I'll wait for you to come out . . .' I said casually: 'I don't know . . . One of these days.' Then, as he seemed to be waiting: 'Tomorrow morning, if you like, same time.' Then, having gone a few steps already, he stopped and said: 'Mind you don't forget!'

The sadness of this reminder on top of all this death! That he should want to go through it again, through this half-hour of – worse than bitterness – of boredom! That he should seem to be attached to me! Once I was alone, I pretended to look at a fallen horse and thus, furtively, watched him moving away with his athlete's stride, his feet parallel. Then, after a moment, he looked back. Then a second time. Then once more.

Tomorrow, surely, I'll do better. Ah, hope! The sail unfurls. On our way again, alas! on our way again.

(He is very sunburnt, but when he bends his head, one can see at the back, where his collar is a bit loose, that his neck is whiter.)

After dinner. I love him, I love loving him, I love suffering him, I love being sad in this languor of the dying day, when a sort of dust rises from the earth towards the sky, and when in spite of everything I am two, myself and he, who does not love me.

August 6th. Waited for him again. I had every reason to approach him without inhibition after yesterday's words: 'When shall I see you again?' Yet this is what happened.

He comes out – and I feel I shan't have the courage. I do not go up to him. I let him go without having seen me. I walk far behind him, not trying to catch up. I feel I am being ridiculous, I feel that in my face, my dress and my whole appearance there is the proof, visible to all, that I am a miserable thing, entirely in his hands and weak because of him; I feel that no one can see me without thinking: who would want to love her? I keep repeating to myself: 'In one second he will look back, recognize me, and go on without stopping.' And is there not something in me that welcomes the idea? Extraordinary, heart-breaking minutes, yet so calm! He walks in front, I walk behind without trying to catch up with him, simply because I don't expect anything from seeing him, because I don't know what to say to him, because we shall talk in a vague bored way; yet I have been waiting twenty-four hours for this moment, I woke up specially early, I hurried, evaded people who wanted to see me, I felt oppressed the whole morning because of this, my morning cocoa made me feel ill, and now we are alone with nothing hindering us, and tomorrow perhaps one of us will have gone! The worst of it is that I am not suffering. After such a failure it seems that my conscience is salved, whereas I would have been tormented all day if I had not come. I follow him until he has disappeared into the massage hut. I find myself alone again; I am not even angry with myself, as though what I had done was quite natural, as though I had come *on purpose to do this*, as though I had derived a morbid satisfaction from throwing this pearl into the sea. Will he pass this way again? Perhaps not again for the rest of the day. There are other exits at the back. Yet I wait for him, wait for him!

I stay. I would stay there till evening. Inertia alone is needed, and it is the only strength of which I am capable at the moment. I cannot leave this place. Does *he* know what parting means? Each step I took away from where he is would be as if someone were tugging at a chain made from my living flesh. I tell myself that perhaps – it's quite possible – after waiting three hours, I shall do the same thing again: I shall watch him go without doing anything. Perhaps; and yet I stay, I wander in anguish and boredom in the midst of the hostile landscape, by the side of the hateful road, intoxicated by the splendour of the summer, and I blame him for my failure to approach him. Shall I have the courage in one hour, or two, or three . . . ? I am afraid of the sun, I am afraid of the journey, I am afraid of this place where we meet, I am afraid of what I read in his eyes when he sees me.

I must . . .

Later. I was sitting alone on a grassy bank, writing this, when a passing gendarme urged his horse into the field, dismounted, and asked me for my papers. As he examined them, he asked me *all* the christian names of my parents (as if one knew *all* the christian names of one's parents!). Then he held out his notebook, made me sign my name, and compared the signature with the one on my papers. Then he apologized: there are so many spies, bogus nurses, etc . . . My heart was thumping. Was I not right in thinking that my appearance is odd, that people give me strange looks as I wander in this lonely countryside?[1]

8 p.m. I saw him again, as he came out of the massage hut.

Brief handshake, which would not have occurred had I not held my hand out first. I haven't the courage to repeat here everything he said to me. For no reason, on the slightest pretext, he laughed at me unmercifully. It was a harsh kind of banter, making everything I said seem ridiculous. Is it because he feels embarrassed? Once I noticed he was looking at me out of the corner of his eye. I thought his lip was trembling, like the mouth of a cat watching a bird. Perhaps I imagined this detail. Honestly, I don't think so.

I left him, or rather he left me, saying he had to be back at a certain time . . . Rubbish!

So we have cleared up nothing, explained nothing, not dared to say anything of what we had decided to say, done nothing to alter the situation; yet we have seen each other, spoken to each other: a kind of peace covers up all these unpleasant things as the neatly levelled earth covers a corpse.

On the way back I made a long detour so as to pass by his billet – knowing that he wasn't there at the time.

(Last night I dreamt that my father came into my room before I went to sleep. I made him put his lamp down on the bedside table; I took his hands in mine and with my eyes closed and my head on his hands I said to him: 'Listen . . . Listen . . . I love this boy . . . . There. Now do something, make him be nice to me . . .')

August 7th. I am leaving.

As soon as I was told, I went to see the Chief Medical Officer. He received me standing, and was scarcely polite. 'I took you on as a supernumerary only to please your uncle, who had asked me to do so. We had no need of your services, and now the pretext we gave for your presence – your knowledge of English – no longer holds good; as you have seen for yourself, there has not been a single American casualty here for four days, and there won't be any more. Besides, I don't know why, but on the few

---

[1] *Dominique has written in the margin of this page, probably after having read it over:* Will the day ever come when I shall write again in this diary things as uninteresting as those I used to write: 'The doctor came, he thinks I've got appendicitis, etc . . .'? Today, each one of my days alone weighs as heavily in the scales as the whole of my past. And yet, how is it that my handwriting hasn't changed? This shocks me.

occasions when you might have been needed, you were never there.'

I am leaving the day after tomorrow, in the morning.

I absolutely must see him this evening.

9 pm. I have seen him, I have seen him, and something new exists.

I only saw him for a minute; he was with some . . . (*illegible*) who were waiting for him. When I told him I was leaving, I saw his face alter. He only said 'Ah!' but he was obviously greatly disturbed.

After a moment's silence he said: 'It so happens that I am going tomorrow to Canly hospital, at Verberie, for a medical, and I have a midnight pass. We could see a bit of each other. You must have some kind of digs outside the hospital?'

I was so bowled over with happiness (I think it was happiness) and even more with surprise that at first I didn't answer and then, thinking the required answer was 'yes,' I said: 'Yes . . . yes . . . I have some luggage in the hotel . . .' And he: 'I must admit I'm tired of our everlasting walking conversations. Since you have a room, it seems to me you could receive me there for an hour. Here, it doesn't matter in the least.' He and I, in a hotel room! I was so astounded that I might have hesitated, made a mess of everything, if someone hadn't called him. Then I told him the name of the only decent hotel in town: 'Central Hotel, what time? – ' 'Nine o'clock.' And he left.

He will come! He suggested it himself! I ought to be overwhelmed with happiness, I ought to bless this departure which at last brings forth between us . . . what? Never mind, some kind of life one can get hold of. Why can't I? I dare not think about tomorrow evening. Yet what a young phrase this *tomorrow evening* is! It seems to me that before today there never existed a *tomorrow evening* on this earth.

At the moment of writing this, I feel faint with something that has seized my soul and does not touch my flesh, yet makes me shiver and feel sick.

Alban! Alban! Alban!

I'm cold.

August 8th. Ah, why, when something unexpected occurs and promises well, why this treacherous desire to make it even more perfect? It is like a temptation from the devil.

I wanted to see him again this morning. As soon as he caught sight of me he turned towards a friend, pretended not to have seen me, and walked away quickly.

Can all that is yet to happen make it so that this had never existed?
It hurts me too much to go on writing.

*   *   *

This last sentence of the diary is an almost illegible scrawl. The hand no longer controlled the pen.

17

No Life at All

WHEN SHE had scrawled these lines, Dominique Soubrier rose. It was four o'clock. Having counted on her fingers – to make quite sure! – the five hours separating her from the time of the rendez-vous, she turned her head away, as from a mountain she had to climb.

She returned in a poor state. She was at that difficult moment, when everything that is not a step towards a better situation in love disgusts you, and when even such steps fill you with nausea because you feel only too certain of their failure. In the mass of possible actions that offered themselves to her, the simplest and most natural won: she set off across the field towards the river.

She knew full well that she had never received anything from nature except weariness and despair; she had not forgotten how relentless this particular river had been towards her, yet she believed that she had only to approach the water to find in it inspiration and rejuvenation. So she looked at it bravely, at the glittering water, iridescent as a printed silk scarf. There were the telegraph wires, as before, but they no longer dazzled her; there were the swallows, as before, but they now flew very low, skimmed over the water and then, in full flight, dived in for a few yards, with a sensation of pure delight. Aloud, she pronounced the soft-sounding name: 'l'Oise'; she opened wide her eyes towards the stretch of land beyond, bleak and melancholy as her own thoughts. And suddenly, with a shiver she turned back to the road and hurried towards Verberie. Her heart was so swollen that she had to stop twice for a deep breath. All the air in the sky was powerless to relieve her oppression.

On her right rose two hills like young breathing breasts. Evening rimmed with russet the eye-rings on the water, like those on a peacock's plumes. She felt infinitely permeable to all these things, so weak, fluttering, as it were dissolving, needing to sit down, to rest her back and head, as if each place she passed, the bushes, the soft slope, the bends of the path, whispered to her: 'He might be here!' – 'He is here! He is here!' she exclaimed to herself. 'In the immensity of France he is at the exact spot where I am. We are in the country, fifty miles away from the constriction of the town. A unique opportunity! Yet what has it produced? And tomorrow I'm leaving.'

She walked faster, having felt all the moisture of tears welling up inside her face, contracting her features; and something went hollow in her as the sea goes hollow around a sinking ship. Striding along like an automaton, she hurried towards the town, for, unable to bear the idea of five hours alone with herself, she had just thought of reading as her salvation. Some negroes who were grave-digging (the empty hospital was being reconstituted under five feet of earth) waved to her. And again, in the town, she noticed she was being stared at: by some roguish-looking Italian soldiers whom she found likeable because of their roguishness, but mainly by horrible gutter-snipes. She felt spied upon, suspected, the effort she made to look casual twisting her features in a strange way: guilt covered her face like a mask. Each person she passed renewed her torture. She went into a store and asked to see the sixpenny novels, chose one, opened it wildly, plunged into this alien world as into a river.

She read as she walked back towards the Oise. The book provided her with a ready-made posture, prevented her from seeing the inquisitive glances of the passers-by, above all prevented her from thinking. She read on, with puckered brows, clinging to her book, stumbling, twisting her ankles on the bad pavement. They hurt, these feet of hers. Glancing down, she thought from the way she was walking that she was slightly knock-kneed. The idea that she had become knock-kneed because she was love-sick forced a smile from her. She plunged back into her book. She could make no sense of the plot, she got the characters mixed up; but what did it matter! It numbed her, dragged her outside herself, so that her mind no longer existed. Once she was seated on the river-bank, she put the open book down on the grass for a moment. Then the flood rose within her, and in a second the tears were on her eyelashes, tears that released her from nothing . . . She took up the book again, and devoured the lines . . .

She read for two hours, only looking away for a glance at her watch. She would have liked to be hungry, so as to while away half-an-hour by eating, but she would have faced death more willingly than a mouthful of food, and moreover her love, after meals, made her feel sick. At a quarter past eight, she got up and went back towards the hotel. The sky was becoming overcast, with great rolling storm-clouds. The imminence of action gave her back some strength, although she shivered in the falling night.

Such was the last of those truly mindless days – for she had indeed, at the time, lost her reason – days that had passed over her like so many tornadoes, leaving her utterly spent. After each of them she should have had the whole of the following day to rest: stretched out without thought or movement, as in the stadium after a race.

As she went through the hotel door, slipping in to avoid attracting attention, the landlady called her:

'The electricity isn't working. I've sent some candles up to your room.'

'Haven't you any lamps?'

'They're all being used.'

She said 'All right, all right,' to get it over quickly. It was the first time she had actually occupied the room, and in half-an-hour a man would join her there; could this woman have any doubts as to what they were coming here to do together? She had cut short the conversation so as to be able to get away, but when she had climbed three stairs, she regretted not having sent out for a lamp from the store. These candles, in this shabby hotel – things could hardly 'look worse'! From a corner of the stairs a revolting stench met her as she passed. In the room itself, the window was open, the shutters closed. At least she would not have to show herself at the window with her white nurse's bonnet, struggling with the shutters in front of the crowd gaping up at her.

She lit two candles, and a flickering light left large areas of the room in shadow. She made an effort to realize that this was the setting in which they would talk together. A small placard on the door reminded her that she 'must not admit any outside visitor' into her room, and she shrank away from the vile implication. Her embarrassment increased. Had she been sure that he would come straight from Canly Hospital, she would have gone out along the road to wait for him; they could have sat in the deserted courtyard of the chateau of Apremont. But she felt unable to risk even a hundred-to-one chance of missing him. Then she cursed him, cursed his lack of delicacy in having suggested a hotel. She thought he must have meant it in a deliberately insulting way. And in her present state of agitation the idea did not entirely displease her.

Nine o'clock struck, so slowly that it seemed as though the strokes could not make up their minds, as though each one of them was to be the last. Ah! the waiting, then, staring at the flame of one of the candles until she was almost hypnotized, seeing it rising and rising forever! She had closed the window so as to be able to draw the curtains, for she was afraid that her shadow might be seen moving through the gaps in the shutters and arouse curiosity; and so she was suffocating with heat, while uncontrollable yawns made her eyes water, for – no doubt because of her exhausted nerves – she felt much more sleepy since she had been in love. Down below, the street flowed on, and the noise, the gossiping, the shouting, the metallic clanking filled her with horror. The Italian soldiers' voices, reminders of the beautiful Neapolitan evenings she had known five years before, added a sweet poignancy to her suffering. One of these noises in particular tormented her as she had been tormented a few days before by the sudden dazzle of the telegraph wires: an iron grid on the pavement creaked beneath each passer-by. Once, there was a growl of thunder. Hearing a buzz of voices, she thought a crowd had formed opposite the hotel. Really out of her mind – at least we must assume she was – she went to the window, put her ear to it as one sees people do in films, and tried to make out what was being said, thinking she heard insults and threats: 'Yah! Filthy nurses . . . They're all tarts . . .' Soon she would hear a stone hitting the shutters.

Ten past nine, and he had not come. What was going on? What if something awful had happened? What if she were to hear the woman's voice downstairs: 'Yes, the young lady's on the second floor and to the right, just go on up . . .' and see her father appear? Or the gendarme who had asked to see her papers? The mere thought of it made her grimace with terror: an atmosphere of guilt piled up around her, weighing her down; for the first time, she realized what it must be like to be 'caught in the act'; she knew she would be unable to keep herself in countenance, that the first person to come in at this moment would have not the slightest doubt on seeing her: 'She is simply here to give herself.' Suddenly, an idea flashed through her mind. Might not this strange rendezvous be nothing but a joke, a means of tormenting her? Might not the young man be in bed at this moment, imagining her anguish and relishing it? Would it be so very much at variance with the attitude he had adopted, since *the day*, of mocking her, toying with her? Just as the coarsest bits alone remain when one shakes a strainer, so, as she frantically stirred up all these thoughts, only the most hurtful were left. Her reason was sinking. Her fingers were cold, and her toes were cold in her shoes, but not her forehead, though she pressed it to the window-pane with her eyes closed. She moistened her lips with her tongue, powerless against this Sahara in her mouth as if she had not drunk since her cradle. An hour such as this can bring one a whole year closer to death. And yet one survives!

Was it possible? Was it possible? Was he as base as that? And she could still think of him without horror? Well, yes! Yes! She accepted and wanted him monstrous in his cruelty, as long as he came. Her love knew no bounds, now that he had twice broken his word to her . . . Suddenly she froze. Someone was coming up.

The dragging feet went past the door, fading away towards the next floor. A shiver ran down the back of her neck. Up above, a door closed. Silence. Then, impulsively, fearfully, despairingly, she crossed the room, went on to the landing, and listened, listened as men will listen to the trumpets of the Last Judgment. There was not a sound in the house, which was filled with opaque darkness as though already plunged in sleep. Suddenly, an excessively violent reflex threw her back. On the wall of the staircase, in the rectangle of light projected by the candles through the open door, she had just seen her own huge shadow . . . Wasn't someone watching her, at this moment, from the next room?

Then, back in her room, she opened the wardrobe, looked under the bed, lifted the trap-door, knocked on the wall to see if it sounded hollow, and tore a page from her notebook to block the key-hole; then she thought she was running a temperature (which she was not), felt her pulse, pictured herself ill and slovenly – yes, all this, poor girl, she did all this. And again there was a turmoil of ideas whirling, loose and muddled, round and round her head that was as empty as the shell of a sucked egg; again the twisting hands, the glances at the watch, the ever-shrinking candles, the intermittent clanking of steps on the iron grid, and that frightful buzzing of the crowd in the street, from which a shout would soon be heard . . .

Half past nine. Nine thirty-five.

'Waiting! Waiting! I am mad to have him here and I don't know what to do. Ah! Everything always boils down to waiting, and one must live on and on, for so long, and on so little! Waiting! Hours struck off your life, really void and dead, the sort of thing the common people mean when they say, with terrifying truth: "That's no life at all." One jumps from one hour to the next like the arch of a bridge, utterly oblivious of the river flowing between, and from each disillusion there rises – ah, woe betide! – an imbecile hope . . . But anything, anything is better than waiting. No suffering for evil done can equal the apprehension of evil yet to come.'

It was over, he would not come. All hope was fading, unless something really had prevented him. In which case, knowing she was leaving the next morning at seven, he might try to see her at the station . . . The childishness of her illusion brought a sad, tight smile to her lips. No, no, the contact was lost. Perhaps after a week she might receive one of those notes in which he demonstrated his skill at being insultingly pleasant, his secret art (which earned him so many enemies) of giving his polite phrases such an affectation of banality that it was impossible not to feel that he intended his indifference to be glaringly obvious: *'Dear friend . . . Most awfully sorry . . . unforeseen circumstances . . .'*

An imperceptible feeling of well-being came over her, now that she had given up all hope. She knew she would never see him again, and this gave her something solid to cling to. She badly needed it. The delayed shock of her nervous exhaustion, and her love-languor too, made her whole body ache as though she had been doing heavy work. She had not a single drop of strength left in her, and was conscious only of burning and sweat. Looking at her suitcases, 'I couldn't lift them,' she thought. She reflected that, should he be killed, ah well! she had accumulated, during the past week and the past hour, the wherewithal to soothe her grief quicker. And should he live, then she felt that this terrible evening was a step towards a decision: such waiting, such bitterness, so much accumulated rage gave her rights over him, or at least bounced her back, throwing her into a state of blind madness through which the ultimate might at last be attained. In this violent state, she could perfectly well picture herself striking bargains with him as with Bouchard: 'Be careful, my family is more powerful than yours. I don't care whether you love me or not; I only want you to pretend you do. Otherwise I can harm you, I can upset all your plans. I am a dangerous enemy . . .'

She heard movements downstairs. She made out the landlady's voice: 'Second floor. You'll see the light.' She recognized the voice which answered: 'Thank you.' Then, terror-stricken, she ran back to the other end of the room, sat at the table, tried to compose some sort of face, her hands drumming on the blotting-paper as on a tambourine.

'May I come in?'

She saw him appear in the frame of the door, not yet in the light.

18

Victory of the Male

THEY ARE not made for regrets, not even for backward glances, those in whose veins there pulses, like sap, the endless power to rebuild. One of Alban's basic characteristics was his capacity to resign himself at once to the inevitable, to 'make the best of it'. Just as he did not 'hark back' to the life and death of Prinet, so he did not hark back to his friendship with Dominique. It had been an extra-ordinary, a unique creation. Now it was finished. On to something else! The masterpiece created by his intellect having been destroyed, his flesh cried out that it, too, yearned for some piercing master-piece. Should he go away then? Should he go back to the front, as he had thought of doing when his clash with Dominique had thrown him back into the male world? Ah, no! Not before he had sacrificed to his desire what was its due.

Since he knew well that the highest point of love is found in the furtive touch of a hand and not in total licence (which soon leads to loathing on the one side and indifference on the other), the sacrifice of possession was but a small sacrifice to him. On the great human 'cello, beautiful airs can be played on three strings. She, the symbol of the pure life, how wonderful it would be to lay her down and adore her! Blaspheming against the intellect yet always ready to accept its aid if only to turn it against itself, he brought it to bear upon his dark organic impulses in order to imbue them with a virulence that the brain alone is capable of activating in the flesh. He was proud of the fact that his toughness had enabled him (after taking in the situation at a glance) to abandon the paths he had followed for fourteen months and fling himself with all his strength in the opposite direction, when so many others would have lamented and equivocated with timid scruples, only to obtain in the end, if it were a victory at all, a victory tainted with sadness.

And yet during that week he had remained undecided. True, there was no change of mind about what had been so firmly expressed on the banks of the Oise. Unjust or not, as long as he measured the world by the scale of martial values, he would find Dominique's love unbearable. This new Dominique, no longer an object of pure affection, could only live on through pleasure. Yes, but was even that quite certain?

He could have sworn it was when the fire in his entrails released fumes which bedimmed his mind. Having recovered his self-control he told himself: 'No doubt the first encounter will be tempestuous. But the second time! How well I shall know her! How little she will have to reveal! How like so many others she will be! The very thought of it makes me sick. Having sought these moments with passionate frenzy, I shall be the first to break them off. While she is getting dressed, and I can't think of anything else to say to her, and I hurry her up so as to be free as soon as possible, and our eyes avoid each other, how, oh how shall I be able to prevent it from being the hundredth time? I shall light a cigarette. She will produce a few scraps of talk which will seem to come from another world. I might even reach for my wallet! I can see it all already, down to the smallest detail . . . Oh imbecile body! wasn't her soul enough?

'And when we have taken leave of each other with a touch of the hand, sick and tired of each other, silently hating each other, I shall not have finished betraying her even then. The time when she was naked and mine will become blurred in my memory like a dream, for I shall be growing older and my pleasures will no longer leave so sharp an imprint. Each body I pass, however mediocre in comparison with hers, will pierce me with the spear of love. Nothing will seem to me desirable except what is not my Dominique. I shall

234

repudiate what I have had by dreaming of what I cannot have. *All of them, at once, and forever,* I shall implore; otherwise I shall always be hungry, always restless. As Tiberius longed for the Roman people to have but one head, so that he might decapitate it at a single stroke, so too would I be satisfied only if the entire female sex had but one body, so that I might possess it once and for all. I shall go on denying and repudiating, and in doing so I shall live only for the next of these joyless moments, for the anticipation which is the only joy. Ah, miserable love! A pint of beer in summer gives more happiness. And yet, when the time is ripe, I shall set you going, shan't I, miserable love? She and I, that splendid memory – all tarnished for the sake of one dizzy moment . . . Yes, that is what I shall do, I know it.'

And he had done it. Threatened by the girl's departure, he had given her that ambiguous rendezvous.

Who can wonder at it? Humanity repeats the *omne animal*; but is there a single human being whom this *tristezza* has ever stopped? In order to obtain it men will give their time, their work, their money, their health, their fame, their honour, their happiness – everything, they will give up everything in order to drown the insistent clamour of the flesh when it has not what it desires.

When Alban appeared in the frame of the door face to face with the prostrate girl, he had recovered the bright-eyed expression of his sixteenth year.

'I've just been chased by a bear,' he said gravely, already seated.

She tensed herself, shivered and tried to smile, foreseeing some of his fearsome tomfooleries.

'It was a black bear,' he specified.

Then, after a pause, delighted to see her flummoxed:

'Spent the whole day walking! This autumn in the heart of summer has something anomalous about it which I find exciting. How could I resist it? There was a certain yellow of the leaves against the white sky which I simply loved! I was thrilled to be able to match the blue-grey of my uniform against that yellow . . .'

She was still trying to smile, unable to find an answer.

'Everything was so mysterious that I kept expecting to see an elephant emerge from the bushes, or a giant, or else a snow-white deer with golden antlers. A bird was singing in an invisible tree on my right, where the lucky omens come from. I listened intently. Its song told me: "You will be permitted every licence."'

She suffered under his gaze.

'And suddenly I gave a start. As though my communion with nature had given me an animal's sharpness of perception, I had sensed the presence of a human being. Thirty yards away – would you believe it? – although the forest hid it from me completely and not a leaf had stirred. I had scented a living creature, sensed its youth, conjured up a voice as fresh and cool as the voice of a sprite. Isn't it strange? I plunge into solitude, yet after a quarter of an hour of solitude I find myself hankering after a human voice. I can remember the beating of my heart, in that no-man's-land in the Hautes Vosges, when after being on the look-out for hours I saw something move under the trees. Was it a Boche, or was it some young wench? I was poised like a snake, not knowing whether, in the next minute, I would have committed an act of murder or of love . . .'

Hearing his words, she began to feel oppressed.

'So what happened just now?' she asked, fascinated by the brutality of his deliberate thoughtlessness.

He opened melancholy eyes:

'Where is she now, that little girl? What became of that little white creature that lit up my life for a moment?'

The little white creature had disappeared into the woods. After that, he said, he had been attracted to a flower, a pool, a fawn, a dog.

He was making it all up as he went along; he had spent the day in barracks, thinking of Dominique. It was not the mating urge which drove him to say these things, so calculated to inflame the girl; nor was it shyness which kept him from using more direct language. The fact was that even now he did not know whether or not he intended to attack her through her body. He could easily imagine

236

himself leaving her tonight without having done justice to his desire. But when he saw her biting her lips, gasping for breath, incapable of hiding her feelings, his merry little tune died away as the wind dies. The gravity of desire spread over his whole face, a gravity so terrifying that it is easier to laugh beside a beloved mother's coffin than in the presence of the woman one desires. He stopped talking and looked at her.

She sat still at first under his stare, pretending to look elsewhere; then, not knowing what face to put on, she smiled awkwardly; then turned towards him with animation; then crossed her legs, waggled her foot, joked without being able to smile any more: 'Is there ink on my face by any chance?' while his eyes remained fixed upon her.

He was completely still. As a tom-cat crouches endlessly in front of the wriggling female, so sure of himself that he can affect indifference, looking to right and left, so Alban waited. He knew that he would get whatever he wanted from her, when he wanted it. Around this certainty, everything was sunk in sleep, as if under some terrible drug. No objection was raised. No threat would have stopped him. Had Dominique's father shouted: 'Open up!' behind the door, he would not have opened it before the time had come.

He got up and went towards her. The sordid flickering of the candles pushed the boundaries of temerity back to infinity. A warmth, an odour marked the moment when he penetrated the atmosphere of her body. She flinched, turning her head away a little as if he meant to kill her.

They stood clasped to each other with all their strength, glued together as though there had been a vacuum in one of them which sucked the other in; he could not have tensed his muscles further had he been clinging to a rock above an abyss. Their faces distorted, looking fifteen years older, she more utterly transfigured than when she was listening to Beethoven, he more than when he was waiting to go over the top, they would not have recognized each other in the street. Feeling the shape of her head beneath her hair, he held

237

this Gorgon tilted back and breathed heavily upon her through his nostrils. She was like a flame upon his face. Had she been a flame, he would have extinguished her. All this in silence.

Ah! this love-tormented face, when would Alban ever forget it? The feverish, sick-bed flush, the parched skin, the apprehension in the eyes, the loosened, blurred features, as if he were seeing her through water, the whole face bursting with its avowal, the indelible accusation spread over it for all to see! Without having touched it, already he had reduced her mouth to pulp. She who had been all spirit and all soul now sweated, sent forth her perfumes, and gasped for breath.

For a second, the distracted look in her eyes had reminded him of Prinet, on the road, when he was afraid. But Prinet was no obstacle.

He said to her:

'Your face is new, like your soul, with every hour stamped upon it. I recognize those morning wrinkles round your eyes; they don't come from the creases in your pillow.'

'Yet I touched up the shadows with powder, so as not to look ill . . .'

The depths of their lives were stirred, but in the midst of all that was dying and all that was being born, only these hoarse murmurs were uttered: voices one imagines very low but which ring out, wild chirpings which are heard through doors like an outburst of violent quarrelling.

He kissed them, these eyelids, which had the slightly sour taste of pippin apples; and then above, where dogs, too, have a warmer little spot; and then below, where a vein passes like a river in the dusk. She had spoken the truth: the rings about her eyes now appeared, a mysterious amethyst, diluted. One would have thought that a thousand mouths had rested there and brushed away the brown of the flesh around the eyes.

He unfastened the top button of her blouse. His hand shook so violently that he could not manage the second one – so violently, this hand that had killed men! 'Help me, then!' he jerked out in a strangled voice. Then she herself, without a word, undid another

238

button. A painful sight, without a word, like an officer being degraded.

He bared her shoulders. His fingers were carried away by these familiar gestures which he had never dreamed of applying to her. The shoulders appeared, soft and firm as the flesh of the grape, and an instinct stronger than desire pulled him up short, caused him to step back 'to get a better look'. For he had just seen, at the tip of the deltoid muscle, two brief ripples of flesh like undulations in a flag.

'What is that?' he asked, unable to name these muscles. And he went in there with his mouth like a frenzied bloodhound following a scent, but his joy was not complete because he did not know the name of these muscles. His anxiety became so acute that again he moved away and looked.

'Ah!' he said with emotion, 'it has not changed.'

'It' was her body. As before, the walls of the *recti* looked like lumps of wax, the shadows of the ridges made him want to burst into song; the delicate creases spreading from the armpit gave the same sensation of virginity as the still visible folds in a material unfolded for the first time. Here was the same delicate strength, the radiant, ethereal form, the perfect thing, the heartrendingly beautiful thing which he had seen blossoming month after month with such inner momentum that sometimes, laying his hand on her back, he almost felt his hand lifting a little, as though it had been resting on a sail filled with wind. And it was as though a detachable head had been stuck on top at random, so striking was the contrast between the inviolate body and the stricken face.

Alban stood motionless, held by a strange compassion. No matter, then, if the great aloof soul had fled, no matter if the convulsion of her inmost being had gone so far as to alter the whole expression of her face, no matter if her body, accustomed to so much care, had been abandoned and assailed; for it resisted, this body, it remained intact, it proclaimed: 'All is not lost, I am holding on, it is not too late . . .' It seemed as though her soul, expelled from inside her breast, had spread itself over its surface. It was no longer the same body, innocent and indifferent, like the body of a young hero; yet

239

it still radiated the glory of a body as yet untouched. As if he had just witnessed a touching act of valour, Alban said to himself: 'Poor body, how brave it is! Can I betray it?'

Faced with her body, now, the gestures of love no longer came to him. How could he lend himself to the transformation of the very prototype of purity into a prototype of impurity! All the languor and, beneath the graceful names, all the diseases of the caressed flesh . . . Could he lend himself to that? Ah, no, he was not such a vandal! Not such a vandal, and not such a perjurer! 'So I am prepared to sacrifice my pleasure? . . . My love is strong enough for such a sacrifice? . . .'

He took her blouse with both hands, and covered up her shoulders.

Immeasurable it must have been, this gesture, for it was understood as soon as begun. A terrible joy stabbed the woman's heart – a happiness akin to death. He saw her go pale, begin to fade, her whole face dissolving as eyes do when they cloud over. 'Hold me,' she murmured, for her legs were giving way. He held her, while she slid down him like water, bending to right and to left, always falling, dragged down by the weight of her breast, heavy as a tree after rain.

'I love you,' he said. 'Do not die.'

From the other end of the world there came a voice repeating: 'Tell me again, tell me again, tell me again,' like that, without being able to stop. Her head – Dominique Soubrier's head – lay loose on her shoulder, as if her neck had been broken between two vertebrae.

'I love you. Do not die. Do not die and do not fear, for I love you. Just listen to these words that I have never spoken, these words that I have never imagined, for I have known affection and friendship and lust, but what I am giving you now is as virginal as on the day I was born. What I am giving you has fled eternally before me like the rayless sun which one ceaselessly pursues through the feverish night. All I have done, all I have learned, all I have known, all I have loved for twenty-two years is now drowned by a terrible roar, covered with black smoke like a burning town. I have just been born. There is not one thing in common between what I was an hour ago and what I am now.'

'Hold me tight, hold me tight, under the arms, like that; I can no longer stand alone upon the earth like all those other women who do not know what I know. Can you feel it? It is autumn already. It is dead now, the sickness of summer. And you are there, and the war is over, and the nocturnal cab rolls through the depths of the Bois. Oh, to be with you in the rain, in the evening rain! I wait for you without pretending not to wait, and you cross the street through the pools of light . . .'

'Don't say that we need the autumn! The seasons no longer need to yearn for one another, since each of them will fulfil its promise. Am I not already smothering you against my heart? I am near you, I touch you, I am immersed in the beauty of your face, I see your mouth with all that it has eaten and drunk, the words it has said and which I have forgotten, the words said and remembered, and those which were left unsaid, the secret ones that blossomed in the night. Ah, cover me once more, drive your love into my flesh, intoxicate me once more, that I may be given a superhuman strength wherewith to possess you utterly.'

Looking down at her, dizzied by the exhalations that rose from her as from an abyss, he saw her love-drenched face, weak with happiness. Love had oozed out of her like sweat after an emotional shock, blurring her so that he could not see her properly. Her mouth came up to him, warm, a thing of the sea half-open in the depths, and it was true that the two of them seemed to be living under water.

He kissed her mouth, knocking against the wet teeth. He lifted her hair from her forehead and kissed the pale skin there, he kissed her ears, which were cold as if they had been covered by a wreath of violets, kissed her eyebrows, her wrists, her fingers, one after the other, and her knuckles, one after the other; kissed everything, endlessly, endlessly, pausing at times for want of breath. Between his kisses she murmured: 'Oh, Alban, love me, love me!' He devoured her words but they were born again, and her mouth

241

remained intact. They came together heaving and swelling like two seas riding one upon the other, surging from their depths and rearing up as they met and mingled. With the gentle hands of his strength, he uncoiled her along the whole length of his life.

When at last, with a mutual accord, they realized they could go no further without entering a realm they had forbidden themselves, she had an inspiration both touching and fatal. She pressed her forehead against his. And they remained thus, with nothing between them but this close but trivial little contact, though he could perhaps also feel, from time to time, the fluttering of her eyelashes on his face.

What obscure motive seized him then? By what devious path did his natural demon, seemingly so well under control, regain its hold on him? Was it merely that he made the comparison, so simple yet so striking, between his offensive vanity if someone caught him undressing her, and the humiliation he would have felt had one single witness seen this gesture of pure tenderness? Did he resent their foreheads touching because, at the same time, a voice cried out to him that their minds were not touching? Was it true, as he believed later, that a furtive glance in the mirror had thrown back at him his own image, the ludicrous image of an ecstatic simpleton? Whatever the reason, it was he who was the first, with a sudden gesture as though of fear, to draw away his head.

'Ah!' he said, 'five to eleven! And I must be back by eleven!'

'You said midnight.'

'I said eleven,' he hissed, surly because he was lying.

'It's thundering. You'll get caught in the storm.'

But suddenly, a splendid inspiration! How unerringly he hit upon the word which would settle everything! What wonderful presence of mind!

'You know I'm going back to the front in a week's time.'

He had found this weapon instinctively. Like a real *agent provocateur*, he had trapped her into degrading herself and by degrading herself making escape easier for him. And yet, no, it was not calculated; his evil-doing had sprung, fully armed, from his panic; like a terrified cat caught by surprise, Alban scratched the woman in his struggle to escape from her. And now, see how she debases herself! Listen to her, perfidious youth, listen to her with both your ears! She implores you, she says she is 'tortured'. She says: 'Am I not enough for you, then?' She says: 'You have done enough to me!' Go on, you don't mind hurting her now.

'Oh yes, it is painful still! She felt so good in my arms. Nothing ever felt so good to me.' In the garden on the banks of the Oise, he had enjoyed watching her destroy herself. Now, after all, she had been pressed to his side like one of his own ribs. He offered her a sword, yet he suffered to see her impale herself on it. 'Be quiet, don't say anything. Accept in silence, Dominique . . .'

'I implore you!'

'And I implore you to say no more. Can't you understand why I'm asking you to stop?'

She wrung her hands, and her head flopped back.

'Stand up! Will you stand up straight! And be quiet, be quiet!'

Ah! It was too late. He pushed her away as she tried to cling to him. Her despair both terrified and fascinated him. For a second he had an impulse to assault her. Alas, here also he was balked; he loved her too much to be able to love her with his flesh, not enough now to love her with his intellect. Only the night could save him. He backed away and opened the door.

The cry she uttered then! His heart broke open and received it. He took one step towards her: 'What did I tell you? Aren't you ashamed to have less courage than the thousands of women who, at this very moment . . .'

She had collapsed once more. God! What was wrong with her? What had happened now in that wind-blown soul? All his love was draining from him, oozing out of his limbs, out of his heart, leaving it like an old shrivelled sponge. He looked at her with her head in her hands. He looked at her crushing her tears. He looked and looked, intoxicated by her self-abasement. The darkness swallowed him up. He was outside.

19

A Magic Storm

'O NATURE, immune to suffering, O vast and imperturbable night, come to me that I may press you to my heart! Winds, wash away the kisses from my mouth. The doors of false love are closed, the obscene, sad arms unbound, and I am my own king, free and pure as in the days of my sixteenth boyhood year!' The ancient paean of deliverance urged him along the road, bareheaded, like an element. Perched on a lorry, a bearded territorial passed him. The joy of it! Someone who did not love him! It did him good to look at him. He could kiss this simple fellow who had no more thoughts in his head than a cabbage, who did not look for hidden meanings in what you said to him, who would sleep in peace, even if Alban had not waved to him. He felt regenerated by life's indifference, like a sudden surge of oxygen into a machine-gun post after a long burst of firing. This was what she had brought him to: a horror of feeling, disgust and boredom with the soul. 'Let me go, demon of souls! Let there be no feeling left on earth!'

Through the night, it seemed to him that he could hear her plaintive cry, weaker and weaker, humbler and humbler. In vain did he try to reassure himself: 'The tantrums of a little girl . . . She'll soon get over it . . . Come on, now, let's get down to serious matters!' In vain did he try to stir up the classic Greek dispute about whether or not women have souls. He had walled her up alive, this woman, and now she bemoaned her fate. He had rolled the tombstone over her. Thinking that at this very moment she was alive, picturing her anguish and despair, he shuddered as though he were watching someone drowning.

There was a rumbling on his right. The front?

The front. In a week's time he would be there. The empty front. Purposeless. Meaningless. Yet he desired it. He desired it! Soft arms, you have made this wild love sweet to him!

Once more, on his right, came the roar, both earthly and celestial. But Dominique was right: it was the storm.

In the darkness, a whirlwind shook the air. The trees went mad. Paler with all their leaves upturned, they cried out, blustered, argued, blessed, reproved. Clouds of dust, accumulated during three weeks of drought, rolled along the road and suddenly reared up, vertically, like geysers. Leaves in their thousands, prematurely dead, were lifted up, soaring high into space or racing past horizontally like a purposeful flight of birds. A ghastly pallor exuded from the sky. Terrified swallows, drifting with outstretched wings at inhuman heights, were swept away, tail first and upside down, like aeroplanes out of control. One of them soared higher and higher . . . Would it disappear? And he, Alban, would he too disappear, like Romulus, during the storm?

A flash of lightning crowned the earth's horizon with a horizon of fire, and Alban made the sign of the cross. He was bristling all over, as he had been under the bombardment; he lifted his head and dilated his nostrils like an old horse in the bull-ring when it senses the bull approaching. The rain burst down. He threw back his head and received it on his face like a gift. Heaven's immoderation assuaged his own.

The notion that he had been the instrument of a great act of justice took shape in his mind. At a time when millions of beings were undergoing the only suffering worthy of interest, that of the flesh, it was right that those who were spared should suffer a little in their souls – an unreal, illusory pain which only existed in their own mental attitude towards it. Here was the basis for an attempt at compensation. And indeed, if God's spite demands a given quantity of suffering, who knew but that the harm done to Dominique had redeemed the harm to be done to another's life, far more useful, more praiseworthy, more deserving than hers: the life of the least of our soldiers? Who knew but that one of our soldiers had been spared a wound because Alban had wounded Dominique? The voices of the dead heard on the banks of the Oise and in the hotel room were clear enough: they demanded a sacrifice. Well, it had been granted them! Let these shades be appeased, as he himself was now appeased, and the spirits of the virile life which he had threatened to betray. The winds could rise at last to carry Alban back to the open sea of the male order. Iphigenia had been sacrificed on the altar.

The storm died down. A thousand imprisoned odours were released. The earth was like a huge flower. The little night-creatures appeared once more. The continuous clicking noise of an insect echoed like a signal in a railway-station. The plain was filled with the sounds of the rural silence: a choir of low, sweet voices.

And then, by a miraculous reversal, the experience of these last hours suddenly began to weigh on Alban. An extraordinary reflux brought him back to the girl. He wanted to say to her: 'Listen, I have eaten and drunk of the pain I have caused you. From it I have kneaded the bread of life. It is yours, I give it back to you. Feed on it . . .' And also: 'I do not need love. I am strong when I give, less strong when I receive. He who gives to me takes from me.' How often had he uttered these terrible words! But now: 'I am strong when I give . . .' – to whom had he given?

He bowed his head. He was struck more forcibly than ever before by the presumptuousness of his cherished motto: 'I am sufficient to myself.' No, he was not sufficient to himself, since he needed to give. Ah, what good had it done him to condemn that *need to love* which debases the love that arises from it, since one gives it to X as one might have given it to Y, because it had to be given to someone and it was X who happened to be there at the time! This need to share with another the fruits of life, what was it if not the need to love? As the body's life is earned by work, the soul's life is earned by love.

He admitted this, and yet, in spite of himself, he rebelled at the very words. At this hour, no doubt, lulled by nature's languor, people everywhere, rotten with sentimentality, were invoking a similar languor. Violently he dissociated himself from them; he wanted to shout for all the world to hear: 'I am not one of them! Do not be mistaken!' For the last time, he repudiated the soft lies, the swooning in destructive arms, for the last time he trampled underfoot the face of false love. And in the same instant he felt in himself the virgin possibility of love, of loving this time in such a way that he would be incapable of hurting. 'Desire is incomplete. Friendship lacks guts. Love as it is generally understood is an inferior thing. Who will draw from me a tenderness which comes from the depths of my being yet which my reason totally approves – a tenderness silent and strong and winged like an eagle!'

Out of the dark night a vague mass emerged: the field-hospital, whence he would be setting out next week, bent beneath his packs, on this same road, for the station and the train up to the front. Here was the railway embankment; here were the telegraph wires, with stars trapped between them like notes on a stave. And suddenly – was it the answer to his question? – suddenly his face was transfigured. A mysterious youthfulness relaxed the tense features now lit up by all his old good nature. With a hint of laughter in his eyes, he laid his hand on a wooden fence as on a frail shoulder:

'I say, young fellow, just look at that . . . Your father's back where he started!'[1]

And dawn broke in his heart.

[1] The author has explained that Alban here is addressing his unborn son (the 'frail shoulder') to whom he will give the sort of tenderness, 'silent and strong', which he has called for in the preceding paragraph. (*Translator's note.*)